All the Lucky Ones Are Dead

all the lucky ones are dead

an aaron gunner mystery

gar anthony haywood

g. p. putnam's sons

new york

*This is a work of fiction. Names, characters, places, and
incidents either are the product of the author's imagination or are
used fictitiously, and any resemblance to actual persons, living or
dead, business establishments, events, or locales is entirely coincidental.*

G. P. Putnam's Sons
Publishers Since 1838
a member of
Penguin Putnam Inc.
375 Hudson Street
New York, NY 10014

Library of Congress Cataloging-in-Publication Data

Haywood, Gar Anthony.
All the lucky ones are dead : an Aaron Gunner mystery
/ Gar Anthony Haywood.
p.   cm
ISBN 0-399-14540-0
1. Afro-Americans—California—Los Angeles—
Fiction.   I. Title.
PS3558.A885A79   1999   99-22586 CIP
813'.54—dc21

Printed in the United States of America

1   3   5   7   9   10   8   6   4   2

This book is printed on acid-free paper. ∞

Book design by Jennifer Ann Daddio

For Damon
My brother. Always was. Always will be.

At the time of his death, less than three months shy of his twenty-fifth birthday, Carlton William Elbridge had a personal net worth of twenty-eight million dollars. He owned two large homes in Los Angeles, a spacious Tribeca loft in New York, and three luxury condominiums, two in Las Vegas, one in Palm Springs. In the garage of his primary residence, an eight-bedroom Tudor hidden behind a wall of Italian spruce trees high in the Hollywood Hills, two Porsches, one Ferrari, a Lexus, and a classic 1961 Harley-Davidson panhead motorcycle sat in constant readiness.

His face had graced the cover of *Time* magazine, as well as the covers of other national and international publications too numerous to count. *The Wall Street Journal* had published an extensive front-page profile of Elbridge in the summer of his twenty-third year, detailing his uncanny business acumen with open admiration. The mantel over his mother's fireplace (in the new three-bedroom home he had bought her in Northridge) was overflowing with his many awards and trophies, a collection he began to amass when he was only seventeen.

On the day of his funeral in Los Angeles, people lined the streets to watch the procession as if it were the motorcade of a President. The vast majority of these people were teenagers, but some were even younger than that: eight- and nine-year-old boys and girls gripping lit candles, their faces either gnarled by anger or stained with tears. For many of these children, Elbridge had been the center of their universe, the single voice in the wilderness they could not only hear but comprehend. While parents pleaded and teachers lectured, preachers prayed and law enforcement officers coerced— Elbridge just spoke the truth to these young people. That this truth was often devoid of hope or optimism mattered little. What mattered was that it came from one of their own, someone the streets had qualified to make bold pronouncements about their present and their future. And—not inconsequentially—in spreading this truth, Elbridge had made himself filthy rich, beating the very odds against achieving economic self-sufficiency they themselves faced daily.

He wasn't the Second Coming, but for most of his countless followers, Elbridge was close enough.

Weeks after his interment, newsstands around the country were lined with magazines paying tribute to Carlton Elbridge, either in cover stories lamenting his death, or in special issues wholly devoted to the telling of his brief life story. All raised questions about his motives for suicide, and discussed at length who might have stood to profit most from his decision to commit such a desperate and unexpected act. Conspiracy theories abounded.

In short, as incredible as it seemed, Carlton William Elbridge—or C.E. Digga Jones, as he was most commonly known—received even more ink in death than he had ever received in life.

But then, such was often the fate of the premier gangsta rapper in all the land.

one

The caller identified himself as "Mike from Gardena," and he said he wanted to talk about Proposition 199, the California state ballot measure that would limit mobile home rent control.

"Go ahead," Sparkle Johnson said.

"I don't think you realize what effect this bill would have on mobile home owners if it's passed," Mike said.

"I think it would have very little effect on them, actually."

There was a brief pause as the caller recoiled from the blatant indifference of Johnson's tone. "But the people who live in these homes are, by and large, older people on fixed incomes. People who—"

"So they're older people. So what? What does that have to do with anything?"

"But we're talking about people who have no other place to live. And if their rent were to suddenly go up by as little as fifteen percent—"

"Oh, please. Spare me. These property owners you're talking about are *business*people, they rent their spaces out to make *money*. What do you think they're gonna do, raise their rents so high they'll drive all their tenants away? That would be stupid."

"Yes, but—"

"Look, if somebody's dumb enough to do that, let his tenants all get together and move out. I mean, what's the problem?"

"The problem is, if all the other park owners raise their rents at the same time—"

"Hey, I'm sorry, but those people should be free to rent their property for whatever, and to *whom*ever, they damn well please. This is America, Mike. Government's got no business telling people what they can or cannot do with their own property."

Stammering with exasperation now, the caller said, "But how about as that applies to racial discrimination? What about all the restaurant owners in the South who only wanted to serve white people before segregation was outlawed?"

Sparkle Johnson almost chuckled. "Let me tell you something, Mike— you don't want to ask me that question, okay? You don't want to ask me that question because you're not going to like my answer to it. You take me there, and I'm gonna have to tell you that *those* people should have been left alone too. They should have been free to serve whomever they wanted to serve.

"Now I know, because I'm black, you think I should feel differently about the subject. But I don't. The Constitution is very clear on the subject, it's not a racial issue . . ."

And that was it for Mike from Gardena. Having served his purpose as a detonator for one of Johnson's trademark tirades against big government, his call to her radio talk show was terminated without further ado. He wasn't told good-bye, he wasn't offered thanks, he was just hung up on under cover of Johnson's latest diatribe, freed to go back to whatever rock the liberal Democrat had crawled out from under in order to turn on his radio and use the phone. This was how all callers voicing disagreement with the vivacious and outspoken Ms. Sparkle were treated. Anyone calling her show expecting to enter into an actual *debate* with the lady was in for a big disappointment.

Aaron Gunner figured he could stomach another five minutes of this bullshit, then he was gone.

He had a nine a.m. appointment to see Wally Browne, 720/KTLK's general manager and the man who was ultimately responsible for putting Sparkle Johnson on the Los Angeles airwaves, but Gunner had been waiting for Browne to show himself in the station's reception area for over thirty minutes now. Even having nothing better to do with his time was not reason enough for the private investigator to subject himself to this, a half hour of sitting on his ass pretending the live broadcast of Johnson's program playing over the station's sound system wasn't driving him to distraction. Especially when what he had to tell Browne he could just as easily have said over the phone as to the man's face.

When Browne finally did appear, moving rapidly toward Gunner with his right arm extended to shake hands, he was beaming, the poor bastard, clearly anticipating something other than the bad news he was about to receive.

"Mr. Gunner. So sorry to have kept you waiting," he said, offering only the shortest of apologies.

He led Gunner upstairs to the runaway opulence of his private office for the second time in a week, and the two men sat down to talk, Browne behind the airport landing strip disguised as his desk, Gunner in one of the two chairs directly facing it. Just as he had four days ago, Browne offered Gunner a cigar, and Gunner shook his head to decline it. They were both getting pretty good at the routine.

"Well?" Browne asked anxiously. "How did it go?" He was an overweight man with unruly brown hair whose puffy face was naturally ruddy, but apparently, nervous apprehension could redden it further still.

"She didn't tell you?" Gunner asked.

"She won't talk about it. I assumed she was still upset that I hired you in the first place."

"Oh, she is that."

"But?"

"But I can't help you." Gunner shrugged, doing the best he could do to create the illusion of grave disappointment.

"What do you mean, you can't help me?"

"I mean that this was a mistake. She thinks you're wasting your money hiring a private investigator, and at this point, I'm inclined to agree with her."

"But—"

"Maybe the answer is another operator, I don't know. All I know for sure is that I don't want the job, and she doesn't want me on it. It's that simple."

"You're saying she didn't like you," Browne said.

Gunner almost laughed at that. The lunch he'd shared with Johnson two days earlier had not been bloody, exactly, but it had been ugly. Johnson had come already convinced that Gunner would despise her, and he had been unable to disguise the fact that he very nearly did. Combined with Johnson's insistence that Browne had hired Gunner in error, their complete and instantaneous dislike for one another seemed reason enough to end Gunner's work on her behalf before it could even begin.

Of course, Gunner had one additional incentive to walk away from the Johnson case, but this was something he could barely admit to himself, let alone to Browne.

"Whether she liked me or not is immaterial," the investigator told Browne now. "What counts is that she can't see the point of going any further with this, and I can't see the point of arguing with her about it."

"Let me talk to her again," Browne suggested.

Gunner shook his head and stood up. "No. Thanks, but don't bother."

Browne raced around his desk in a panic, said, "Listen, she's just being stubborn. She gets threats of one kind or another all the time, she thinks they're all the same. But these are different. She doesn't want to admit that, but they are."

"Different how?"

Browne swallowed hard, about to broach a subject he knew he should have mentioned four days ago, and asked, "You ever hear of a group calling itself the Defenders of the Bloodline?"

Gunner almost winced. His unspoken incentive for walking away was no longer unspoken. "Unless there's something you haven't told me yet, there's no evidence they're involved in this, Mr. Browne."

"No, that's true. There isn't. But—"

"Maybe she's right. Maybe these threats *are* like all the others. You ever think of that?"

The question gave Browne pause. "Of course. But this guy who's been calling—"

"The Defenders don't mess around with pseudonyms, Mr. Browne. They hate you, they want you dead, they tell you straight up, no phony names required." He went on before Browne could interject. "And they don't generally threaten your life more than five or six times before trying to make good. Something your caller has yet to actually do, correct?"

"Correct. But I still—"

Gunner shook his head again. "Like I said, I'm sorry. But it's not going to happen. Right or wrong, the lady doesn't share your concern for her safety, and she doesn't intend to be a cooperative surveillance subject until she does. Which, quite frankly, gives me all the excuse I need to find something less aggravating to do with my time. Have a good day."

Browne opened his mouth to protest further, but Gunner's back was already turned to him for good.

Driving back to his office a few minutes later, Gunner wondered if he'd just made a huge mistake.

As he had two days earlier, while making the trip out to Sparkle Johnson's Orange County townhouse for lunch. On that occasion, the potential mistake he'd been contemplating was his *acceptance* of Browne's work offer, rather than his ultimate rejection of it, and listening to a tape of Johnson's program in the car during the long drive south had only reinforced his sense of doubt. He had heard Johnson's shtick before, but that drive was the first time he'd endured her company for longer than fifteen minutes. Gunner was far from a political animal—his idea of political activism was endorsing at least one petition worthy of his signature annually—but the oxymoron that was black archconservatism had always been able to get a rise out of him. It was simply a concept he didn't get, African-Americans like himself sharing ideologies with the far right, to whom the desegregation of the South back in the early sixties represented little more than the first stirrings of political correctness.

But then, people had a right to believe whatever they wanted to believe, and no one was more willing to grant them the privilege than Gunner, with the single proviso that all their propagandizing be done outside the range of his faculties. Suffering the company of fools was something the investigator did best only from a distance, though this wasn't always possible. On occasion, pressed into a corner by financial straits, Gunner found it necessary to work for a wrongheaded blowhard like Sparkle Johnson in spite of his wishes to do otherwise. It wasn't easy, but he could manage.

So when Wally Browne approached him four days ago to look into a series of death threats his star radio personality had received over the last three weeks—more than a half-dozen phone calls, and twice as many typewritten letters, all from a man identifying himself only as "M"—Gunner had not rebuked him out of hand. For the kind of money Browne was offering, in fact, he figured there was nothing Johnson could say or do that would make working a case on her behalf anything more than a slight annoyance.

Then he actually met the lady.

They'd come together Saturday afternoon not far from Johnson's home, at a lushly foliated bistro near the Huntington Beach coastline, where the dress code was name-brand sports apparel and artificial tans, and designer sunglasses no one ever lifted above their eyes, even while indoors. It was a crowd the thirty-something Johnson fit right into. She was statuesque, with flawless brown skin, straight black hair, and cheeks that dimpled deeply when she smiled. A manufactured beauty, to be sure, but maybe as close to the best money could buy as Gunner had ever seen.

"Tell me, Mr. Gunner," Johnson had said eventually, after putting away a Chinese chicken salad and two glasses of iced tea with extraordinary dispatch. "Do you ever listen to my show?"

"Your show?" It was one of several key questions he had sincerely hoped she'd never get around to asking. He shrugged and said, "Sure. I'm not a fan or anything, but—"

"And?"

"And what?"

"And what do you think? About me, and the opinions I express? Do you generally agree with me, or . . ."

"I don't generally agree with you, no. But then, I could say that about a lot of people." He smiled to be polite. "Why do you ask?"

Johnson smiled back, said, "Because of your vibe, Mr. Gunner. I picked up on it right away."

"My *vibe*?"

"That's right. Hostility's coming off you in waves. I know, I get it from black folk like you all the time."

"Black folk?"

"Come on, Mr. Gunner. Let's not play games. You don't like me. You think I'm a bootlicking Auntie Tom who doesn't know the first thing about being black, and the only reason you're here is because you see a fat, easy paycheck in all this. Isn't that right?"

Gunner almost laughed, until he realized Johnson was deadly serious, her accusation heartfelt. "Look. Let's try and leave our likes and dislikes at home, all right? If your life's in danger, I can help you, whether I think you're the spawn of Satan, or a girl just like the girl who married dear old Dad."

"But my life *isn't* in danger," Johnson said.

"No?"

"No. Hate mail and ugly phone calls are part of my everyday life, Mr. Gunner. And Wally knows that. You do what I do, the way I do it, pissing some idiots off just comes with the territory."

"But Browne doesn't think this Mr. M of yours is just another idiot."

"That's true. But you know what? That's Wally's problem, not mine. Because this guy *is* just another idiot. A little more articulate and well-read than the rest, maybe, but an idiot just the same."

"And you know this because?"

"Because I do. I have a feel for people, like I said. If this person were really a threat to me, I'd be the first one to know about it. The *first.*"

Gunner studied her in silence for a moment, said, "You seem pretty certain about that."

"I *am* certain."

"Actually, I mean you seem to know it for a *fact*. Like it's more than just conjecture on your part."

Johnson's face shifted briefly, betraying something that looked to Gunner like unease, then quickly reverted to the iron mask it had been. "I never said it was conjecture, Mr. Gunner. I said it was a sense I have. One is just a function of the mind. The other is a function of the spirit."

And so it went. Gunner had never tried to sell ice to an Eskimo, but it seemed certain he would've had more luck at that than he did selling Johnson on the value of his assistance. The sister just wasn't interested. She was convinced Wally Browne was throwing his money away, paying Gunner to investigate something she had no doubt was benign, so she politely declined to answer any more of his questions, until the frustration finally broke him down, precipitating his unconditional surrender.

Now, almost forty-eight hours later, Gunner had made that surrender official, and he was left to wonder if he hadn't given up too easily. He didn't need Johnson's help to do what Browne wanted done. He had worked around uncooperative co-clients before. Why had he allowed Johnson to bully him out of a job he had no immediate replacement for?

In the end, he decided the answer was every bit as simple as Johnson had thought: He didn't like the lady. She was a loud, self-obsessed peddler of the rose-colored glasses that conservatives liked to turn on the failings of their nation, so as to better ignore all the little brown bodies that kept getting caught up in its internal mechanics, and money alone was insufficient incentive for Gunner to work a case for such a person when all he could expect in return was aggravation.

Had he been flat broke, rather than merely reluctant to live on his savings until his next gig, things might have been different. But he wasn't. For a few weeks, at least, he was solid. So he put Wally Browne behind him, pushed his burbling red Cobra north to South-Central along the California sun-soaked 405, and kissed Browne's retainer check good-bye, with only a modicum of lingering regret.

Unaware that he would remain gainfully unemployed for all of the next twenty-seven minutes.

two

"You got any plans to come in today?" Lilly Tennell asked.

Gunner hadn't been at his desk ten minutes when his favorite barkeep had called. "Who wants to know?"

"Pharaoh's got somebody he wants you to meet. He asked me to call, see when you'd be comin' by."

"It's not even noon yet. I wasn't —"

"Get your ass over here and stop actin' like you wasn't comin', fool. This is important."

The big black woman hung up.

Gunner knew he should be insulted, being treated like a nine-year-old at Lilly's beck and call, but all he could do was laugh.

At twelve-thirty on a Monday afternoon, Lilly's Acey Deuce bar was as black and silent as a bad dream. The only customer in the house—if someone drinking coffee could really be thought of as a "customer" in this place—was Gunner, sitting at a corner booth flipping through a battered copy of the *L.A. Weekly*. Pharaoh Doubleday, the tall, reed-thin part-timer

Lilly had hired to help her tend bar, stood behind the counter drying beer mugs, making the only noise in the room as he stacked the glasses on a shelf behind him. Lilly herself was in the back office, supposedly going over the Deuce's books.

Pharaoh had told Gunner very little about the man he wanted Gunner to meet here, other than that he was a friend of a friend who was in the market for a private investigator. Gunner had tried to get him to elaborate, but Pharaoh demurred, saying he felt it would be best if his friend explained everything himself.

Twenty minutes into the *Weekly*, and halfway into his second cup of coffee, Gunner looked up, saw a short, narrow silhouette stepping into the bar's shadowy cool, moving with the unmistakable hesitancy of a man with brittle bones. The man approached Pharaoh at the bar, shook his hand, then followed the bartender over to Gunner's booth, like a patron being shown to his favorite table by an underdressed maître d'.

"Aaron Gunner, this is my friend Benny Elbridge," Pharaoh said when the pair reached the investigator. "Benny and I attend the same church. Benny, this is Aaron Gunner. The investigator I told you about."

Gunner stood up to shake the older man's hand, examining him with undisguised professional curiosity. Elbridge was a wiry black man in his early fifties, who was dressed impeccably and most appropriately for a Saturday night on Central Avenue in 1946. He wore a gray sharkskin suit, a black silk shirt, and a thin red tie knotted tightly at the collar, and his black-and-white Oxfords were polished to an almost blinding sheen. His eyes were red and milky, like those of a sick dog, and his beard was full of coarse, unruly gray hair.

"Pleased to meet you, Mr. Gunner," he said, sounding tired and heart-broken.

"Same here," Gunner agreed.

For several seconds, both Elbridge and Pharaoh Doubleday looked upon Gunner in silence, as if expecting him to say something they each considered inevitable.

"Can I get either of you gentlemen a drink?" Pharaoh finally asked, when Gunner failed to speak.

Gunner shook his head, and Elbridge did the same.

"Well then, I'll leave you two to talk business." The bartender smiled and moved off, as Elbridge and Gunner sat down opposite each other in the booth.

"Tell me how I can help you, Mr. Elbridge," Gunner said, anxious to find out what kind of trouble this man had in mind for him.

"I want to hire you to find out somethin' for me," Elbridge said, and again he paused afterward, as if waiting for Gunner to offer him an obvious, specific response.

"Okay. What would you like me to find out?"

"I want you to find out who killed my boy. Carlton."

"Carlton?"

"That was his real name, yeah. C-A-R-L-T-O-N, Carlton. But you probably only knew 'im as the Digga." Elbridge gave Gunner yet another expectant look.

"The Digga?" Gunner appraised the older man more closely now, straining his eyes against the Deuce's dim light, and recognition finally kicked in. "You're Digga Jones's father? The rapper?"

Elbridge nodded again, betraying an almost unnoticeable trace of pride. "Yes sir. His mama don't want no one to know it, but his real name was Elbridge, same as mine. Carlton Elbridge. Jones was just somethin' them record people called 'im to make 'im sound more like a gangster or somethin'."

Gunner didn't know much about C.E. Digga Jones under any name, other than that he was a gangsta rap superstar who'd allegedly committed suicide a little over a week earlier, sending his millions of fans—primarily young, inner-city kids—into a funk from which they were still struggling to extricate themselves. Gangsta rap wasn't Gunner's thing, and he only barely understood how it could be anyone else's. That he'd heard of "the

Digga" at all was proof of the intensity with which the music industry bombarded his community and others like it with this particular form of angst-filled, obscenity-laced music; you lived in the hood, the hype was everywhere. A kid couldn't open a magazine or turn on a radio, walk past a construction-site fence plastered with posters, or watch five minutes of MTV without being sold the bill of goods its manufacturers liked to innocently call the "gangsta life."

"I know the boy liked to play up to all that foolishness," Elbridge said, "to act like he was as bad as they made 'im out to be, but Carlton wasn't really like that, Mr. Gunner. He was just playin' a role. Young man can't make it in the music business these days if he don't."

"Sure," Gunner said, completely unconvinced.

"Them other fools, most of them are the real thing. They just as soon shoot you in the head as make another record. Which is why they killed Carlton, see. 'Cause he wasn't like the rest of 'em, and they knew it. He was—"

"Hold it, hold it. I thought your son committed suicide."

Elbridge shook his head angrily, said, "That's a lie. That's just what they set it up to look like, suicide. Carlton didn't have no reason to kill himself, he was happy as a young man could be."

"I'm sure that's true, Mr. Elbridge, but—"

"My son was murdered, Mr. Gunner. I don't give a damn what the police or nobody else says. That's why I'm here, talkin' to you. I want you to find out who killed Carlton, and see to it they get what's comin' to 'em. All you gotta do is tell me how much you need t'get started."

He reached into his pocket, took out a wad of bills that had the well-worn look of a man's life savings, and started peeling back fifties one by one. Waiting for Gunner to say when.

"Hold on a minute, Mr. Elbridge," Gunner said, holding a palm up to ward Elbridge off.

"What? You don't want the job?"

"I didn't say that. I said hold on a minute."

"I'm in a hurry here, Mr. Gunner. You ain't the man I should be talkin' to, just say so."

"Look. We're getting a little ahead of ourselves here, that's all. Before we can start talking about my fee, I need to hear a little more about what you're asking me to do for it."

"You wanna ask questions? Fine. Ask me anything you wanna know, I'll tell you," Elbridge said. He put his money away and leaned forward in his seat, crossed his hands atop the table like a kid on the first day of school.

Gunner let him sit that way for a long while, trying to decide what to do. He'd already heard enough to know the work the older man was offering him was the kind he often regretted accepting later. The cast of characters he'd have to rub elbows with in order to look into the circumstances of a gangsta rapper's death was obvious: thugs who knew how to sample and rhyme, so-called security men eight days out of San Quentin, and power-mongering record execs who spent more time cutting lines of coke than they did distribution deals.

But Gunner was not the overly discriminating judge of prospective cases he used to be. Whereas the thought of having to deal with such an unsavory group might once have sent him running for cover, even if nothing awaited him there but a mountain of unpaid bills and a half-empty carton of oatmeal, today it merely caused him to proceed with caution. Over time, and with experience, he had learned to appreciate the challenges that sometimes came with an otherwise undesirable work assignment. And since he had already turned his nose up at one job offer today . . .

"All right," Gunner said. "Let's start off with an easy one. You have any actual *evidence* your son's death was something other than suicide? Any witnesses, any letters or documents . . ."

"No."

"No?"

"No sir. I don't have nothin' like that."

Gunner took in a deep breath, held it for a moment. "His body was discovered in a hotel room, I believe."

"That's right. Over at the Beverly Hills Westmore. Real nice place."

"And he was there because?"

"Huh?"

"Why was he staying in a hotel room? He lived here in Los Angeles, didn't he?"

"Oh. Yeah, that's right. He did. But the boy liked to go to the Westmore to write sometimes. You know, just for a coupla days or so, to get away from the wife and kids."

"He was there alone, then?"

"Alone? Sure, he was alone. Who—"

"So there was no one else in the room with him when he died."

"No. I mean—"

"I don't understand, Mr. Elbridge. If there were no witnesses to his death, and no evidence to suggest foul play, what exactly are your suspicions based upon?"

Elbridge took umbrage at the very question, said, "They're based on what I feel right *here*"—he pounded his chest with a fist—"and what I *know* right here!" Now he poked his right temple with an index finger. "That's what they're based upon!"

With considerable effort, Gunner suppressed the impulse to sigh. "I see."

"You're a detective, ain't you? An investigator?"

"Yes sir, I am, but—"

"Then what do I need with *evidence*? You're supposed to find *me* the evidence!"

"Technically, Mr. Elbridge, that's correct. But without reason to believe such evidence *exists*—"

"If my money ain't good enough for you, Mr. Gunner, all you got to do is say so."

"This isn't about money," Gunner said, starting to get angry himself now. "If you'd just hold up a minute—"

"Whatever you heard the boy's mother say about me is a lie. Ain't a word of truth in nothin' her and all them newspapers been sayin' about me, not *one damn word*!" He was shaking with rage now, and Gunner could see there were tears in his eyes as well. "Coretta thinks a man can't love his son just 'cause he wasn't there when the boy was growin' up," Elbridge went on, wiping his eyes with a monogrammed handkerchief he'd removed from his left trouser pocket. "So she goes around tellin' everybody I was only after the boy's money, comin' around 'im now that he's grown and makin' millions.

"But you don't see *her* here, do you? Offerin' to spend her own goddamn money to find out what happened to him? Hell no! Why should she? He left practically half of everything he had to that woman, she couldn't care less how he really died!"

As Elbridge spoke, fragmented memories of the news reports that had made him vaguely familiar came back to Gunner, all portraying the man before him as the quintessential whipping boy of the African-American community: the absentee father. A man who'd conceived a child in his youth, abandoned its mother soon after the child's birth, and only returned to the scene of the crime long after all the hard work of parenthood had been done. Gunner was now even able to recall how Carlton Elbridge's mother—a tall, gangly woman with a fierce, unsettling scowl that never seemed to leave her face—had been accusing her former lover of all these offenses and more, to any reporter who might ask, ever since their son's body had been discovered in that hotel room eight days before.

Did Elbridge deserve to have his character so assassinated? Gunner couldn't say just by watching the man cry, and he didn't know how much it should matter to him if he did. Working for people who had done less than right by their immediate family was, after all, about as rare in the private investigation racket as wearing laced shoes.

"Maybe the boy's mother just doesn't share your belief that he was murdered," Gunner said.

Again, Elbridge became outraged. "The hell she doesn't! Every time she opens her mouth, she's tellin' somebody how Carlton was killed! She knows as well as I do he never would've taken his own life like that!"

"Maybe. Or else she could just be in denial about it. Most mothers would be in her position, right?"

"Coretta ain't in no denial, Mr. Gunner. She knows the truth, same as me. Only difference is, all she wants to do is *talk* about it."

"All right. So what is this 'truth'? If Carlton was murdered, who murdered him?"

Elbridge shook his head, said, "I don't know. I wish to God I did."

"You don't have *any* ideas?"

"Ideas? Hell yes, I got ideas. But—"

"Let me hear one, Mr. Elbridge. Please."

Elbridge glanced over at Pharaoh at the bar, acting like he was suddenly in need of a drink, then turned back to Gunner and said, "Me, I think it was probably 2DaddyLarge."

"2Daddy who?"

"2DaddyLarge. The East Coast rapper. You know about all that, right? East Coast, West Coast?"

Gunner did, but only vaguely. According to his limited understanding, there were two separate and distinct planets in the gangsta rap universe— East Coast and West Coast, New York versus "Cali"—and rarely did the twain ever meet. At least, not without some exchange of trash talk and/or, on some occasions, automatic gunfire.

"And you suspect this 2Daddy because what? He was East Coast, Carlton was West Coast?"

"That's all it was. These kids today don't need no other excuse to start shootin' each other."

"There wasn't something personal between Carlton and 2Daddy?"

"Personal? Not for Carlton there wasn't. All that East Coast / West Coast foolishness didn't mean nothin' to *him*. But 2Daddy and his crew— they take it serious as a heart attack. 2Daddy *hated* Carlton, Carlton used to say the boy couldn't do an interview with nobody without talkin' 'bout how he was gonna serve Carlton up at least once."

Gunner started jotting down notes on a large legal pad, said, "Any chance this 2Daddy—Large, was it?—could've had more reason for hating Carlton than that? This East Coast / West Coast business?"

"More reason? I don't—"

Keeping his eyes turned down to the legal pad, Gunner asked, "Is 2Daddy a gangbanger, for instance?"

The question caught Elbridge off guard. "A gangbanger?"

"Yes sir. Representing the wrong coast isn't the only thing can get a kid thrown down on these days. His colors can get him killed just as easily."

"That might be right. But I wouldn't know."

"What about Carlton?"

"He wouldn't'a known neither."

"He had no gang affiliation?"

"No. Carlton didn't mess with no gangs."

"And you can say that with such certainty because . . ."

"Because I was his *father*. That's how."

Gunner smiled to take the edge off, said, "I hope you'll forgive me for pressing what's clearly a delicate point with you, Mr. Elbridge, but where exactly did your son grow up? Here in Los Angeles, or—"

"That's right. Los Angeles. He grew up less than ten blocks from where we're sittin' right now, his mama's old house is over on Ninety-seventh and Beach. But what's—"

Gunner cut him off. "Not to say it isn't done, sir, but that must have been pretty tough for him, don't you think? Living here in the heart of the hood without ever messing with gangs?"

Elbridge glowered at him, furious. "You tryin' to say he did?"

"I'm trying to say not every rapper's fronting when he drops lyrics about 'banging. A lot of these kids are the genuine article, Crips and Bloods through and through."

"Maybe they are. I don't know, like I said. All I know is, Carlton wasn't like that."

"He never even played to that perception?"

"No. If you mean did he ever *claim* to be a Crip or a Blood, the answer's no."

"And the lyrics to his music—I guess they never referred to gang-banging either?"

"Look—there was a lot of *violence* in the boy's music, sure. Talk about guns, and women, and jackin' people up, and such. But none of that mess was *real,* Mr. Gunner. The boy was just givin' his fans and his record company what they wanted. It was business, that's all."

And Gunner knew it could easily have been just that. In the gangsta rap arena, the image of a hard-core "killa" was an invaluable marketing asset; you couldn't sell the anger and venom in the music with the reputation of a Boy Scout, after all. If Carlton Elbridge had been a harmless kid wearing the face of a thug like C.E. Digga Jones strictly for the purposes of commerce, he wouldn't have been the first gangsta rapper to do it. And he certainly wouldn't be the last.

"Okay. Let's get back to the boy's mother," Gunner said. "You say she's just as convinced Carlton was murdered as you are."

"Yes. That's right."

"So who does *she* think murdered him? 2DaddyLarge, like you, or somebody else?"

Elbridge began to fidget in the wake of the question, as if answering it would bring him almost certain embarrassment. "Coretta got a lot of ideas about who killed the boy," he said.

"Give me a for instance."

Elbridge shrugged and made a face, trying to dismiss the validity of what he was about to say. "She mostly thinks it mighta been Bume."

"Excuse me?"

"On accounta the boy was thinkin' 'bout leavin' his record company for another one. But Bume—"

Gunner sat up abruptly. "Bume? Bume Webb?"

"Yeah. Bume Webb. How many other niggas named Bume you ever heard of?"

Gunner just looked at Elbridge forlornly, wondering why he hadn't been fully prepared for this particular name to come up. For few and far between were the rap music controversies that did not in some way involve the legendary black recording mogul whose first name was pronounced like a cannon shot. The six-foot-six, 280-pound Webb spelled it B-U-M-E, rather than B-O-O-M, but it was a fitting handle for him all the same, as it was said the street thug turned entrepreneur and the sounds of heavy artillery were quite often all but inseparable.

"Carlton recorded for Bume?" Gunner asked, trying to make the question sound wholly innocent.

"Yeah. But he was thinkin' 'bout changin' companies, like I said."

"Where was he thinking about going?"

"He hadn't decided yet. But there was this new company he was talkin' to, called New Millennia, he was thinkin' 'bout goin' over there."

"Because?"

"Because Bume was goin' to jail, that's why, and Carlton didn't wanna be the last one still workin' for 'im when he got out. At least, that was part of it."

In a highly publicized turn of events even Gunner hadn't missed, Bume had been busted on a weapons charge three months earlier, the latest in a long line of such offenses, and a no-nonsense judge had sentenced him to a five-year stretch at the California Institution for Men out in Chino as a result. The big man had only been away for a little over six weeks, but in that short stretch of time, Body Count—the multimillion-dollar record label he had single-handedly built from scratch—had all but fallen into bankruptcy, so lost was the enterprise without his heavy-handed leadership.

Key to Body Count's demise, of course, had been the defection to other labels of all but a handful of the company's major recording acts. Making a move many believed could only be dared in Bume's absence, rapper after rapper, group after group had jumped the Body Count ship to escape the allegedly suffocating control of its incarcerated CEO. As a result, the label as it existed today was nothing but a shadow of the industry giant Bume had left behind. Surely, Gunner thought now, had Carlton Elbridge/ C.E. Digga Jones lived to carry out the move he'd apparently been considering, he would have provided the last nail in the Body Count coffin. Which meant Bume Webb, imprisoned or not, had at least one possible motive for wanting him dead.

Gunner turned to look at Pharaoh, just as Elbridge had done moments earlier, and raised a hand to wave the bartender over. He'd never met Bume Webb himself, and so had no reason to fear him—but just learning he was involved, however peripherally, in the case Elbridge was trying to sell him had an unsettling effect on the investigator all the same.

"You ready for a drink yet?" he asked Elbridge.

"Yeah," the older man said, nodding. "As a matter of fact, I am."

three

One of the major drawbacks to having an office at the rear of a barbershop was the reluctance some people felt about meeting Gunner there. The first thing others thought of when they heard the word "barbershop" was a place filled with local gossip, where anything said in confidence could be spread to the far corners of the earth by the next rising of the sun. Which was exactly what Mickey's Trueblood Barbershop was, of course. The oddball group of characters who let Mickey clip their hair on a semiregular basis could be counted on for nothing if not the broad and instantaneous dissemination of every word they heard spoken in his establishment, especially if said word was best kept hush-hush.

This was why, when Gunner called his old high school partner Slicky Soames to ask for a meeting Monday afternoon, and Slicky actually agreed without argument to come down to Mickey's, Gunner was totally amazed.

As Gunner often was, to a lesser extent, at the success Slicky had achieved since their days in school together. The kid who had once been the most comical and unreliable loser in Gunner's stable of Dorsey High School homeboys was today one of the preeminent concert promoters on the southern California music scene. All the top hip-hop, rap, and R&B acts worked with Slicky almost exclusively.

"Hard to believe, ain't it?" Slicky asked, grinning from ear to ear. The grin was the same one Gunner remembered from the old days, but everything else was not: the flamboyant clothes, the four gold rings on his hands, and the close-cut hair pasted back on his head with a gleaming coat of gel were all new.

"I'm not sure I do believe it," Gunner said.

They were seated across from each other at Gunner's desk, finishing off the bottle of Wild Turkey Gunner had purchased a few minutes earlier, just for the occasion.

"People used to say I was 'clever,'" Slicky said, his smooth, child-like face caught in the tiny halo of Gunner's desk lamp. "But what I was was *smart*. They'd've measured my IQ back then, they'd've known that."

"Right. Stupid them. Not being able to see the genius behind all those F minuses."

The two men reminisced in the relative dark awhile longer, then got around to discussing the actual purpose of their meeting. Gunner told Slicky everything Benny Elbridge had told him at the Deuce, and explained that he was hoping his old friend could give him some background on the players involved in the case he'd just taken on. Maybe even offer him a little advice on where to start things off, as a bonus.

"Don't," Slicky said immediately, completely straight-faced. "Tell the Digga's daddy you made a mistake and refer him to somebody else."

"And why would I want to do that?"

"Because you don't wanna mess with Bume, that's why. Unless you're ready to spend the rest of your life hooked up to one of them machines in a hospital someplace."

"You're saying he's dangerous."

"Shit. You tellin' me you don't already know that?"

"I don't know it personally. What I read and hear about the man's pretty bad, sure, but—"

"Brother, if I saw that nigga comin' down the street, I wouldn't just cross to the other side—I'd move to another state. What more do you need to know?"

"Then you do think it's possible he had the Digga killed."

"Possible? With Bume, all things are possible."

"Even though the kid's father tells me he and Bume were tight? That Bume liked to treat him like a son?"

"Even though that's true, yeah. Hell, that's all the more reason for Bume to take it personal, the Digga was gettin' ready to take his music across the street like people say he was. Right?"

Gunner had a taste of Wild Turkey, nodded to concede the point. "How well do you know him, Slick? Bume Webb, I mean."

Slicky shrugged. "We've worked together a couple times, that's it. I did some shows for two of his acts, Godfather Royal and this girl they call Tynee Itty Bit. They were good shows, man, but Bume was in my face every minute. Got kind of funky there, one time."

"Funky?"

Slicky took a deep breath, said, "There was a little dispute about some money. Damages to the facility his contract with me held him responsible for. He didn't wanna pay, and disliked the fact I didn't either. So he tried to force the issue."

Gunner refilled his own glass, let Slicky decide for himself to go on.

"Couple of gorilla-lookin' niggas came by the office one day, busted in on me in the middle of a conference call. Both strappin' Tec nines. One of 'em takes the clip out of his, sets it down on my desk and says, 'With Bume's compliments.' Then they both leave." He shoved his empty glass toward Gunner, beads of sweat starting to appear at his scalp line. "Like I said, I ain't never doin' business with that fool again."

Gunner took note of his old friend's distress, then said, "You may not get the chance. Way Elbridge tells it, Body Count's as good as dead."

"Yeah, it is. While the cat's away, the mice will play, right? But Body Count goin' away ain't gonna be the end of Bume. Anybody who thinks that is crazy."

"And why's that?"

"Because the nigga's connected, that's why. Same money he got to build Body Count's gonna be waitin' for 'im when he gets out. All he's gonna do is rebuild."

"What money is that?"

Slicky grinned and shook his head. "Hell, Gunner. You weren't that ignorant even in high school."

"You're talking about drug money."

"See? I told you."

"Whose drug money?"

Slicky hesitated, considering the delicacy of the question, and said, "Nobody knows for a fact, but it's supposed to be an O.G. named Ready Lewis. Major player, owns a dance club over in the Crenshaw district, they call it Ruff 'n Ready's."

Gunner almost dropped his glass into his lap.

Slicky grinned. "Friend of yours?"

"You might say that. He's my nephew."

Slicky stopped smiling. "No shit. Ready? That right?"

Ready Lewis's real first name was Alred, and his late mother, Ruth, had been Gunner's older sister. When Ruth died eight years ago, her death certificate had attributed her passing to congenital heart failure, but everyone in the Gunner clan knew that wasn't true; Alred had murdered her. Twenty-one years of heartbreak wasted on an oldest son who couldn't—or wouldn't—care for anything or anyone but himself had finally broken the boy's mother down. Her death had stung him for a while, but only briefly; in the end, he found it liberating. In the eight years since her passing, he'd become the fully developed sociopath he'd always wanted to be: Ready Lewis. Player. Killer. Rock dealer extraordinaire.

To say that Gunner and his nephew weren't close was to flirt with unparalleled understatement.

"Damn, man," Slicky said after Gunner had explained things to him. "I never knew."

"You wouldn't. He wasn't somebody whose picture we kept up on the mantel."

"You ever talk to him?"

"Once, little over a year ago. I had a favor I needed to ask."

"And?"

"That was it. He helped me because he owed me one, now we're all even. End of story."

Slicky nodded, rightfully deciding that was probably as far as Gunner wanted the subject to go.

"How sure are you about this, Slicky? About 'Red being Bume's banker?"

"I told you. I'm *not*. Might be him, and it might not."

"But?"

"But all the talk says it is. Him and Bume are homies, right? They go out together, run with the same crowd. Only natural they'd be in business together too."

"You think he could have had something to do with the Digga's death?"

"I don't know. Never met the man. All I got to go by is word on the street."

"And word on the street is . . ."

"He's just as capable as Bume. Maybe more."

Gunner nodded, agreeing. He didn't want to believe Alred could be that far gone, but he did all the same.

"What was your take on the Digga's suicide, Slicky? Did you buy it?"

"Did I buy it?" Slicky paused to think it over. "That's hard to say. I was surprised to hear about it, I guess, but the shit didn't shock me, if that's what you're askin'."

"Why not?"

"I don't know. Why should it? I mean, just 'cause the boy had money don't mean he was happy."

"It's a long way from not being happy to putting a gun in your mouth, Slick," Gunner said.

"Yeah, that's true. But it's like this old expression we got in the business: 'All the lucky ones are dead.' Which means all the shit that comes with fame an' fortune ain't always worth the struggle. The Digga had a lot of pressure on 'im, man. All them big stars do. They got people comin' at 'em from every angle, Gunner—fans, managers, media types, record execs— all tryin' to get a piece of 'em. And if you're only nineteen, twenty-somethin' years old . . . you might be able to handle it, and you might not."

"Was this particular kid supposed to be that soft?"

"Soft?"

"I mean fragile. His old man's telling me he was a pussycat, of course, but I rather doubt he could've been all that."

"A pussycat?" Slicky shook his head and chuckled. "Naw, man. He wasn't no pussycat. I don't know no *female* rapper you could call a damn pussycat."

"Question I'm really asking is, was this kid just fronting tough, or was he the real thing?"

"You mean, was he a 'banger?"

"Either that, or someone who could've easily passed for one, yeah."

"He wasn't a 'banger that I know of. But that don't mean he wasn't one. It's for sure he could act the fool like one, he felt like it. I can think of a couple times at least he threw down with niggas in public."

"Would one of them happen to be 2DaddyLarge?"

"2Daddy was one of 'em, yeah. The Digga's pops told you the truth about that—2Daddy and his boy didn't have no love for each other. That was a well-known fact."

"Because 2Daddy's East Coast, and the Digga was West Coast."

Slicky shook his head again. "That was only part of it," he said.

"So what was the other part?"

"Other part was the same thing almost had me in *your* ass once. Remember?"

He was talking about a girl named Lindsey Waddell. A long-legged eighteen-year-old with a pretty face and a killer smile they'd both tried to date in high school. First Slicky, then Gunner, after Lindsey had decided eight weeks in Slicky's company was more than enough for a lifetime.

"This sister named Lindsey too?" Gunner asked, fighting to keep the name from bringing a self-satisfied grin to his face.

"No. This one's name is Danee. As in Danee Elbridge."

"The Digga's wife?"

"And 2Daddy's ex—main squeeze. Yeah."

Gunner sat back in his chair, turning contemplative. "Funny. But Mr. Elbridge failed to mention that. And he was so hell-bent on selling 2Daddy as a prime suspect too."

"Might be he don't know," Slicky suggested. "You said he was late on the scene, right? Only been around the boy 'bout a year or so?"

Gunner nodded.

"And it ain't like it was public knowledge. People in the business knew about it, but that was about it."

Gunner wasn't satisfied with that answer, but he decided to move on, let Benny Elbridge himself respond to the question later.

"All right. So 2Daddy had a motive for killing the Digga. That mean he had the wherewithal to act on it?"

"No. Not necessarily it don't."

"But you think he did."

"Lemme just put it to you like this, home. Most of these kids we been talkin' 'bout are like the Digga was—more rapper than gangsta." Slicky shook his head. "But that ain't 2Daddy."

The solemnity with which his friend had spoken made it clear to Gunner that nothing more needed to be said. If 2DaddyLarge hadn't murdered Benny Elbridge's son, it wasn't for lack of potential.

"I figure to start out by talking to the Digga's manager, Slicky," Gunner said, standing up. "Man by the name of Desmond Joy. You know him?"

"Desmond? Sure." Slicky stood up too.

"How forthcoming can I expect him to be, under the circumstances? Is he going to want to help me here?"

"If he trusts you? I don't see why not. But if he don't . . ."

"Then maybe it would help if he knew *you* trust me before I dropped in on him. Feel like calling ahead, letting him know I'll be coming by?"

"I can do that, yeah." Slicky reached out, pounded Gunner's right fist with his own. "But only for one reason."

"What's that?"

The smile on Slicky's face widened. " 'Cause you didn't last no longer with Lindsey Waddell than *I* did."

Gunner laughed at the painful truth in that, then showed his old friend to the door.

four

Despite the fact he'd told Slicky Soames otherwise, Gunner actually began his work on the Elbridge investigation with the police, not Desmond Joy.

He simply walked into the Beverly Hills Police Department's fancy new digs on Rexford Drive early Tuesday morning and told the desk sergeant out front he wanted to speak with the officer in charge of the C.E. Digga Jones suicide case. The sergeant hadn't given him much hope that his request would be granted—the uniform's reaction to the black man's credentials had been understated, to say the least—but the cop picked up the phone to call the homicide desk, and thirty seconds later, a plainclothes detective named Kevin Frick appeared.

A thin-lipped thirtyish redhead with freckles under both eyes and a crew cut you could use for a desktop in a pinch, Frick played the uninterested, I'm-too-busy-for-this-shit public servant for a while, then led Gunner back to a small conference room where, he said, they could talk in private.

"Actually, I'm not surprised to see somebody's on this," Frick said as soon as the door had closed behind them, providing Gunner with his second mild surprise in less than twenty-four hours.

"Say again?"

"I said I'm not surprised you're on this. I'd've been related to the kid, I might've put somebody on it myself."

"That right?"

"Not that it would change anything, necessarily. I still believe he did himself, don't get me wrong." Frick followed Gunner's lead and sat down. "But I'm a curious kind of guy, and there were a few things about the kid's suicide a man could be curious about."

"Such as?"

"Such as the number of people who might've wanted to see the victim dead, for one. He was a gangsta rapper with damn near as many enemies as he had fans, and his wife was a little on the jealous side. Meaning she once took a carving knife to him. And finally, if that's not enough, Elbridge was in business with Bume Webb. You know who Bume Webb is, don't you?"

"Oh, yeah."

"Apparently, the Digga's manager, a real smoothy named Joy, had been negotiating a deal for the kid with another label. A development that would've no doubt pissed Bume off to no end."

"But Bume was in prison when the Digga died."

"Right. He was. But I understand his connections are such that if he'd wanted the kid dealt with, he could've hired the work out, no sweat."

Gunner let a moment pass, about to broach a sensitive subject, then said, "So how is it you didn't follow the homicide angle up, you had so many likely suspects?"

Frick never blinked. "Very simple. We didn't go homicide because all the physical evidence pointed to suicide. Our victim was found inside a locked hotel room, alone. Next to a suicide note written in his own hand-writing. Holding the Glock nine that killed him, from which we were able to lift only one set of prints—his own. Do I need to go on, or are you getting the picture here?"

"The locked door was the only way in?"

"Right. Both the dead bolt and swing bar were engaged from the inside. Hotel security had to break the bar off the jamb to get in."

"And they did that when?"

"Sunday morning around nine. Joy hadn't heard from the kid in over twelve hours, and he was worried about him, so he had them open up his room to check. We got the call out a few minutes after that."

"Any chance the scene had been disturbed before you got there?"

"No. I don't think so. The security guy who let Joy in was with him the whole time, he said neither of them touched a thing."

"Who was this?"

"You mean his name? I believe it was Crumley. Ray or Rod Crumley, something like that."

"And Elbridge had been dead how long when they found him?"

"Almost ten hours. Coroner set time of death at eleven-thirty p.m. Saturday."

"But the gunshot—"

"Nobody heard any gunshot. Round was fired through a bathroom towel wrapped around the Glock's muzzle."

Gunner found his notebook, started scribbling some hasty notes. "So who was the last person to see the Digga alive?"

"His wife. Danee Elbridge. She visited him in his room shortly before nine Saturday night, stayed about thirty minutes."

"She say what kind of mood he was in when she left?"

"She said he seemed fine. She, on the other hand, was a little pissed."

"About?"

Frick grinned, said, "About the two women who'd apparently been in there to see her husband earlier."

Gunner raised an eyebrow. "Two women? You saying he didn't just take that room to write, like his father says?"

"Not entirely."

"She drop any names? Or didn't she know them?"

"She seemed to know at least one of 'em. I remember her referring to one by name. But who they were didn't really concern her as much as *what* they were. She said they were both "ho's" of the highest order."

"Professional, or amateur?"

"She didn't say, and we didn't ask. But since she knew one, we guessed the latter."

"You ever talk to them?"

"Who, the ladies?" Frick shook his head. "Why would we? Both Mrs. Elbridge and Crumley agreed they'd come and gone long before the Digga died—what would we have wanted to talk to them about?"

Finding himself unable to answer that, Gunner shifted gears to ask the detective about the note he'd said Carlton Elbridge left behind.

"The note? There isn't much to say," Frick said, "except it didn't make a whole lot of sense. Few of 'em ever do."

"But it did make some mention of his intent to kill himself."

Frick shrugged. "I guess."

"You guess?"

"What I mean is, it all depends on your interpretation. Way my partner and I read it, the inference was there the kid was looking to off himself, yeah. But what do *we* know? We're just a couple of white-bread cops from Beverly Hills, and he was a gangsta rapper. The three of us barely spoke the same language."

Gunner nodded, seeing his point. "How many people knew about this note's existence?"

"Its existence? Its existence was a matter of public record. It was its content we kept hush-hush. Until we closed the case out as a suicide, we withheld that info from everyone except the people who already had it, and they were instructed to keep it to themselves."

"And who were those people?"

"Just Joy and Crumley. They both read the note when they discovered the body."

Gunner was slightly annoyed. This alleged suicide note was something else Benny Elbridge had neglected to tell him about the day before.

"Any chance I could see this note now?"

"Not unless Ms. Trayburn, the kid's mother, wants to show it to you," the detective said. "Once we ruled out homicide, it ceased to be evidence and became a personal effect, so it's been turned over to her." He finally looked at his watch, a move Gunner had been expecting him to make for several minutes now. "Sorry to break this up, Gunner, but I'm afraid that's about all the time I can give you here. Duty calls, and all that."

"Sure. No problem." Gunner offered the cop his hand as they both stood up, and Frick took it, shook it warmly.

"You have any more questions later, give me a ring, I'll try to answer 'em for you if I can."

"Will do. Thanks." Gunner was looking at Frick like a yellow octopus he'd just seen crawl out of a UFO.

"Something wrong?"

"Not a thing. Just always throws me a little. Finding a cop I've never met so willing to treat me with a modicum of respect."

Frick smiled and opened the conference room door. "Forget about it," he said. "Far as I'm concerned, you're just another schmuck trying to keep his head above the slime, same as me. Bein' private doesn't change that."

Amazing, Gunner thought. A real human being in Beverly Hills.

Gunner met with Desmond Joy at the Bad Rock Recording Studios in Hollywood shortly before noon, but only after a cute little sister in a bronze Lexus almost took the front end off his Cobra in the parking lot outside.

She was flying out of the driveway as Gunner was turning in, and she stood on her brakes just in time to avoid a collision that would have cut Gunner's sports car in half. The investigator gave her a hard look, trying to penetrate the black lenses of her sunglasses to reach her eyes, but he needn't have bothered; no sooner had the short-haired beauty brought the big GS400 to a halt than she was flooring the gas pedal again. The Lexus swerved around the Cobra, dropped off the edge of the curb, and squealed away north down Highland Avenue, doing what had to be fifty-plus in a thirty-five-mile-per-hour zone.

Gunner wondered what someone could have done to piss her off so completely.

Inside Bad Rock, he sat in a small reception area near the studio's front door and waited for Joy to join him, idly watching a recording session in progress on a closed-circuit TV. Joy had left word with Mickey earlier that he'd be here supervising a session featuring a kid named DeadRinga, and Gunner figured the stocky, bullet-headed young brother on the monitor overhead was probably him. Shouting into an oversized mic in an otherwise empty recording booth, a large pair of headphones draped across his gleaming head, the 'Ringa was dropping lyrics to a heavily sampled sound track that as near as Gunner could tell, told the story of a jealous girlfriend getting in the 'Ringa's face over a woman he'd just had sex with at a party. The rapper wasn't pleading innocent, exactly, but he *was* making the argument that he was only a man, and as such, there was no way he could be expected to decline a fine piece of ass if someone was going to offer it to him with no strings attached.

It was an argument Gunner had heard made many times before, though never with any positive effect.

Still, Joy's client emoted through two takes of the song before a disembodied voice called for a short break. Minutes later, a door opened to Gunner's left, and a middle-aged black man wearing white-on-white stuck his head into the room and said, "Come on back, Mr. Gunner."

Desmond Joy shook Gunner's hand and introduced himself, then led the investigator down a narrow corridor to a large control room, where a black man Gunner assumed was a recording engineer sat alone before a massive bank of knobs and slide switches, a canned soft drink in one hand, half a sandwich in the other. The recording booth DeadRinga had occupied only moments before stood on the other side of a giant pane of glass, empty and silent.

"We're going to need a few minutes, Larry," Joy said curtly.

The other man departed without comment. Joy closed the door behind him, then asked Gunner to take one of the three large swivel chairs in front of the console before taking one for himself. Between the white-on-white outfit and shoulder-length, dreadlocked hair, he looked like the kind of exaggerated character the comedian Eddie Murphy might have played on *Saturday Night Live* back in the early eighties.

"Well? What did you think?" Joy asked, his diction as pointedly perfect as a British magistrate's.

"About what?"

"About the 'Ringa. You were listening to those last couple of takes, weren't you?"

"Oh, that. Yeah, I guess I was."

"So?"

"So the kid seems to be very talented."

Joy laughed. "Shit. You don't have to jive me, brother. Only talent that boy's got is in his pants. He knows how to sample other people's shit, and rhyme 'ill' with 'chill.' That's it."

"If you say so," Gunner said.

"Refresh my memory for me. You're working for Mr. Elbridge, right?"

"I don't believe I mentioned who my client was."

"But it is Mr. Elbridge, correct?"

As Benny Elbridge had given Gunner permission to disclose this information at his discretion, the investigator nodded his head.

"I knew it. He just can't let it go," Joy said.

"What's that?"

"Come on, man. You know what. He thinks the Digga was murdered."

"And you don't?"

"No. Hell no."

"How can you be so sure?"

"Because it isn't possible, that's why. He was in that hotel room alone the night he died. He locked the door himself, from the inside."

"Or somebody made it appear that way, you mean."

Joy shook his head.

"Then the Digga *had* been entertaining ideas of suicide just before his death."

"In his way he was, yeah."

"I don't understand."

"It's like this. Killing himself was never very far from the Digga's mind. I never really thought he'd do it, but the possibility was always there."

"Why?"

"Why? You mean—"

"What reasons could he have had for being that despondent, yeah."

Joy smiled and shook his head. "Sorry, Brother Gee, but I'm afraid I can't say."

"You can't?"

Joy shook his head a second time.

"Would it help me to read the alleged suicide note he left behind?"

"Oh. You know about that, huh?"

"The note's common knowledge. What isn't is what it said. Or, for that matter, whether it was really a suicide note, or just the latest flava the Digga was getting ready to drop on his fans."

"You're talking about song lyrics, right?"

Gunner nodded.

"Yeah. That's what the cops thought it was too, at first. But no." Joy paused for emphasis. "It was a suicide note."

"You're sure about that."

"As sure as I need to be. I mean, the note might've *looked* like some lyrics, yeah. All it was was some lines on a sheet of paper, no punctuation or caps, same way the Digga always laid his lines down. But if you concentrated on what the note was *saying*, instead of what it *looked like* . . ."

Gunner looked at him expectantly, hoping he'd go on on his own without being prodded.

But Joy recognized the ploy, said, "I'm sorry, Brother Gee. But that's as much as I can say. You asked me if the boy could have been considered sui-cidal before his death, and I said yes. What his reasons might have been for bein' that down are, in my opinion, private and immaterial."

"Not if they involved a second party who may have murdered him they aren't."

"They didn't. You can take my word for that."

"I'd like to. It'd make for a shorter work week. But that isn't what Mr. Elbridge is paying me for, is it?"

"I already told you. I don't know *what* Mr. Elbridge is paying you for."

"You don't think the Digga was murdered. No problem. Every man's entitled to his opinion. But I think we both owe it to the kid's father to at least consider the possibility for a few minutes, don't you?"

After a long pause, Joy shrugged and said, "All right. Why not? You want to know names, right? People who might have wanted to kill the Digga?"

"As many as you can think of."

"Bume Webb," Joy said, without hesitation.

"But Bume Webb is in prison."

"Raymont Trevor isn't."

"Who's Raymont Trevor?"

"Raymont Trevor's the brother who's been running things for Bume since Bume went away. He's kind of a full-service second-in-command— bodyguard, errand boy, hatchet man. Whatever Bume needs, Raymont is."

"And his motive for killing the Digga would have been?"

"Damage control. What else?"

"What kind of damage control?"

Joy glanced at his watch impatiently, said, "Have you been following the troubles of Bume's label lately?"

"You mean Body Count? Sure."

"Then you know it's a sinking ship about to go down."

"I know it's suffered one hell of a talent drain since they took Bume away, yeah."

"And do I have to tell you why that is?"

"Bume's a tyrant. Now that he's gone, his subjects are going over the wall as fast as they can scale it."

"Exactly."

"So?"

"So the Digga was the last name rapper Bume had left, and he was halfway out the door. We only owed Body Count one more record, and we delivered it a month ago. In another two weeks, I was going to move the Digga to another label. We had a deal all ready and waiting to be signed."

"Only the Digga died before that could happen."

"Yes. Which makes him just as unavailable to Body Count as he would have been otherwise, of course, except for one thing. This way, Bume saves some face. Better to lose his last bankable act to an unforeseen tragedy than watch him become yet another defector."

"And this Raymont Trevor would have done the job for him if Bume had wanted the Digga killed?"

"Raymont? Oh, yeah." Joy shrugged again and smiled. "But this is all speculation, remember? I'm not actually accusing Raymont of doing any-thing."

"What about 2DaddyLarge?"

"2Daddy? What about him?"

"Mr. Elbridge seems to like him for the Digga's murder even more than you like Bume. And frankly, so do I."

"Yeah? Why's that?"

"Two reasons, really. This East Coast–West Coast rivalry they had going on, and the little matter of the Digga's wife."

Joy raised an eyebrow. "Danee? What's she got to do with anything?"

"I understand the Digga wasn't the first rapper she's spent quality time with. Before him, there was 2Daddy."

"Who told you that?"

"Not my client, if that's what's worrying you. I don't think he even knows."

Joy had thought he had his displeasure in check, but was unsettled now to learn that Gunner had noted it. Checking his watch again in a fully ineffective attempt at misdirection, he said, "I'm afraid we're going to have to wrap this up, Brother Gee. Lunchtime in here is almost over."

"Sure. But why don't you finish telling me what you think about 2Daddy murdering the Digga, first," Gunner said.

Joy started to object, then changed his mind and said, "I don't see it. 2Daddy might have had motive to kill the Digga, sure. He may have even had the opportunity." He shook his head from side to side. "But he doesn't have the smarts to do it the way it would've had to be done. Aim and shoot, that's the only way that fool could ever kill anybody."

"You're saying he's a dummy."

"With a capital *D*. Lays all his lyrics down in crayon."

"But you say he may have had the opportunity to commit the crime, if nothing else?"

"That's right. He was here in L.A. the night the Digga died. He'd been on the Coast for three weeks, shooting a video, I believe."

"Then he's back in New York now."

"As far as I know."

Gunner nodded, then asked Joy if the Digga had really been staying at the Beverly Hills Westmore to write, as Benny Elbridge believed.

"For the most part, yes," Joy said.

"And the other part?"

"He was there to chill out. Do some reading, swim in the pool . . ."

"Get jiggy with a couple of ladyfriends other than his wife?"

When Joy just stared at him blankly, Gunner told him about the two women the Beverly Hills Police Department's Kevin Frick had said the Digga entertained in his hotel room only hours before his death.

"Okay. So he had some company," Joy said simply.

"Were they friends of yours?"

"Friends of mine? Why would they be friends of mine?"

"You were his manager. Some managers might consider that sort of thing just another service within their purview."

"Not this one. My clients do their own pimping. Any more questions?"

"Just a small one. There was a freak in a bronze Lexus pulling out of the parking lot as I was pulling in a few minutes ago. Almost tore my car in half, and looked disappointed when she didn't. *She* wouldn't be a friend of yours, would she?"

Joy frowned, as if the question were the one he'd least wanted Gunner to ask. "That would've been Danee," he said.

Gunner didn't know why, but that was exactly what he'd thought Joy would say.

For the cost of one night at the Beverly Hills Westmore, a man could fly from L.A. to New Orleans and back and still have change. Some considered it the premier luxury hotel in Los Angeles, and anyone who'd ever set foot on its grounds would be hard-pressed to argue the point. Set back from the northeast corner of Sunset Boulevard and Beverly Drive, behind a fortresslike wall of green landscaping, the Westmore was an old, Spanish-style monument to comfort and overindulgence that catered only to the rich and famous.

As Gunner was neither of these things, his Tuesday afternoon visit to the historic hotel was his first, and most likely last. But that was all right with him. He had lived this long without having his tea served from a sterling silver tray, and he could go right on doing so.

He had made the trip in order to talk to the security man named Crumley, who, Kevin Frick said, had read the Digga's alleged suicide note along with Desmond Joy. But Crumley—whose first name turned out to be Ray, not Rod—wasn't there. Tuesday was his day off.

"You should've called ahead," his supervisor said. He was a middle-aged, potbellied white man wearing an ill-fitting version of the security staff's blue blazer. His name was Bob Zemic, and he greeted Gunner's arrival with all the hospitality of a border patrol officer.

"I thought I'd surprise him," Gunner said.

"Looks like you surprised yourself. What's this all about?"

When Gunner told him, Zemic scowled and said, "You wouldn't be trying to make a case for liability here, would you, Mr. Gunner?"

"Not at all. Should I be?"

"Only if you enjoy wasting time. The hotel did everything that could have possibly been done for Mr. Elbridge, I assure you."

He had said "Mr. Elbridge" as if the rapper had no more deserved such lofty recognition than a bug he might scrape from his shoe.

"I'm sure that's true," Gunner said, filing the man's obvious distaste for the Digga away for future reference. "But like I said—liability isn't my interest here. I only came by to hear Mr. Crumley's account of his discovery of the body, and maybe ask him for a short tour of the room, if that's possible."

"The room is occupied at the moment," Zemic said.

"I see. Maybe you could just walk me quickly past the door then."

"The door?"

"Call it going through the motions. My client's getting charged for the time, the least I can do is take a quick look around, right?"

It was a rationale that fit in perfectly with Zemic's low opinion of Gunner and those in his profession. Calling himself being generous, he shrugged after a moment and said, "Sure. No harm in that."

The last room C.E. Digga Jones would ever sleep in—number 504— was, predictably, up on the hotel's fifth floor. It was one of ten large suites arranged symmetrically on either side of a freshly painted mauve hallway. To reach it, Zemic had to guide Gunner past a gauntlet of fine southwestern art pieces and kaleidoscopic flower arrangements, and wrought-iron light fixtures that mimicked the soft radiance of kerosene lamps.

Zemic stopped at the appropriate door and said, "This was Mr. Elbridge's suite here. Five-oh-four."

"Sure we can't go in?" Gunner asked.

"I'm afraid so. Like I said, the room's occupied."

"Really? How do you know? I never saw you check."

"I don't have to check. Part of my job here is always knowing what rooms are vacant, and what rooms aren't."

Before the white man could stop him, Gunner reached out with his right hand, rapped on the door three times. "Let's just make sure," he said.

Zemic was furious. "That wasn't smart, Mr. Gunner. The Westmore doesn't appreciate having our guests disturbed unnecessarily."

When no one answered his knock, Gunner said, "You can't disturb guests who aren't in." Letting the security man see he never believed they were there in the first place.

"All the same. We can't go in there," Zemic said.

Gunner peered down the hall, saw a housekeeper's cart parked outside an open suite door. Zemic watched him start toward it, moved quickly to follow him.

"What are you doing, Mr. Gunner?"

Ignoring him, Gunner reached the open suite, stepped inside just far enough to get a look at the interior side of the door. A uniformed housekeeper stood in the bathroom nearby, eyeing him warily, as Zemic appeared alongside him.

"I asked you what you're doing," the security man said testily.

"Just wondered what the locks look like. This the same setup as the one in five-oh-four?"

"Yes. But I'm not sure I care for the question."

The door featured a dead bolt with a large, wedgelike knob, and above that, the latest replacement for the old standby chain lock: a swing bar. A thick U-shaped brass bar that swiveled on a hinge when the door was closed to interlink with a brass ball mounted to the jamb. Gunner was no expert in such things, but it didn't look to him like an arrangement that could easily be manipulated by someone working on the outside of the closed door.

The investigator stepped out of the suite as Zemic watched, and found the twin camera domes he knew had to be there, this being the high-cost establishment it was. They were mounted to the ceiling at either end of the hallway. The domes' mirrored skeins made it impossible to see how the cameras inside were aimed, but it seemed safe to assume that one of them must have had a fairly decent view of the door to suite 504 the night Carlton Elbridge died.

Following Gunner's gaze, Zemic said, "We have surveillance cameras like that on every floor here. Security at our hotel is the finest in the industry, as you can see."

"The video feed is recorded, as well as monitored?"

"Of course."

"And are the tapes recycled, or archived?"

"They're archived for thirty days, then recycled. But look—"

"Any chance I could see the ones for this floor recorded the night Elbridge died?"

"No. No way. We already let the cops borrow one, no way I'm gonna run 'em now for *you*."

"The cops borrowed one? What do you mean?"

"I mean they asked Ray if they could take one down to the station for a while, and he let them. If we hadn't gotten it back a few days later, he'd be looking for work right now, and so would I."

"Hold on a minute. You're saying Beverly Hills PD took a copy of the tapes we're talking about off-site? For what?"

"You'd have to ask them, not me. I imagine they were just being thorough, not wanting to rule Mr. Elbridge's death a suicide until they were absolutely certain that's what it was."

Gunner was somewhat surprised. Kevin Frick hadn't said anything about having viewed any surveillance tapes, and in fact had led the investigator to believe he wouldn't have cared to. He and his partner had been convinced from the first that Carlton Elbridge had committed suicide, Frick said. Wouldn't so closely monitoring who Elbridge's visitors were the night of his death have been more appropriate behavior for a cop who smelled a *homicide*?

"They only took one tape?" Gunner asked Zemic. "Not the whole series?"

"You mean—"

"I mean for the entire period between the time Elbridge last entered his room on Saturday and Crumley entered it on Sunday, when you say he and Joy discovered Elbridge's body. That couldn't have all fit on one tape."

Zemic shook his head, said, "No, of course not. That would have been five, maybe six tapes at the least. If Ray had given them all that—"

"But you say he didn't. He only gave them one."

"Yes. That was plenty."

Another curiosity, Gunner thought. To adequately rule out the possibility that someone had entered the Digga's room to murder him, then slipped out afterward, Frick and his partner would have wanted to examine the full series of tapes Gunner had just described to Zemic; one tape alone would have told them nothing, unless it caught the murderer entering and exiting the scene of the crime just before, and just after, the Digga died. The two cops could have taken a shot with the single tape covering that time frame, hoped it alone showed them what they were looking for, but it would have been damn shoddy police work to do so. And if there was one thing Frick *hadn't* appeared to be to Gunner, it was a cop who liked to do shoddy police work.

"Crumley gave them the tape without your consent?" Gunner asked.

"Absolutely. It was against all hotel policy to do so without checking with legal first. I personally would have never allowed it."

"So how did you find out he'd done it? I don't suppose he told you himself."

"Actually, he did. But only in reply to direct questioning. I'd noticed the tape missing from the shelves in our office, and asked him if he knew where it was. He told me then he'd given it to the detectives who were investigating the Elbridge suicide. The only reason I didn't fire him on the spot was because he thought he was doing the right thing, cooperating fully with the authorities."

"Do you recall which tape it was, exactly, that he gave them? What time period it covered?"

"Of course. It was early evening that Saturday, I believe. Sixteen hundred to twenty hundred hours."

"That would be four p.m. to eight p.m."

"Yes."

"But Elbridge reportedly died around midnight. You're saying they took a tape that ended a full four hours before that?"

"I'm simply answering the question you posed to me, Mr. Gunner. The tape they had ran from four in the afternoon that Saturday to eight in the evening. Why they chose that particular tape, I couldn't tell you."

Again, this was something else that didn't add up. If the Digga had been killed only thirty minutes shy of midnight that Saturday, and Frick and his partner only took *one* surveillance tape—it should have been the one relevant to that specific time frame. None of the others, recorded either before or after the Digga died, would be capable by itself of proving who had or had not been in the room with him when he was shot.

"When did you say you got the tape back?"

"A few days after they took it. Two or three, tops."

"And was it returned to you personally, or . . ."

"It was returned to Ray. Ray went down to the station when they were done with it and brought it back here himself. He gave it to me and I refiled it, after checking it over to make sure it was the right tape, of course."

"You viewed it?"

"Yes. Not in its entirety, naturally, but I scanned through it. Four hours of what was mostly an empty hallway, I certainly wasn't going to look at the whole thing in real time." Zemic eyed Gunner suspiciously, said, "I don't know where all of this is leading, Mr. Gunner, but I'm afraid I'm going to have to get back to my office now. I trust I've answered all your questions?"

"All but one." Zemic looked annoyed, having already taken one step toward the elevators. "I'd still like to have that talk with Mr. Crumley, if I could. Would it be possible to get his home number from you?"

"I've got a better idea. I'll take yours, and have him call *you*."

Gunner smiled good-naturedly, said, "You could do it that way, sure. But my way would look more like cooperation on your part, if anybody were to ask me later how helpful the Westmore's been to my investigation. Don't you think?"

Zemic visibly stiffened, stung by the veiled threat. Carlton Elbridge's death on the premises had already brought Zemic's beloved hotel all the negative publicity it could ever use; if stories were to start circulating now that the Westmore's staff was impeding Gunner's investigation into the rapper's alleged suicide, rumors that the hotel was engaged in a cover-up of some kind wouldn't be far behind.

"Follow me down to my office, I'll give you Ray's number there," the security man said.

Biting down hard on every word.

Gunner used a pay phone in the lobby to make three calls before leaving the Westmore. His first one went out to Kevin Frick, who wasn't at his desk at the BHPD; Gunner left a message on the cop's voice mail for him to call. Next, Gunner tried Ray Crumley, but the security man too was out; Gunner left the same message he'd left with Frick on Crumley's answering machine. Finally, the investigator checked in with his unofficial secretary, Mickey Moore, looking for messages of his own.

"It's about damn time you called," the barber said immediately, clearly in a panic.

"Why? What's up?"

"You got the biggest brother I ever seen waitin' for you over here, that's what. Damn near blotted out the sun when he walked through the door."

"He give you his name?"

"He says his name is Jolly. Jolly Mokes."

"Jolly Mokes?"

It was a name Gunner had nearly forgotten. The last time he had seen William "Jolly" Mokes was on television, during a news report of the giant black man's arrest for the murder of his wife, Grace. He had strangled his pretty little woman to death in a drunken, jealous rage the day before, and would soon offer the police a full confession to the crime. When they shipped him off to prison shortly thereafter, Gunner thought he'd never see his old Vietnam War partner again.

But that had been nineteen years ago. Time enough for Jolly to make like a model citizen inside and maybe earn himself an early release. He wouldn't be the first convicted killer to get off so lightly.

Gunner told Mickey he'd be right in, then hung up the phone. Later, sitting in the idling red Cobra, he checked and reloaded the clip in his nine-millimeter Ruger before putting the car in gear.

Mickey was waiting for him out on the street upon his arrival. The barber ran up to the car as Gunner pulled it to the curb and said, "He's still in there. Lookin' like somebody shot his mother. You sure I shouldn't call the cops?"

"I'm sure," Gunner said, joining his landlord on the sidewalk. "I told you, he's a friend."

"A friend, huh? Baddest-lookin' friend I ever saw. Whoever named 'im Jolly must've had one helluva sense of humor."

"Anybody else in there right now?"

"No. I closed up early. If what I think is gonna happen when you go in there happens, I don't want nobody around to get hurt and sue me afterward. I can't afford that kind of trouble, I'm sorry."

The two men entered the silent barbershop together; then Gunner went straight back to his office, waving at Mickey to stay put out front. He stepped into the muted light of the room and Jolly jumped up from the couch like a man caught sleeping with another man's wife. Gunner noticed immediately that he hadn't changed much in nineteen years; prison food had thinned him out some, but he still stood six-foot-six in his stocking feet, and was as wide across the chest as a small forklift.

"So there you are," Jolly said, smiling nervously.

"Jolly. What's up?" Gunner answered.

The eyes in his friend's peanut-shaped head turned to the nine-auto Gunner was training on his midsection, and the big man's smile lost a fraction of its enthusiasm. "Hey, man. It ain't like that, is it?"

"I don't know, partner. You tell me."

"I didn't come here to bust you up, if that's what you're thinkin'," Jolly said, angry now. "I just wanna talk to you, that's all."

Gunner searched his smooth, babylike face for deceit, couldn't really find any. He took a calculated risk and slipped the gun back into the front waistband of his pants. "What do we have to talk about, Jolly?" he asked, starting forward to take the chair behind his desk.

Jolly let him take two steps, then lunged at him to throw a right hand, nearly broke Gunner's jaw with a blow that barely landed. Gunner hit the back of his head on his desk as he fell to the floor, tried to draw the Ruger from his pants before the big man could reach him, but Jolly wouldn't have it. He pounced like a cat, seized the Ruger with his left hand and Gunner's throat with his right, then slowly drew the investigator to his feet, intent on looking Gunner straight in the eye when he broke his neck.

"You should've stopped me, Gunner," Jolly said.

Mickey burst into the room seconds later, armed with the only weapon he ever kept in the place, a Louisville Slugger signed by Ken Griffey, Jr.—

but he was too late. All the excitement was over. Jolly was sitting on the couch again, hunched over and breathing heavily, while Gunner lay in a heap on the floor, right where the giant black man had dropped him.

"It's okay, Mickey," Gunner said, rising slowly to his feet.

"I told you this was gonna happen! Didn't I tell you?"

"Nothing happened. We're okay. Get the hell out of here, will you?"

But Mickey wasn't easily reassured. Still holding the bat at the ready, his body poised for attack, he glared at Jolly, who had yet to even glance his way, and said, "Nothin' happened, my ass! He tried to kill you, just like I said he would!"

"No. He didn't." Gunner crossed over to take Mickey by the arm, guide him forcefully to the door. "Man just needed to let off a little steam, that's all. You can leave us alone now, he's all right."

Mickey gave Gunner a long look, questioning his sanity, and finally eased back out of the room. Jolly continued to just sit there, head turned down toward the floor. Gunner looked around, saw his Ruger in a distant corner where the big man had discarded it, and moved to retrieve it. Then he sat down at his desk and waited patiently for Jolly's gaze to turn his way.

"It wasn't my fault, Jolly," he said.

"You could've stopped me," Jolly said bitterly, eyes brimming with tears.

"It wasn't my job to stop you."

"She said she asked you for help! You were supposed to be my friend!"

"And if I'd talked to you for her, what then? What were you going to do? Stop beating her because I said so?"

"No! But—"

"She was *your* wife, Jolly. Not mine. I wasn't going to waste my breath trying to make you respect a woman when you had no respect for yourself."

It was a harsh thing to say, but it was true. And it shut Jolly up, which was Gunner's intent. The big man was rubbing his nose in something the investigator had been trying for years to forget. Justifiably or not, he'd always held himself at least partially responsible for Grace Mokes's death, and he didn't like Jolly reinforcing those sentiments now. He had enough guilt to deal with.

"You're right," Jolly said, nodding his head slowly. "I didn't have no respect for myself."

"Didn't?"

"That's right. Didn't. I know you ain't gonna believe this, Gunner, but I'm a different man now. I've been saved."

"Saved? You?"

"I found Jesus back in the joint, and he found me. I know now that it's wrong for a man to lay his hands on a woman in anger, especially his wife. The Word says so, Ephesians chapter five, verse twenty-eight: 'Husbands should love their wives as their own bodies. He who loves his wife loves himself.' "

Gunner didn't know what to say. The big man wasn't just mouthing the words, he seemed to wholeheartedly believe them. "I'm happy for you, Jolly. Really. But if you came here looking for converts . . ."

"Converts? Naw, man. I ain't lookin' to convert nobody."

"Then what are you doing here?"

"I'm lookin' to make restitution. For what I did to Grace, and all the other folks I done wrong in the past."

"I'm not following you."

"Lord says I got some serious service to do here in the community. He even got me out early so I could get started. I could go work with a preacher, or one of them youth groups, but I'd rather work with you."

"Me?"

"You ain't a cop, I know, but you do the same kinda work, right?"

"No. I don't—"

"I need a job, Gunner. Otherwise, they're gonna send me back inside. When I asked the Lord where to find one, he told me to come see you. So here I am."

The big man fixed his eyes on Gunner's and defied his old friend to turn away. Gunner didn't even try.

"The Lord tell you to try and kill me too?" he asked.

"No. That was on me. I really did use' to blame you for what I done to Grace, man. 'Fore I was saved, I mean. I guess seein' you again kinda brought it all back for me." He shrugged, said, "I'm sorry."

"Forget about it. I'm sorry too. Because I can't help you, Jolly."

"You can't?"

"I don't have any work for you. I don't have any work for *anybody*. I run a one-man operation here, as you can see."

"Maybe somethin' will come up."

"I don't think so. At least, I wouldn't count on it. I'm sorry."

Jolly stared at him a moment longer, measuring Gunner's words for falsehood, then lifted himself to his feet. He lumbered over to the investigator's desk, stopped just in front of it. "Lemme have a pen and some paper," he said.

Gunner found a pen in a desk drawer, handed it to Jolly along with a small notepad.

"I'm gonna leave you my address over at the apartment I got downtown," the big man said, scrawling out the address. "I ain't got a phone, but all you gotta do is come over, you decide you need me. I'll be right there waitin'."

"Jolly . . ."

"Anytime day or night, don't matter. I'll be there." He handed the pad and pen back, took one more look at the determined expression on Gunner's face. "Lord says you got work for me to do, Gunner, and the Lord never lies. You'll see."

Jolly turned and stalked away.

Gunner watched the beaded curtain in his office doorway sway to and fro in Jolly's wake, didn't realize his phone was ringing until it was almost too late to answer it.

It was a man who identified himself as an LAPD homicide cop named Steven La Porte, no one Gunner had ever heard of before.

"What can I do for you, Detective?"

"You're Aaron Gunner. The private investigator, is that right?"

"That's right. How can I help you?"

"I was wondering, Mr. Gunner, if you knew a man by the name of Ray Crumley?"

"Ray Crumley?" Gunner felt the stirrings of a queasy stomach fast approaching. "I don't know him, no. But about forty minutes ago—"

"You left a message on his answering machine at home. Yeah, we know."

"We?"

"My partner and I, plus a few of our friends from the division. We're over at Ray's place right now, tidying up a bit. You wouldn't mind dropping by to give us a hand, would you?"

"I wouldn't know the way. I never met Crumley, like I said. What the hell happened, Detective? You gonna clue me in, or what?"

"What happened is, ol' Ray is dead. And he didn't die of natural causes," La Porte said. "But don't take my word for it, Mr. Gunner. Why don't you come on down and see what's left of 'im for yourself?"

six

The late Ray Crumley had been renting a clean little one-bedroom apartment in the Mid-City area of Los Angeles, on Burnside Avenue just north of Olympic. Situated in the heart of a quiet, ethnically diverse neighborhood where trouble rarely reared its head, his apartment building was a two-story, white-with-yellow-trim number that looked like all the other such rental properties surrounding it, except for the buzzing police activity out front: squad cars and yellow tape, news crews and an ambulance, and a host of uniformed patrolmen with answers to nobody's questions.

Gunner was out in the hallway beyond Crumley's open apartment door when the familiar stench of a runaway bloodletting told him what he'd find inside. Actually seeing the crimson splatter someone had made in the dead man's ransacked living room in the process of killing him proved almost anticlimactic.

"Looks like somebody had a real thing for red, don't it?" Steven La Porte asked, grinning.

He was a tall reed of a blond, with an angular face beneath a mound of curly hair. His brown suit fit him like something he'd inherited from a larger uncle, and his smile was filled with the yellowed, unappealing teeth of a lifetime smoker.

"Aaron Gunner, right?"

Gunner nodded, still surveying the bloody, disheveled room. Oblivious to the two crime scene technicians flitting about it, a body lay under a sheet on the floor beside the couch, staining the white fabric red in several places.

"Detective Steven La Porte. This is my partner, Detective Chin."

Gunner looked over, caught the nod of the stocky, grim-faced Korean La Porte was referring to.

"What happened?" Gunner asked.

"From the looks of things? Burglarus interruptus. Which is to say, Mr. Crumley walked in on somebody robbing his apartment, got his head bashed in for his trouble. Come on, take a look." La Porte led Gunner over to the corpse on the floor, crouched down to lift the sheet away from its head. Or what remained of its head. Crumley had been beaten so badly only the left side of the black man's skull was not a caved-in mass of bloody pulp and bone. "Had to be a druggie. Nobody else would expend this much energy killin' a guy, right? Just to get his wallet and the change in his pockets?"

Gunner nodded, taking the sheet out of the cop's hand to cover Crumley's face again. He hoped he didn't look as sick as he was starting to feel.

"You okay, Gunner? You don't look so good."

"I'm fine. Showing a little respect for the dead, that's all."

He caught La Porte throwing a sideways glance at his partner, anticipated the cop's next question.

"I didn't know the man, La Porte," Gunner said. "I called him once an hour ago, and left a message on his machine. That's as close as I ever got to meeting him."

"Yeah, we know. You told us that. But maybe we'd be more inclined to believe you, you told us what your reasons were for calling."

Gunner gave them the general idea of the case he was working on, no more and no less. La Porte seemed to be satisfied.

"When did all this go down?" Gunner asked, surveying the room again.

"Late last night sometime," Chin said, speaking for the first time. "Coroner's first guess is ten, ten-thirty, and a couple of neighbors in the building seem to confirm that."

"You've got wits?"

La Porte shook his head for his partner. "They just heard all the commotion. Nobody saw anything, or anybody."

"What about a weapon?"

"Hasn't turned up yet."

"And the body? Who found it?"

"His girlfriend. One Lori Fields. She's a stewardess for United who just got back from Chicago, she says. Came by to fix Crumley breakfast this morning, and got a little surprise."

Gunner looked around, didn't see anyone fitting the description. "So where is she?"

"Hospital," Chin said. The two cops were making like a tag team now. "She did a dead faint when she saw the body, banged her head on the coffee table over there when she fell. She was cut pretty bad, so we had the paramedics take her in for treatment."

"You let her go?"

"We released her for medical reasons. She isn't going anywhere. Besides, her story checks out. United says she worked the red-eye from Chicago last night, didn't get into LAX until a few minutes shy of eleven a.m."

"Mind if I ask a question?" La Porte cut in, talking to Gunner. "What was your interest in Crumley? What'd you think he could tell you about your rapper's suicide you didn't already know?"

"I wasn't sure. Maybe nothing. But his supervisor over at the Westmore said something this morning I thought was a little odd, so I thought I'd ask Crumley about it."

"Yeah? Like what?"

"Like Crumley had told him he'd turned over one of the hotel's surveillance tapes of the floor Elbridge's suite was on the night he died to the

Beverly Hills PD. Which he may indeed have done, except that the cop in charge of the investigation never mentioned having viewed such a tape to me."

"And you think that means . . ."

"Either Crumley lied to his supervisor about turning the tape over, or the supervisor lied about Crumley having done so. One or the other."

"Funny. I thought sure you were gonna say it was the cop who had to be lyin'."

Gunner looked at La Porte evenly, taking the obvious dare, said, "There's that possibility too, of course. But since I never asked him any direct questions about the tapes, it'd probably be more accurate to say he never volunteered any info about 'em, if in fact he actually had any to volunteer."

"What exactly are you thinking this surveillance tape would've shown?" Chin asked, taking his turn at bat again.

"Visitors to Elbridge's room several hours before his death. Beverly Hills PD says all the visitors he had that weekend came and went long before he died, but maybe this tape proves otherwise, somehow." Gunner turned to look over the shambles of the room again. "Any idea what all is missing here, yet?"

Chin shook his head. "Nothing obvious is missing that we can see. TVs and such are all still here. Either our perp was only after the small stuff to begin with, or he panicked, took off after killing Crumley with only what he found on Crumley himself."

Gunner saw a big-screen TV sitting on a maple stand nearby, only a cable box resting atop it; there was no VCR in sight. Without asking for permission, he left the living room, found a smaller television among the wreckage of Crumley's bedroom, on top of the dead man's dresser, facing the bed. A second cable box sat beside it, a black-faced VCR rested beneath it, and a host of assorted videotapes were scattered to all sides of the three.

Gunner was hitting the eject button on the VCR with the end of a rollerball pen when La Porte and Chin caught up to him, the white cop getting red all around his shirt collar.

"What the hell do you think you're doin'?" he asked.

"Looking for the dupe of my tape," Gunner said, using his pen now to lift the VCR's cartridge door open manually. There was no cassette inside.

"You're an invited guest here, Gunner. Not an investigating officer. Put your hands in your pockets and keep 'em there, or I'll have my friend Pete here show you how his cuffs work."

"Sure thing. Sorry." Gunner put his pen away, faced the two cops directly. "This it for VCRs?"

"Unless he had one hidden in his pants," Chin said.

"Look, Gunner," La Porte said. "We're just getting started here, Pete and me. And we appreciate your anxiousness to help. But I think maybe we should do the rest of our talking down at the station, if that's all right with you. Away from all these distractions."

Gunner frowned. "Come on, La Porte. I told you before, I'm not your man."

"Of course you aren't. But I wouldn't be doing my job if I didn't ask if you can prove that. You do have wits who can vouch for your whereabouts around ten, ten-thirty last night, right?"

Naturally, Gunner didn't. He'd spent all of the night before at home, soaking in a hot tub while listening to Donald Byrd, then watching an old Jim Brown movie—*Tick . . . Tick . . . Tick . . .*—on cable from his bed. Alone, save for his faithful dog, Dillett. Who wasn't at all the kind of company he would have preferred.

"I don't need wits," Gunner said angrily. "What the hell do I need with wits when I don't have a motive?"

"Maybe this tape you've been talkin' about is your motive."

"What?"

"What my partner's saying is that people try to run that game on us all the time," Chin said. "Volunteering theories about the hows and whys of a homicide, acting like they're talking about some third-party perp, when they're really only talking about themselves."

"You've gotta be kidding."

"Do we look like we're kidding?" La Porte asked.

"For Chrissake. I left a message on Crumley's answering machine this morning, remember? What do you think, I killed him without leaving a clue to my identity, then called to leave my name and number on his machine the next day just to throw you geniuses off the scent?"

"We think there's some chance of that, yeah. However remote. Clever guy like you just might've thought that'd make one hell of an argument for your innocence after the fact."

"I'm neither that smart nor that stupid, La Porte."

"Maybe. But Pete and I won't know for sure until we get you in an interview room, see how you do on an IQ test, will we?"

"You mean the same one you flunked to get your badges?"

"Never mind the IQ test," Chin said, angrily ripping the handcuffs from his belt. "You've just *proven* you're an idiot."

Gunner threw his hands up to ward the Korean off, said, "Okay, okay! That was uncalled for, my bad." He looked at La Porte. "But fucking with me is just gonna be a waste of your time. Surely you know that."

La Porte's silence said that he did, but neither he nor his partner could bring themselves to admit it.

Chin, his face hard enough to break, said, "I'll tell you what we know, Gunner—that anything's possible. Okay, so maybe we've got no reason to suspect you for this right now. But that could change. In a heartbeat."

"Especially if you can't prove where you were at the time our homicide took place," La Porte added. "Which, judging by your lack of response to my question earlier, we have to assume you can't."

The two detectives waited as one for Gunner to say differently, but the black man just stared back at them instead. There was nothing else he could do.

"You're free to go," La Porte said. "We need to talk to you again, we'll give you a call."

He was lucky to be getting off so easy, all things considered, but the dismissal rankled Gunner all the same. "Thanks. You guys are two of the good ones," he said.

On his way out the door, he glanced at Crumley's bedroom one last time, saw something on the floor that made him stop and stare. When La Porte and Chin stepped forward to follow his gaze, he said, "Maybe one of you officers should make a note of that, huh?"

"What?" Chin asked, visibly agitated.

"Looks like all the tapes there are prerecorded. I don't see any blanks."

Before either man could ask him what the hell that suggested, he left them to figure it out on their own.

That night, Gunner met his cousin Del Curry at the Deuce, and together, excluding Lilly and Pharaoh Doubleday, the two men made up all of a third of the bar's entire crowd. While Gunner and Del sat at one end of the bar keeping Lilly company, Howard Gaines and Beetle Edmunds played dominoes at the other, a nephew of Howard's Gunner had only met once before—he believed the kid's name was Justin something or other— watching at his uncle's side. Pharaoh, meanwhile, was flitting back and forth between the bar and the Deuce's only occupied table, servicing the needs of a good-looking black woman no one claimed to know or recognize.

"There. She's doin' it again," Lilly said, referring to the stranger.

"You're nuts," Gunner said.

Del looked over his own left shoulder, discretion be damned, and said, "She's right, Aaron. The lady *is* lookin' at you."

Gunner raised his eyes to the mirror behind Lilly's bar, examined the woman's reflection in the glass just as his cousin could have, had he possessed the smarts. She was an unspectacular beauty in her early thirties, light-skinned and compact in both height and general shape; some men would never look twice at her, but many, like Gunner, would look once and have a hard time turning away. She was neither dressed for trouble nor posed in any way that might invite it—but she had a natural, unforced sex appeal that filled the room like a sound wave.

And yes, she did appear to be returning Gunner's gaze with something more significant than a smidgen of interest.

"Well?" Del said.

"Well, nothing. Only eight people in the whole house, who else is she gonna look at, you?"

"It's more than that, brother."

"So it's more than that. I'm not interested." Gunner picked up his glass, eased some more Turkey down his throat.

"He's bein' a good boy tonight," Lilly said to Del, chuckling and winking simultaneously. "But it ain't gonna last."

"How much do you wanna bet?"

"Shit. That lady of yours is what? Two thousand miles away? And you ain't seen her in how many months?"

"Weeks, Lilly. It's only been six weeks."

"Yeah, but they been six loooong-ass weeks, haven't they?" The big bartender laughed heartily, and Del joined right in with her.

Nobody believed Gunner could make it work, this long-distance love affair he and Yolanda McCreary had been engaged in now for going on six months. Yolanda lived in Chicago, and the two only saw each other when their schedules and finances permitted, which so far meant about every five weeks. It would have been a difficult arrangement to pull off under the best of circumstances, but further complicating matters was the fact that Yolanda was a former client; Gunner really had no business seeing her at all.

Yet here they were, the PI and the LAN administrator, falling harder for each other every day.

They spoke on the phone nightly, and traded amorous e-mail messages laced with sexual innuendo on their computers, and on those weekends they actually managed to see each other—either Gunner flying east to Chicago, or Yolanda jetting west to L.A.—they came together like interlocking puzzle pieces, as physically and emotionally inseparable as a mother and her unborn child. What their sex together lacked in regularity, it more than made up for in intensity, and they had found no subject yet they could not discuss openly and honestly.

In short, despite the distance between them, theirs seemed a relationship teeming with promise.

Unfortunately, that distance did exist, and with it came pressures that did nothing but work against them, not the least of which were loneliness and sexual deprivation. Two things Gunner was having a harder time dealing with than Yolanda ever would.

And didn't both Lilly and Del know it.

"Never mind the lady," Gunner said, pushing his empty glass across the counter for Lilly to see and refill. "We were talking about gangsta rap, remember?"

"You were talkin' about it. I wasn't," Lilly said.

"Sure you were. You said it wasn't music."

"It ain't. It's just a lotta noise and bad language. 'Muthafucka' this, and 'muthafucka' that, boom-boom-boom." With this last, the big woman was trying to imitate a heavy bass line, lowering her voice to a deep rumble that nearly shook the stacked glasses behind her off their shelves.

"It isn't all like that, Lilly," Del said.

"All that shit I ever heard is. You call that music?"

"But if it's socially relevant . . ." Gunner started to say, continuing to play devil's advocate.

"Socially relevant? What the hell is socially relevant 'bout singin' songs about bitches and 'ho's, and niggas can't do nothin' but smoke crack and kill each other? How the hell is that socially relevant?"

"If it's based on real-world observations, it's as relevant as any other form of art. At least, that's what some people will tell you. They'll say, just because the kids use the language of the street—"

"Damn right they use the language of the street," Del said. "You play some of that mess too close to a dry weed, you're likely to start a brush fire."

"It ain't good for children to be listenin' to all that shit, day after day after day," Lilly said. "That don't do nothin' but mess with their minds."

"And you see what it does to the rappers themselves," Del added. "Another one's getting shot or killed every day. Take that boy Kaleel. Look what happened to him."

Kaleel Takheem was a West Coast rapper who'd been murdered in the main parking lot at Disneyland several months earlier. The news stories Gunner had read said he'd been leaving the park with his manager when a lone assailant—described by witnesses as a black man in his early twenties, driving a late-model white Honda Accord—perforated the rapper's car with automatic gunfire, then sped off. Takheem's manager had managed to survive the attack, but the rapper himself was a DOA before the first 911 call could ever be made.

"They find his shooter yet?" Gunner asked, not having heard anything about an arrest in the case.

Del shook his head. "Hell no. And I bet they never will. Whoever killed that boy is going to get whacked himself before the cops ever come close to finding him. You watch."

"It's one of them vicious circles," Lilly said, splashing bourbon all over the bar as she refilled Gunner's glass. "East Coast child kills a West Coast child, some other West Coast child kills him. And so on and so forth."

"And here you are now, jumping right in the middle of it all," Del said to Gunner. "Just asking to catch a bullet by mistake."

"Or maybe not by mistake," Lilly said.

Gunner snorted to show them how seriously he was taking the threat. "Come on. It's not like that."

"Yeah, it is. You're stickin' your nose into the Digga's murder, ain't you? Leavin' your business card all over town so the fools who killed 'im will know where to find you when they decide to shut you up?"

"Nobody said the Digga was murdered yet, Lilly."

"Nobody has to say it. He worked for Bume, didn't he?"

"What's that got to do with anything?"

"What's it got to do with anything? Lord have mercy, Gunner, Bume is a damn gangster, that's what! And I don't mean the kind that makes records. If he ain't out killin' somebody, somebody else is out tryin' to kill him."

"Says who?"

"Says me. You ever known me to be wrong about somethin'?"

She only asked the question because she knew what his honest answer had to be—no—but all Gunner said was, "You mean today?"

Del started to laugh, but had to reconsider when Lilly caught him in the act. "This ain't funny, fool," she said. "People who get too close to that big ugly nigga always end up dead. And it ain't never 'cause they wanted to kill themselves."

She didn't know it, but all Lilly was doing was building a case for something Gunner was fast becoming certain of on his own. Because Kevin Frick of the Beverly Hills Police Department had returned his call late that afternoon to report that at no time had either he or his partner removed any surveillance tapes from the grounds of the Beverly Hills Westmore Hotel.

"Somebody said we did?" Frick had asked, clearly annoyed.

"Bob Zemic. The Westmore's security chief. He said the tape recorded on Elbridge's floor between four and eight o'clock the Saturday he died was turned over to you by his man Ray Crumley, and that you returned it to Crumley roughly seventy-two hours later."

"Sorry. Mr. Zemic's mistaken. We neither asked for any tapes nor received any, from Crumley or anyone else."

"That's what I thought you'd say."

"It doesn't make any sense. Why would we only take one tape, and the wrong one at that?"

"I couldn't figure that out either. Only thing I could guess was that Crumley was lying."

"Either him or Zemic, yeah."

"I wouldn't blame Zemic. Unless I'm reading him wrong, he was only telling me what Crumley had told him."

"In that case, it sounds like Lloyd and I should have a little talk with Mr. Crumley."

"Not unless you believe in séances, you won't. Crumley's dead. Somebody hollowed out his skull at his apartment late last night, left his brains all over the furniture."

After Gunner recounted what little he knew about Crumley's murder, Frick grew silent for a moment, then asked, "You're thinking Crumley took this tape himself to copy it, then somebody killed him to get the copy, is that it?"

"Evidence at the scene certainly seemed to support robbery as the motive, and nothing larger than a pack of cigarettes appeared to have been taken. Add to that the lack of blank tapes at the scene—"

"Come on. That's a nonissue. Lots of people don't own a blank tape, they only use their VCRs for playback."

"Yeah, but—"

"Besides. You say Crumley returned the tape. If the reason he took it in the first place was to copy it, he would've needed two machines, right? And you said he only had one."

"One was all we found, yeah. But that doesn't mean—"

"Come on, Gunner. You're grasping at straws here. Even if we assume Crumley had a way of copying it, that surveillance video as you describe it shouldn't have been worth *stealing,* let alone killing a man over. So it shows somebody entering Elbridge's room four hours before he died, so what? What's that supposed to prove?"

"Maybe it doesn't prove anything. Maybe the tape he took wasn't the one Zemic said it was at all, but the one that was recorded during the actual time of Elbridge's death. *That* one could have been worth killing for, right?"

"You're saying Zemic lied about which tape it was?"

"Either that, or he was misled. He sounded too certain to be simply mistaken. All Crumley would have had to do was swap or replace the labels on two tapes to make Zemic think the one you borrowed was for the earlier time period."

"That's true, sure. Only—"

"Why would he do that? Yeah, that's a good question."

"Sounds like he was gonna be in hot water if Zemic found out the tape was missing, no matter which one it was, right? Why go to all the trouble of changing labels?"

"Because Zemic would have been unduly suspicious otherwise?"

Frick paused to think that over, said, "Possibly. But I still think that's a stretch."

Gunner's silence said he agreed. "All right. Let's consider another option then. One we haven't even mentioned yet."

"You wanna know if there's any chance my partner got the tape from Crumley without my knowing about it."

"Yes."

"The answer's no. But thanks for taking so long to ask."

"You understand I'm not accusing either one of you of anything. I'm just wondering—"

"You don't have to wonder. I just told you. It didn't happen. You wanna leave it at that, or get on my bad side?"

"Sorry, Detective. I didn't mean any offense. I'm just trying to find a scenario here that follows some kind of logic, that's all."

"Yeah? Well, how's this one? Zemic's the head man over there, right? Put yourself in his shoes for a minute. Some private ticket you've never seen before comes around asking to see something you don't particularly feel like showing him—a series of hotel surveillance tapes the ticket might be looking to use in a wrongful death lawsuit against your employers—what are you going to tell him? The cops have already seen them. They had one down at the station for three days, didn't see a damn thing on it."

"That's a fine theory, Frick, except for two things. Zemic brought Ray Crumley into the mix on his own, number one, and he gave me more detail than I asked for, number two. If all he'd wanted was for me to go away, he'd have told me he personally gave you guys every tape in the sequence, not just one, and left Crumley completely out of it."

"If he could think that fast on his feet, you mean. Not everybody can."

And that was true. Most lies were told on the fly, without the benefit of premeditation, so it wasn't unusual for a string of them to add up to something that, when viewed as a whole, made little or no sense. Caught off guard by Gunner's request to see the Westmore's surveillance tapes, and determined to dissuade him from doing so, a panicked Zemic could indeed have concocted an argument against the investigator's need to view the tapes that included the very gaps in logic Gunner had just mentioned. And yet . . .

"I just don't think he was lying," Gunner said. A gut feeling that returned him and Frick right back to square one: Why would Ray Crumley take the tape Zemic claimed had been missing if it couldn't prove someone besides Carlton Elbridge had been inside his room at the time of his death?

"The hell if I know," Frick said.

"Then you agree there's something here worth investigating."

"For you? Oh, yeah."

"Wait a minute, Frick . . ."

"No, Gunner, *you* wait a minute. Our investigation is closed, remember? We've already decided what happened to Elbridge. He committed suicide."

"Yeah, but—"

"Okay, so maybe it's a little funny, Crumley lying to Zemic about us having that tape, then getting his head bashed in ten days later. If I could drop what I'm doing now to help you solve that little conundrum, I probably would, I'm that curious about it myself. But I can't. My plate's too full. You had some concrete evidence to support your theories, maybe it'd be different, but you don't. Do you?"

"Assuming Crumley's corpse doesn't count? No. I don't."

"Crumley's corpse *doesn't* count. Why the hell should it? All his murder's proof of right now is that somebody wanted *him* dead, not Elbridge."

"But if he was murdered over the tape—"

"A, we don't know that he was, yet, and B, what of it if he was? There could've been a million things on that tape somebody might have wanted to kill him over, Gunner. It didn't have to relate to Elbridge's suicide at all."

"No, but—"

"Listen. The Elbridge kid wasn't the only guest staying on the Westmore's fifth floor that night. As I recall, there were eleven others, and I bet you more than a couple of 'em had been walking the halls all weekend with people other than their husbands and wives. If Crumley was the blackmailing type, as you suspect, he could've used that tape against any number of people, and if he was unfortunate enough to choose the *wrong one* . . ."

Frick couldn't see it, but Gunner was nodding his head, conceding the fact that the cop's suggestion was a sound one. For the moment at least, they had no reason to believe that Ray Crumley's homicide was related to the death of Carlton Elbridge, short of Gunner's questionable sense of instinct, and profound lack of faith in coincidence. Two things, for all Gunner knew, the LAPD's Steven La Porte and Pete Chin would prove completely invalid tomorrow.

"I hear you talking, Detective. But I still wish to God Zemic would let me see that tape," Gunner said forlornly.

"So go ask him to see it again. Nicely, this time."

"To hell with that. I'll just tell him *you* sent me. That ought to scare a little cooperation out of his ass."

"Tell him anything you like. Just don't mention me by name," Frick said.

That had been over four hours ago.

Now Gunner was here at the Deuce with Lilly and Del, allowing all their impassioned admonishments to feed his nagging fear that, despite all of Frick's rationalizing to the contrary, Ray Crumley's murder not only was connected to the case he was working, but was somehow indicative of the far-reaching power of Bume Webb.

"All right," Gunner finally said to Lilly with great impatience. "So there are safer things to do than play in Bume's sandbox. I get that. But you're the one who got me involved in this mess in the first place, remember? If something happens to me, it's not gonna be my fault, it's gonna be yours."

"My fault? What the hell did *I* do?"

"You were the one who called me down here to talk to Pharaoh's friend Benny Elbridge yesterday, weren't you?"

"Yeah, but—"

"But what?"

"But Pharaoh never told me what they was gonna ask you to do. All he told me was he had a friend from church needed a private investigator."

"So you recommended me."

"You needed the job, didn't you?"

"That's beside the point, Lilly."

"Shit. Not if you wanna keep comin' in here drinkin' my liquor, it ain't." She broke out laughing, and Del followed suit, both of them finding endless amusement in the disgruntled look on Gunner's face.

"From the lady," Pharaoh said, suddenly appearing among the trio to slide a fresh drink under Gunner's nose. He was grinning like somebody who'd just heard the punch line to a very ribald joke.

"Aw, shit," Lilly said to Gunner playfully. "What'd we tell you?"

Gunner was the last to look over, see the strange beauty behind him waiting patiently for his reaction to her offering. He lifted the glass of bourbon for her to see, nodded thanks, and she returned a nod of her own, smiling pleasantly.

"Is that all you're gonna do?" Del demanded when he and his cousin had turned around again.

"You don't at least go over there to say hello, she's gonna think you're very rude," Lilly said, her red lips turned up in a smile filled with wicked satisfaction. Even Pharaoh was still standing there, watching to see what Gunner was going to do in the face of such an enviable gift.

Gunner frowned at them all, threw back a long swallow of Wild Turkey, and started over to the lady's table, taking his drink along with him.

When he had finally reached her, she laughed and said, "They made you come, didn't they?"

She had a full, throaty laugh that Gunner found hard to resist. He chuckled himself and said, "It was that obvious, huh?"

She nodded and held her right hand out for him to shake. "Brenda Warren."

"Aaron Gunner." He shook her hand and sat down, conjuring up an image of Yolanda McCreary and affixing it to a corner of his mind, just to remind himself of his limitations. "Many thanks for the drink."

"It's going to sound like a line from a really bad movie, but I don't do this very often. Only under special circumstances."

"Yeah?"

"It's a self-defense mechanism. Whenever I come to a strange place like this, somewhere I've never been before, I'm almost always approached by somebody, and it's usually somebody I'd just as soon not be bothered with. I've learned if I make a move first, pick somebody out who looks halfway interesting, before somebody else can step up to the plate . . ."

"I get it. It's a preemptive strike."

"Exactly."

"Well. Lucky me," Gunner said, tipping his glass to her again.

"Not all that lucky. I'm only here for the conversation. I hope that doesn't disappoint you."

Gunner was surprised to discover that it did. Maybe his intent to keep this meeting short and uneventful had been less genuine than he thought. "Frankly, that suits me just fine," he said. "Only I'd be lying if I said my pride isn't a little bit hurt."

"Please. Don't take it personally. Conversation's all I'm ever looking for lately." She smiled, but her eyes did something altogether different.

"I'm sure there's a good reason for that," Gunner said, stepping lightly.

"Yes. There is."

"A husband back home, maybe? Or a boyfriend?"

"A husband. But not at home. Almost never at home. We don't need to mention his name."

"No. Let's not."

"He's a good man. When he's around. I only do this to save my sanity in his constant absences, that's all. I'm not looking to get laid, Mr. Gunner."

"I understand."

"You really do, don't you? Damn. Now *my* pride's a little hurt." She laughed her throaty laugh for him again.

"If you were thinking the thought never crossed my mind, forget about it," Gunner said. "You're all that, and more. Thing is, I've got reasons of my own to be good tonight. And we don't need to mention her name either."

"Wife or girlfriend?"

"Girlfriend. For now."

"For now, huh? Sounds serious."

"I think it is." Gunner took a deep breath, braced himself for the monumental move he was about to make. "Which is why I'm going to stand up now, get the hell out of here before I do something stupid to screw it all up." He pushed himself to his feet. "Because I would, given half a chance. Conversation's a wonderful thing, Ms. Warren, but . . ."

"Yes, I know. Sometimes, what you want from someone goes a little farther than that."

For the first time that night, she gave him a look fully intended to deliver a sexual message, and it was enough to make Gunner take a step back, fight to maintain his balance.

"Thanks again for the drink," he said. "I owe you one."

Then he proved himself a man of his word and went home.

Leaving the Deuce that night, Gunner had the feeling he was being followed.

He'd sensed the same thing earlier that day, during his long drive from
Mickey's out to Ray Crumley's apartment, but he'd shaken it off as a by-
product of the dread he was already feeling, knowing the scene of an ugly
homicide awaited him. Now he had no such excuse.

But neither did he have any evidence to support his suspicion. Nothing
in his rearview mirror struck him as unusual, or particularly familiar. Just
headlights and parking lamps moving north along Vermont Avenue, winking on and off as they went their own way.

Still, to ease his mind, he played some of the tricks he knew to shake
an unwanted tail out of hiding—making illogical turns to see who would
follow, pausing at the curb to catch someone else abruptly doing likewise—
but such efforts proved futile. No one appeared to take the bait; no one did
anything even mildly incongruous.

If there really was someone back there, Gunner finally decided, they
had to be better at hiding than he was at flushing them into the open.

seven

"So? What you got for me?" Benny Elbridge asked Gunner the next morning. It was only a few minutes after seven, and the sound of the ringing phone had nearly fried the investigator's brain waking him.

"Nothing but a few questions," Gunner said into the phone, willing himself up to a sitting position on the bed.

"Questions? What kinda questions?"

To start, Gunner asked Elbridge why he hadn't told him about the alleged suicide note his son had left behind.

"'Cause it wasn't no suicide note, that's why," Elbridge said predictably, seemingly aggrieved by the very suggestion. "The police tried to say that, but that wasn't nothin' but some lyrics to a song the boy was writin'. Any fool coulda seen that."

"You saw the note yourself?"

"I didn't have to see it. Coretta saw it, and she told me what it was."

"You think Coretta might show this note to me, if you asked her?"

Elbridge paused before answering, apparently taken aback by the request. "She might if *you* asked," he said. "But if *I* ask, it's for sure she won't even talk to you. But what you wanna talk to her for, anyway? I already told you she don't know anything."

"She was your son's mother, Mr. Elbridge. I would think she knew some things about him no one else did, including yourself."

"Yeah, but—"

"You have some problem with my talking to her?"

"What?" Elbridge grew silent again, but Gunner could hear his mind grinding out a response even over the phone. "No, I don't have no problem with it. It's just . . . She don't know I hired you, see, and if she finds out, I ain't never gonna hear the end of it. 'Cause she's gonna think this is all about money, 'stead of about the boy."

"I hear what you're saying, and I sympathize. But if for no other reason than to get a look at that note, it would really help my cause here to talk to her."

"Do you have to tell her who you're workin' for?"

"I don't have to, no. But if she asks, and I refuse to say . . ."

"She won't wanna talk to you. Yeah, that's right," Elbridge admitted.

"Tell you what. I'll keep your name out of it if I can. But it won't be easy. In the meantime, I've got another question for you."

"Shoot."

"Your daughter-in-law Danee. She's something of a hothead, isn't she?"

"How do you mean that, 'hothead'?"

"I mean she had a jealous streak a mile wide, and she liked to swing knives around when it flared up. Or didn't you know that about her?"

"Little girl has a temper, that's true," Elbridge said, somewhat reluctantly.

"I guess that was something else you forgot to mention Monday. Carlton's wife once trying to cleave him in half with a carving knife."

"I didn't forget about it. I just knew it wasn't important. So the girl got crazy on the boy once, so what?"

"Was she trying to kill him, Mr. Elbridge?"

"No! I mean . . ." The older man's voice trailed off as he thought about it. "That ain't what it sounded like to me. Carlton said she'd just had a little too much to drink that night, that's all."

"How long ago did this happen? Recently, or . . ."

"A month or two, maybe. Not much longer than that. But if you're askin' 'cause you think she had somethin' to do with Carlton gettin' killed . . ."

"I'm just looking at all the possibilities, Mr. Elbridge. That's what you're paying me for, right?"

Gunner's client let him listen to another short stretch of silence, then said, "Yes. I guess it is." Making the concession sound like something that hurt him to his very core.

"One more thing before I let you go. The name Ray Crumley mean anything to you, by any chance?"

"Ray Crumley? No. Who's he?"

"Nobody, really. Just another dead man. I'll talk to you again tomorrow, Mr. Elbridge."

Without issuing a formal good-bye, Gunner hung up the phone.

"I'm sorry, Mr. Gunner, but I told you yesterday," Bob Zemic said. "Unless you have a court order for me, I can't allow you to see our surveillance tapes. It just isn't going to happen."

He was sitting in his office at the Beverly Hills Westmore, hands clasped firmly together atop the blotter on his desk, striking the ultimate pose of a man who was never in a thousand years going to change his mind.

"I understand your reluctance here, Mr. Zemic, and I admire your dedication to duty," Gunner said, smiling in lieu of breaking the security man's neck. "But I would think in light of Mr. Crumley's murder—"

"Please leave what happened to Ray out of this," Zemic snapped. "It's immaterial to this discussion."

"I think that remains to be seen. In fact, I feel just the opposite. That's why I'm asking you again to let me see the tape you say he had. So I can establish with some certainty whether or not it had some bearing on Mr. Crumley's death."

"That's not for you to determine, Mr. Gunner. That's for the police to determine. And as I already told you, the two detectives who were here earlier this morning had no interest in viewing the tape. At least, they didn't ask to."

He was talking about La Porte and Chin, who had apparently been by to see him just over an hour ago.

"They don't know what I know," Gunner said.

"And that is?"

"That Crumley may have been using a copy of the tape to blackmail somebody. Somebody who just might be responsible for both his murder and Mr. Elbridge's."

"Except that Mr. Elbridge wasn't murdered," Zemic said. "He committed suicide."

"That is what everyone originally thought, yes. Even me. But it's funny—the more I hear some people say it, the more I think they're afraid to believe anything else."

Zemic sat up, readjusted the torque holding his hands together. "Was that an accusation of some kind?"

"An accusation? No. It was a cry for help. I need your assistance here, Mr. Zemic. I have a job to do, same as you, and it's got nothing to do with helping anybody sue the Beverly Hills Westmore for negligence. You've got to believe that."

"Do I?"

"You do if you don't like the idea of somebody getting away with murder. Possibly even *two* murders. And I suggest to you that that may be exactly what happens if you record over or otherwise destroy that tape before the police and I have had a chance to examine it."

"There is nothing on that tape to indicate Mr. Elbridge's death was anything but a suicide," Zemic said. "I reviewed it, remember? I know."

"I seem to recall you saying you only scanned through it. That it was basically four hours of an empty hallway, so why watch the whole thing?"

Zemic flushed, having failed to anticipate this flaw in his own argument. "I think I saw enough of it to make a reasonable judgment of its contents," he said firmly.

"Okay. So what did Crumley want with it, then? He risked his job to take it home for two days, then lied about having it when you found it missing. Why? Why would he do all that over a tape with nothing on it?"

"I didn't say there was nothing on it," Zemic said, becoming increasingly irritable. "I said there was nothing on it relevant to Mr. Elbridge's suicide."

"Say again?"

"What I'm trying to say is that there may indeed have been something on the tape Ray was interested in, but not because he was looking to blackmail anyone. I don't think that was Ray's intent at all."

"Then?"

Zemic paused, obviously conflicted. "Ray was a bit of a voyeur, Mr. Gunner. From time to time, he—we—would see things on our surveillance monitors here that piqued his interest. I don't have to explain what kinds of things I'm referring to, do I?"

Gunner shook his head. The picture was fairly clear.

"Guests here at the Westmore are generally very discreet people, but sometimes they forget themselves. If the tape we're talking about happened to depict someone in a, shall we say, compromising position, it's possible Ray may have found that worth a second look. I'm not saying that's what happened, of course, but it is a possibility."

It was better than that, Gunner thought. It was as good an explanation for Crumley's behavior as any, and almost twice as likely.

"I can see that, sure," Gunner said to Zemic, trying to sound infinitely reasonable. "Unfortunately, I can't afford to simply assume that was the case. In order to be certain Ray's motives for taking the tape had nothing to do with the events I'm investigating, I've got to know for a fact what those motives were or weren't. So I'd like to suggest a compromise, if I may."

Zemic raised an eyebrow, instantly suspicious. "Compromise?"

"Let's forget about my viewing the tape for the moment. *You* view it again, instead. In its entirety this time. Then call me and let me know what you find. Can you do that for me, at least?"

After a long pause, Zemic said, "I suppose."

"Good. Think you could get around to it this afternoon sometime?"

"I can try. I'll run it during my lunch hour." He shook his head. "But it's not going to do you any good. I'm not going to find anything to support the idea that your Mr. Elbridge was murdered."

Zemic smiled. Just in case Gunner was thinking he was turning soft, or something.

Later, over a huge breakfast at Rae's, a popular Santa Monica diner on Pico just west of the Santa Monica Freeway, Gunner decided to look up yet another old friend, Fetch Bennett. He had worked the Carlton Elbridge case for two days now, and it was time to answer a question he knew he should have addressed long ago: Had the "murder" of Carlton Elbridge even been humanly possible?

The police had already decided that it wasn't, as had Bob Zemic. Both Kevin Frick and Zemic seemed completely satisfied that Elbridge's locked hotel room had ruled out any chance of foul play. And maybe they were right. Maybe there was no way for someone to enter a Westmore room, commit a murder made to look like suicide, then lock the door behind when exiting, all without being detected. But if it could be done—if the mechanics for such a convoluted act actually existed—Bill "Fetch" Bennett would know how to do it.

Because Fetch was a thief par excellence. He'd been a retiree from the business now for almost ten years, but the big man still knew more about breaking and entering than half the people presently practicing the discipline. Whenever Gunner needed instruction in the methods of gaining entrance to places equipped to keep him out, Fetch was the first person he called.

Standing a shoeless six-foot-seven and weighing almost twice what Gunner did at a whopping 375, Fetch was now a security troubleshooter for Sunrise Suites, a West Coast motel chain that catered primarily to the business trade, headquartered in a cylindrical glass office tower just off the 405 Freeway in Torrance.

"Hell, man, that's easy," Fetch said after Gunner had run the setup out at the Westmore down for him. The white-haired giant had a small office on the third floor that barely allowed him to bend either arm at the elbow without punching a hole in the wall.

"Okay. Tell me why," Gunner said.

"What you're talkin' about is what they call a swing bar tie-down. Door has to be closed to engage it, and you can only engage it from the inside."

"That's right."

"Unless you've got some piano wire, or a long human hair. A hair would actually work best."

"A hair?"

Fetch laughed and nodded. "You tie the end of it around the bar, step outside, and slowly close the door behind you. Then, just before the door latches shut, you pull the hair, swing the bar closed, and snap the hair off so nobody'll find it. Piece of piano wire would work too, like I said, but you'd probably have to leave some of that behind."

Gunner stepped through it several times in his mind, realized it could have been done exactly that way. "Damn," he said.

Fetch just laughed again.

"Could the dead bolt crank be rigged the same way?"

"You mean to lock from the outside?"

Gunner nodded.

"Sure. Why not? That'd just take a little more time and care, that's all.

Door would have to be all the way closed, and the clearance for the hair through the jamb would be tight. And you'd probably have to use a little piece of tape to keep the hair secured to the crank so it didn't come off till you were ready for it to come off. But you could do it, sure."

"Would it take a pro, or could an amateur do it?"

"An amateur like you, you mean? An amateur could do it, I guess, long as they knew what they were doin'."

Gunner asked Fetch how long he thought the process would take, once the person doing it was standing outside the closed door.

"For a nonpro? Could take a minute, could take a little longer. But a pro like me could get it done inside of thirty seconds, easy."

Gunner fell silent, trying to picture Desmond Joy or Danee Elbridge standing outside the Digga's hotel room door, following the course of action Fetch had just described. It was easier to see a smoothy like Joy exhibiting the patience for such a thing, but that didn't mean the widow Elbridge was incapable; anybody could muster sixty seconds of calm and concentration, they felt the stakes were high enough.

"What's this all about, Gunner?" Fetch asked, too curious now to respect his friend's code of discretion a moment longer.

Gunner shook his head and smiled. "Sorry, Fetch, but I'm gonna have to keep the lid on this one for a while. Not that I think you'd spread it around, but if the wrong people hear I'm working it, they could make life fairly complicated for me."

Fetch shrugged, taking no offense. "Fair enough. You can tell me all about it when it's over, then."

Gunner shook the big man's hand and promised he would do just that.

It wasn't often that the U.S. Weather Service got something right, but they'd called Wednesday in Los Angeles perfectly. They'd forecast temperatures in the L.A. basin in the high eighties, and every bank message board

Gunner passed on his way from Fetch Bennett's office to Coretta Trayburn's home in Northridge said they'd only underestimated by four or five degrees. They called what they did science, meteorologists, but Gunner couldn't see the science in it; predicting a hot and smoggy day in Los Angeles in the middle of July took about as much technical expertise as hammering a nail into a two-by-four.

Right up until the moment he pulled the Cobra into her driveway, Gunner wasn't sure why he wanted to talk to Carlton Elbridge's mother before the young man's wife. Thanks to her ex-husband, he already had a good idea who Coretta Trayburn would say she believed was responsible for the "murder" of her son—Bume Webb, naturally—and it didn't seem likely that she would offer him any proof of that theory, or suggest any alternatives to it. Danee Elbridge, on the other hand, seemed to promise much more in the way of new and useful info relative to Gunner's investigation. Carlton and his mother may indeed have been close, but he and Danee had been sharing a home, and a bed, and that was a level of daily intimacy with the deceased no one else could claim. If Danee Elbridge didn't know how or even if her husband had been murdered, it was doubtful that anyone did.

Still, Gunner went to see Trayburn first. One, because he wanted a look at the so-called suicide note both her ex-husband and Kevin Frick of the Beverly Hills PD claimed she was in possession of, and two, because he was anxious to see for himself if she was in fact the closed-minded, money-grubbing shrew Benny Elbridge said she was.

That she looked the part was never in question. Just as she had on her brief television interviews, Coretta Trayburn in the flesh exuded all the charm and sensitivity of a rusty hacksaw blade. She was taller than most men Gunner knew, and her lean build almost bordered on the skeletal. But there was nothing frail about her. From her high-cheekboned face to her narrow ankles, she looked like someone you could pound with a mallet for an hour and only get tired for your trouble.

At Gunner's ring of the bell, she came to the door herself—a sure sign of a woman who lived alone and had no qualms about doing so—and led him into her living room with a minimum of discussion. He'd arrived halfway expecting to have her door slammed in his face, but had only had to state his name and the nature of his business to win her approval. Initially, anyway.

"Who you workin' for, Mr. Gunner?" she asked as soon as they were both seated. He couldn't remember a cop ever asking a question more directly.

"I thought you might hit me with that question at the door," he said.

"I could have. But you looked like a good man to me. I didn't think I needed to know everything about you right away."

"You could tell I was a good man that quickly?"

"I can spot the bad ones faster than that. Answer my question, Mr. Gunner."

"My client was kind of hoping to remain anonymous, Ms. Trayburn. Would you mind if I just said it's somebody who, like you, believes there may be more to your son's death than suicide, and left it at that?"

She considered the offer carefully, her eyes trying to read him from the inside out. Finally, she said, "All right. I think I can guess who it is, anyway. Tell me what I can do to help you."

"You believe your son was murdered, and that it was Bume Webb who murdered him. Is that correct?"

"Yes."

"You have any proof of that theory, Ms. Trayburn?"

"No. Would we be sitting here now if I did?"

Gunner smiled, rightfully embarrassed, and said, "You're right. That was a stupid question. I'll see if I can make the next one a little smarter."

Trayburn folded her hands in her lap and waited for him to try.

"The prevailing train of thought seems to be that Bume had Carlton killed to keep him from abandoning Bume's record label, Body Count. Is that your feeling too?"

"It is."

"Yet the two of them were supposed to be quite close."

Trayburn had no response to that.

"What, that isn't true? Bume and Carlton weren't close friends?"

"A 'friend' is what the Devil always pretends to be before he puts the knife in your back, Mr. Gunner. Surely you know that."

"Yes, ma'am, I do. But—"

"My baby's dead because he didn't understand that. He thought a smile was just a smile, and that everyone who showed him one meant him no harm. He wouldn't listen to me when I tried to tell him that that monster he was workin' for was no good. He thought I was just bein' jealous."

Gunner could see she was building up to a good-sized outrage; all he had to do was slip up once, give her some excuse to cut loose with it.

"I don't mean to suggest you aren't right about Bume, Ms. Trayburn," he said. "But my understanding is that Carlton's decision to leave Body Count hadn't really been made yet."

"So?"

"So Carlton was practically the last major rapper Bume had left under contract. In fact, he was all that was holding Body Count afloat, by most accounts. If his departure had been a done deal, I could see how Bume might've thought killing him would serve some purpose. But before then? When there was still a chance Carlton might re-up?" Gunner shook his head. "Why would Bume want to do that?"

Trayburn almost smiled at the inanity she found in the question. "You've never met Bume Webb, have you, Mr. Gunner?" she asked.

"No. Can't say that I have."

"When I called him the Devil a moment ago, I bet you thought I was exaggerating. But I wasn't. Bume Webb is as purely evil as any man who has ever walked this earth. He has one love—*money*—and for that love, there is nothing, and no one, he will not destroy. Do you hear what I'm tellin' you?"

"Yes ma'am. I only meant—"

"It doesn't matter what you meant. When I tell you it was Bume Webb who killed my son, you can take my word for it."

"Carlton had no other enemies outside of Bume?"

"Enemies? Of course he had enemies. Young man with money always has enemies. But that don't mean any of Carlton's had the backbone to kill him."

"No, but—"

"Most of 'em are just children, same as Carlton was. All talk, and no action. They like to act big and bad, but that's all they can do. Act."

"You talking about other rappers?"

"Yes."

"Like 2DaddyLarge, for instance?"

Trayburn made a small sound deep in her throat, as if the name alone were something beneath her contempt. "2DaddyLarge," she said, sneering. "That little fool's the biggest coward of 'em all."

"Yeah?"

"Oh yes. He likes to carry himself like a killer, sure, especially when he's got that so-called 'crew' of his all around. But soon as he finds out you aren't afraid of him, that you aren't gonna run off just 'cause he said boo to you, he don't want any part of you anymore. I know, Mr. Gunner, 'cause I sent 'im runnin' with his tail between his legs once myself."

"You did?"

"Sure did. It was last year in Detroit, at the Soul Train awards show. They nominated Carlton for three awards, and he took me out there with 'im. He was gettin' ready to go on backstage when 2Daddy got in his face, started yellin' and screamin' about what him and his boys were gonna do to Carlton when the show was over. I stepped in between the two of 'em, told that crazy fool he'd better turn his ass around and leave my boy alone before I put my high heels in his behind, and I wish you'd've seen how fast he shut up, went on back to his dressin' room like he had some sense."

Gunner smiled and said, "You don't think your being a woman could've had something to do with that?"

Trayburn laughed outright this time. "Are you serious? These children don't have any respect for women, Mr. Gunner. They think we're all bitches and 'ho's, they'd just as soon knock one of us down as hold our hand. Only reason 2Daddy ran off that night was 'cause he knew I was gonna rip his eyes out of his head if he didn't. Not because I was a woman, or a mother, or anything else."

"And that's what leads you to believe he couldn't have been responsible for Carlton's death. The fact that he ran away from *you* once."

"Yes."

Gunner paused, forming the language of what he was about to say next with great care. "I'm sorry, Ms. Trayburn, but I'm afraid that places you in a very distinct minority. Most people I've talked to up to now say 2Daddy was more than capable of murdering your son. Maybe not in the way it would've had to be done, but—"

"I don't care what other people think, Mr. Gunner. I know what I know. And what I know is, 2DaddyLarge was neither brave enough nor stupid enough to ever touch my son."

"So all the threats you say he made against Carlton at the Soul Train awards were just talk."

"Yes."

"And they were precipitated by what? Did something get him started, or . . ."

"Did something get 'im started? No, didn't nothin' get 'im started! The boy was just bein' evil, that's all. Lookin' to shake Carlton up before he went on stage, so maybe he'd go out there and embarrass himself or somethin'."

"That was it? He was just being evil?"

"Yes. That was all."

"It didn't have something to do with Danee?"

He could have slapped her across the face and angered her less. Her eyes caught fire and her back stiffened, and Gunner was certain the order to leave was coming, when she said, "No. It certainly did not."

"The question seems to have upset you."

"It upset me because I know why you asked it. Someone told you that

Danee had been messin' round with 2Daddy behind Carlton's back. Isn't that so?"

Gunner didn't answer, preferring to see where Trayburn would go from here on her own.

"Of course it is. That boy's been spreadin' that lie around for months now, you couldn't've helped but hear it from somebody."

Gunner paused a moment, proceeding with caution, and said, "Are you sure it *is* a lie, Ms. Trayburn?"

Trayburn affixed her gaze on Gunner's own, spoke with an even timbre that had the strength of tempered steel. "I have never been more sure of anything in my life," she said. "Dance's been through with that fool for years, Mr. Gunner. She doesn't want nothin' more to do with 'im."

"You don't think—"

"No. I don't. Danee has been the finest wife my son could've ever asked for, she's been faithful and loyal to him to a fault."

It was an odd thing to hear a son's overly possessive mother say about her daughter-in-law, but there was no question in Gunner's mind that she believed it.

"And Carlton? What about him?"

"Pardon me?"

"Was he faithful to Danee to a fault? Or was that strictly a one-way street?"

Trayburn rubbed her hands together in her lap as she glared at him, scrubbing them clean beneath an invisible tap. "Carlton was a fine young man, Mr. Gunner," she said, "but he wasn't perfect. He had flaws and weaknesses, just like anybody else."

"Meaning . . ."

"Meaning I'm not going to be the hypocrite you think I am, sit here and tell you my son didn't sometimes forget he was a married man."

"I see. And Danee was okay with that?"

"No woman is ever 'okay' with it. But the good ones learn to deal with it over time. It's either that, or learn to be alone." She smiled sadly, said, "Are we about through? I think I've answered all the questions I feel like answering right now."

"I only have two more."

"Yes?"

Gunner asked her if the name Ray Crumley sounded familiar to her, and she shook her head in response, having betrayed no sign of discomfiture in the process. Afterward, he said, "Final question, then. It's my understanding you have the suicide note your son wrote before he died. Is that correct?"

"It's not a suicide note," Trayburn said sharply.

"You're right. I shouldn't have called it that. What I meant to say—"

"It's a rap poem, that's all. I told the police that a thousand times, but they wouldn't listen to me."

"Do you think I could have a look at it? Would that be possible?"

"Why? I told you, it's just a poem."

"Yes ma'am, I know. But I'd like to judge that for myself, if that wouldn't be a problem."

Trayburn shook her head, said, "I'm sorry, no. That note is the last thing my son ever wrote, Mr. Gunner. I might release it to the public someday, but for now, I'd like to keep what's in it private."

"Even if it could help determine what really happened to Carlton?"

"I already know what happened to Carlton. And I think you do too. You're just pretending not to so you can keep Desmond on the clock."

"Desmond?"

"That's who's payin' you, isn't it? Desmond Joy?"

Finding the assumption intriguing, Gunner asked, "What makes you think that?"

Trayburn smiled knowingly. "Well, you aren't workin' for free, are you? Who else has got the money to hire somebody like you to prove my boy was murdered?"

It was a question Gunner should have long ago thought to ask himself, but somehow never had. He showed Trayburn a smile of his own, hoping to mask his embarrassment, and said, "I like the way you think, Ms. Trayburn." He took a business card from his wallet, reached across the space between them to hand it to her. "You change your mind about showing me that note, give me a call. Could be there's more to it than you realize."

Carlton Elbridge's mother rolled the card around in one hand as she studied it, looking on both sides for the hidden strings she suspected were attached, and nodded before Gunner found his own way back to her front door.

eight

The gates leading onto the grounds of Carlton Elbridge's Hollywood Hills estate on Woodrow Wilson Drive were the kind no one ever left open, so when Gunner found them standing that way later that afternoon, he considered it a bad omen.

And more were yet to come. No one responded to his calls from the gateside intercom, and his drive up the red brick driveway to the front door of the mammoth Tudor home went completely unimpeded. The bronze Lexus coupe Danee Elbridge had tried to run him over with the day before sat nearby, its hood as cold to the touch as the water in the ornate stone fountain that graced the front lawn. Gunner looked to the winged female nude atop the fountain for clues as to what was going on here, but the figure remained silent, unmoving.

"Thanks," Gunner said.

He turned to start for the portico when the first shot rang out, a slight buzzing noise filling his left ear as the bullet passed within a few inches of his head.

"What the f—!"

He ducked for cover behind the Lexus, reached under his left arm for a Ruger that wasn't there as his attacker fired on him again, succeeding only in punching an ugly hole in the crown of the Lexus's left front quarter panel. Less than twenty-four hours earlier, Gunner would have had the Ruger with him, but not today; he'd put the gun back in its drawer at home the previous evening upon learning the giant who had had Mickey so spooked was only Jolly Mokes. One day, Gunner chided himself now, he'd learn to carry the damn thing twenty-four/seven just for occasions such as this.

"Hold your goddamn fire!" he shouted, trying to give his voice all the authoritative power he could raise above his fear. "I'm unarmed!"

But a third round sounded all the same, shattered the Lexus's side glass just over his head after entering the car's interior through the roof. A clear and unsettling indication that the gunman he was facing was perched above him, on a second-floor balcony, from where he was no doubt at least partially visible.

"Hey! I said I'm unarmed!" Gunner barked again.

"Bullshit!"

A fourth shot followed the tiny, childlike cry, struck nothing but air and green grass this time. Gunner poked his head up, caught a quick glimpse of the diminutive black woman leaning over a balcony railing, both hands clutched tightly around the grips of a silver-plated automatic: Danee Elbridge.

"I'm telling you the truth, Ms. Elbridge! I'm not armed!" Gunner steeled himself, gradually raised one empty hand into the air, then the second, jerked both back simultaneously when the Digga's widow fired two more rounds in his direction, hit the driveway an inch from his right foot with the first, the hood of the Lexus with the second. "Shit! Put the goddamn gun down already!"

He was still alive only because the lady couldn't shoot straight, but that was a shortcoming she could eventually overcome, if he gave her enough chances. He quickly ran over his options in his mind, realized he had only two: stay where he was and hope she'd keep missing him forever, or make a run for it, either away from the house and out the main gate the same way he'd come in, or toward the house and the safety of the portico beneath her.

Jumping back into the topless Cobra to try and save his car as well as his skin was out of the question.

As impatient as she was silent, Danee Elbridge fired her silver automatic at him again, actually scored a hit this time: the bullet grazed Gunner's left calf, ripped a hole in his pants leg as it gouged a painful if benign trench through his flesh. He yelped, furious, and instantly made his decision: he would go for the portico. If he could get that far now.

He slid quickly toward the rear of the Lexus, head down and body low, and provoked the woman above him to fire three more rounds at him wildly in a desperate effort to halt his advance. None hit anything but the Lexus, the resale value of which was plummeting by the second. When the last bullet zinged off the trunk lid, Gunner made his move, sprinted as fast as his bad left leg would allow through the space between the Lexus and the Cobra, up onto the front porch. He had to dodge two more slugs to get there, but he managed to make it without suffering any further injury.

Now out of reach of Danee Elbridge's vision, he moved immediately to the front door, tried to push it open. But it was locked. He could hear her footsteps pounding along the floor above him as she ran, no doubt hoping to race downstairs and catch him breaking in. Which of course, he had no intention of doing. Just as he had no intention of fleeing, the prospect of getting shot in the back being as real here as it had been down in the carport, if she decided to come out after him. And he had no doubt she would. She wasn't running down those stairs inside to escape; she was coming to get him, looking to put a permanent end to whatever threat she thought he represented.

Gunner had all of four seconds to think of something to do with her when she got there.

He eventually stood directly in front of the door, and waited. It was a solid slab of white, ornately paneled but windowless, so he couldn't be seen standing there from within, except through the narrow decorative windows on both sides. If she chose to peer out through one or the other before exiting . . .

But she didn't. The gun and her eagerness to use it made her careless, encouraged her to go straight to the door and yank it open. The second it cleared the jamb, Gunner shoved on it with both hands, drove its weight into the face of the unprepared woman behind it. Wood and bone met with a loud bang, and Danee Elbridge hit the white tile floor on her back as if struck by a speeding Peterbilt, the automatic in her left hand spitting one final round into a nearby wall. Gunner stepped forward quickly, snatched the gun from her listless grasp before it could go off again. The Digga's widow never even knew he was there.

He released the clip of the lady's weapon—a .45 caliber Smith & Wesson, he noted—and put it in his left-hand trouser pocket before stuffing the body of the gun into the front of his waistband, taking a good long look at the woman fighting unconsciousness at his feet as he did so. She was the same short-haired, caramel-colored beauty he'd seen flying out of the Bad Rock recording studio parking lot the day before, only now she was marred by a growing lump on her forehead, and her wardrobe was far more casual. She was wearing a peach baby doll negligee as transparent as water, and there was nothing whatsoever beneath it but the skin she'd been born in. Had she not been trying to kill him, he might have noticed this last about her right away.

Bravely refusing the opportunity to pass out, the widow Elbridge eventually brought a hand to her head, moaned an unladylike curse, and gazed up at the black man standing over her like someone trying to read a newspaper through a dirty screen door.

"Who the fuck are you?" she asked, fighting to get the words out.

"I would've thought you knew. Or do you try to kill just anybody who dares to drop in on you unannounced?"

"I *asked* you a question."

"My name's Aaron Gunner. I'm a private investigator." He got his wallet out, turned it open to his license, and handed it down to her. He glanced around the house as she studied it, said, "No kids around today?"

"They're at my mother's. Not that it's any of your bus'ness." She looked his credentials over the way she might an advertisement for toothpaste, pushed his wallet right back at him. "Bullshit," she said.

"Bullshit?"

"You heard me. Bullshit. What the hell would a private investigator want with me?" She finally saw how much trouble he was having keeping his eyes trained on her face, tucked her legs up underneath her and covered her breasts with her arms. Accomplishing very little, actually, other than to draw more attention to herself.

Gunner smiled as he put his wallet away, said, "I've been hired by a friend of your late husband to look into the circumstances of his death. Either to confirm it really was a suicide, or to produce evidence it was a homicide."

"Homicide? You mean murder?"

Gunner nodded. "You don't think that's possible?"

She didn't answer the question, just let her eyes bore into his for a long, painful moment. "I don't believe you," she said.

"I can see that. But maybe if we got you up off the floor, found some ice for your head, you'd be a little more inclined to."

"I don't need any fuckin' ice."

"I respectfully disagree. That bump's changing colors by the minute. Come on, let's get up, find our way to the kitchen."

He extended his hand, let her take all the time she wanted to think the offer over, accept it in the spirit given. When at last she did, she stopped at a hallway closet to grab a powder-blue silk housecoat, tossed it on over her immodest dress before leading her guest past an elaborately furnished dining room into the largest kitchen he had ever seen. It was all iceberg-white with marble trim, and a small yacht could have been parked within it without marring any of the cabinet doors. Only the island in the center of the Mexican-tiled floor bearing a six-burner stove and a giant butcher-block surface would have had to be moved to accomplish the feat, and that with nothing less than a fifty-foot crane.

With Gunner's hand on her left arm to keep her steady, Danee Elbridge went straight to the brushed-aluminum refrigerator, reached for the handle on its freezer door. But Gunner stepped in to stop her, said, "Here. I think you'd better let me."

Shortly thereafter, the two of them sat in the Elbridge living room to talk, she holding a damp dish towel filled with ice cubes to her head, he holding the same to the wound on his left calf.

"If this leaves a mark, I'll kill you," she said, grimacing.

"You already tried that. Twice. Maybe you should try to kill somebody else for a change."

"What do you mean, twice? I ain't never seen you before in my life."

"Actually, you have. First time was yesterday, out at Bad Rock. I was pulling in, you were pulling out, somewhere in the neighborhood of seventy miles an hour, as I recall. You don't remember?"

She studied him more closely, smiled through her pain. "That was you?"

"That was me. Desmond say something to insult you?"

"Desmond? What's Des—" She stopped, getting a sudden thought. "Oh. I get it. That's the friend of Cee's you was talkin' about workin' for a minute ago. Desmond."

"Tell you what. Let's leave who I'm working for for later, talk right now about who you thought I was when I first arrived. That okay with you?"

The Digga's widow moved the makeshift ice pack around on her forehead, said, "I don't know what you're talkin' about."

"Come on. You were layin' down ground fire out there like a Huey tryin' to take out a bridge. People don't throw ammo around like that unless they've got a specific target in mind."

"You were trespassin' on my property! I don't have a right to protect myself?"

"Sure you do. Only, if that's all you'd been interested in, protecting yourself, you'd have given me some chance to escape. Told me to get my black ass back in my car and get the hell out of here, rather than shoot at me like somebody you needed *dead,* not gone." When she acted as if he had to be talking to himself, Gunner went on: "You were expecting somebody else, Mrs. Elbridge. Somebody who either scares the living hell out of you, or makes you see some serious red. One or the other."

Still, Danee Elbridge refused to speak.

"If you're in trouble, I might be able to help. You never know."

"Help? Why should *you* wanna help *me*?"

"Call it a hobby of mine. Sticking my neck out for beautiful, half-dressed women in distress. And you are in distress, aren't you?"

The Digga's widow teetered on the brink of lying, decided to nod her head instead, tears pooling up in her eyes.

"Why don't you tell me what kind?"

"I got a nigga tryin' to get in my pants don't wanna take no for an answer. All right?"

"You mean 2DaddyLarge?"

Danee Elbridge blinked at him incredulously. "How did you know?"

"I haven't had a conversation in three days in which his name hasn't been mentioned at some point. And you two were a couple at one time, right? Before Carlton came along?"

"We weren't never a couple. We weren't anything. I went out with his ugly ass a couple times, that's all. He wants to make a thing outa that, that's his problem."

"Only he doesn't see it that way."

"No. Nigga's hardheaded." She started crying. "I tell 'im I don't wanna be with 'im, that it ain't nothin' personal, but he don't listen. He says we're gonna be together whether I like it or not."

Gunner watched her find a tissue in one of the pockets of her robe and blow her nose gracelessly into it. "Is 2Daddy here now? In Los Angeles?"

She nodded. "He's waitin' for me at some hotel somewhere. He said the name, but I don't remember it."

"You talked to him today?"

"He got my cellular number somehow, called me in the car on my way home from the gym, said he was gonna send one of his boys over to pick me up, take me to see 'im. I told 'im I wouldn't go, but he just laughed."

"So *that's* who you thought I was. His boy."

"Hell, what would *you* think? Strange nigga comes crashin' through your front gate . . ."

"Actually, the gate was open. You didn't leave it that way?"

She shook her head, re-creating her arrival in her mind. "No. But then, it ain't been workin' right lately. It's supposed to close automatically when you pull in, but sometimes it don't. I shoulda looked back to check it, but I was so crazy . . ."

"Hello?" a voice called out from the direction of the front door.

Gunner and Danee Elbridge turned to see a pair of LAPD uniforms step tentatively into the room, sidearms drawn, faces fixed with nervous concentration. The lead man, a red-nosed white man older than his black partner by at least ten years, studied the pair before him, said, "A neighbor reported shots being fired at this address. And there's a car out front all full of holes."

"That's my car," Danee Elbridge said. "It was all a mistake. I thought—"

"You the owner of the house, ma'am?"

"Yes. This man—"

He cut her off again, still holding his weapon at the ready, said, "And you, sir? Who are you?"

Gunner told him, kicking off what turned out to be a thirty-minute break in his conversation with the Digga's widow. The story he and she offered the two officers was disjointed and incomplete, but in the end, the uniforms didn't have much choice but to buy it and retreat. They were able to confirm that Danee Elbridge was indeed the owner of the home, and that the gun she had allegedly used to do all the shooting was registered in her name. And she was insistent no harm had been done, the ugly bump on her head notwithstanding.

When they were at last alone again to pick up where they'd left off, Danee Elbridge and her guest resumed their original positions on her living room couch, sans the makeshift ice packs, and decided after some consideration that their last subject of discussion had been 2DaddyLarge, and the man he had promised was on his way to bring Danee to him. By force, if necessary.

"Funny thing is, I almost gave my shit up," she confessed, opening the collar of her bathrobe slightly to draw Gunner's eyes to the negligee beneath it. "I mean, I thought maybe if I finally let the nigga have a taste, didn't do nothin' to make it special or anything, he'd see it wasn't workin' and lose int'rest. I was all dressed and ready to go . . . and then I saw your car comin' up the driveway. An' I said uh-uh, fuck that. I done held that motherfucker off this long, I ain't gonna just bend over for 'im now."

"Sounds like maybe someone should have a little talk with him," Gunner said. "See if they can't encourage him to look for companionship elsewhere."

"You mean *you*? Man, why should he listen to you? He never listened to Cee, and Cee was my husband."

"True. But maybe Cee never managed to catch him alone. I hear 2Daddy's a lot more agreeable when his homies *aren't* around than when they *are*."

The Digga's widow laughed. "Ain't that the truth."

"Your mother-in-law, in fact, seems to believe he's completely harmless."

"Coretta? She said that?"

"In so many words. I asked her if she thought 2Daddy could've had anything to do with Carlton's death, and she all but laughed in my face at the thought."

Danee Elbridge's expression darkened, told him he'd struck a chord with this last.

"What do *you* think about that idea?"

"What idea?"

"That 2Daddy may have been involved in your husband's death some-how."

"I think it's crazy. Cee committed suicide."

"You sound quite sure about that."

"I am."

"Mind if I ask why?"

"Why? Because that's all it coulda been, suicide. All these people sayin' Cee was murdered don't know what the hell they talkin' about."

"Because?"

"Because they wasn't there, that's why."

"You mean at the hotel. To see the note he left behind."

The Digga's widow tipped her head slightly to one side, the better to view him with renewed distrust. "Coretta told you about Cee's note?"

"No. Joy did."

"But he didn't tell you what it said, right?"

Gunner almost had to laugh. "No. And neither did your mother-in-law, if that was going to be your next question. Would you like to be the first to clue me in?"

Danee Elbridge just shook her head. Greatly relieved.

"No. I didn't think you would," Gunner said.

"Hey, I'm sorry, Mr. . . . . what'd you say your name was?"

"Gunner. Aaron Gunner."

"I'm sorry, Mr. Gunner, but that's just how it is. Wasn't nothin' in that note you or anybody else needs to know about."

"No, apparently not. At least, that's what everyone who's ever seen it keeps telling me, aside from Ray Crumley, of course. Did you know poor Ray?"

If she did, her face never showed it. "Who?"

"Ray Crumley. He was the security man at the Beverly Hills Westmore who discovered Carlton's body along with Joy. You never met him?"

She shook her head again, said, "No. I mighta seen 'im at the hotel that day, but . . . we didn't talk or anything. Least, I don't remember talkin' to 'im. Why? What's he gotta do with me?"

"It's beginning to look like he took home a hotel surveillance tape that may have shown someone entering or exiting your husband's room the night he died, kept it a couple of days, maybe even made a copy before returning it. I'd tell you why he'd want to do something like that, except I never got the chance to ask him. He's dead."

"Dead?"

"As in murdered in his apartment last night, yeah. Somebody broke in and trashed the place, then beat him to death when he discovered them there."

A short, painful silence ensued as he waited for the Digga's widow to offer some response.

"So? I already told you I didn't know the man. Why you tellin' *me* all this?"

She was either telling the truth, or faking it better than almost anyone Gunner had ever seen. "Because I was hoping you could tell me what it all means," the investigator said. "Crumley's supervisor says the surveillance tape he took was recorded between four and eight o'clock p.m. that Saturday, more than four hours before your husband was determined to have died. It should have been worthless in terms of proving he was murdered, and therefore useless as a means for blackmail, yet it's my guess somebody killed Crumley trying to retrieve the tape and keep its contents secret. The question is, why?"

"I don't know," Danee Elbridge said.

"Beverly Hills PD tells me *you* visited your husband's room that night. Around what time was that?"

"I don't remember."

"You don't remember if it was between the hours of four and eight p.m.?"

"It coulda been. I told you, I don't remember."

"Do you remember if Carlton had any other visitors around that time besides yourself?"

A full five seconds went by, then: "No. I was only over there for a few minutes, I didn't see who else came by."

"That isn't quite true, Mrs. Elbridge. Your husband had at least two other visitors that night the police say you were aware of. Both of them were female."

"Okay. So he had a couple bitches in his room 'fore I came by. What about it?"

"Could *they* have been there between the hours of four and eight that evening?"

She held on to her answer like it was something he was unworthy of, finally mumbled, "Maybe. I'm not sure."

"The police say you knew one of the ladies by name."

Another long, angry pause. "Yeah."

"And that name was?"

"Antoinetta."

"Antoinetta. Antoinetta what?"

"I don't know the bitch's last name."

"How about the other young lady?"

The Digga's widow shook her head. "I didn't know her. That was the first time I ever seen her."

"But you knew Antoinetta."

"Yes."

"In what way? She a personal friend, or . . ."

Danee Elbridge laughed bitterly, shook her head. "See? I knew it. You ain't no goddamn investigator! Look at these questions you askin'!"

"She was in your husband's hotel room the night he died. She might know something—"

"Get outa my house, Mr. Gunner. Now!" She stood up, pointed a long-nailed finger at the door. "Take your ass back to whatever newspaper, or magazine, or TV show you workin' for, and don't ever come back around here!"

"You're jumping to false conclusions, Mrs. Elbridge," Gunner said, getting to his own feet. "I'm not a reporter."

"Bullshit!" She stepped up to him, pushed him full in the chest with both hands. "Get out!"

"Take it easy!"

"I said get out!" She pushed him again.

"Look—how about if I told you who my client is? Would you believe I'm who I say I am then?"

"No! Get out!"

"I'm working for your father-in-law. Benny Elbridge," Gunner said.

Sometimes, given no other choice, you had to *give* a little love to *get* some.

"Say what?" Danee Elbridge asked, stunned.

"My client's Benny Elbridge. What, did I stutter the first time?"

"Cee's father? *That's* who you workin' for?"

"Yes. I don't—"

"Oh no. Now I *know* you' lyin'."

"Excuse me?"

"That old man ain't got a dime to his name! How the hell's he gonna hire somebody like you to do anything?"

Gunner didn't immediately know how to answer that. "I had the impression he was spending savings of some kind," he said.

"Savings?" Danee Elbridge laughed openly. "He ain't got no savings! Savings from what? Mr. Elbridge ain't held a job longer'n three weeks his whole life."

"What?"

"Aw, damn. You really *are* workin' for 'im, ain't you? Only you just now findin' out it's for *free*!" She was laughing in earnest now, indifferent to the possibility that Gunner might take offense.

But there was no way that he could, of course. He deserved to be ridiculed. For while he was actually innocent of the crime she believed him guilty of—taking a destitute man's case without seeing some money first— he *had* waited until now to wonder where else the five-hundred-dollar cash retainer Benny Elbridge had paid him two days ago could have come from, other than Elbridge's own pocket. It was an incredible example of shortsightedness that suddenly left him feeling quite stupid.

"Free or otherwise," he said, working hard to keep his embarrassment beneath the surface, "my services are being provided here at Mr. Elbridge's request. So does that buy me a little trust from you or not?"

Once again, she made him wait to hear her answer. "Depends on what you ask me."

"You mean you still won't talk about the note."

"No."

"Even if it might indicate that your husband *didn't* commit suicide?"

"It don't matter what it indicates. Cee wrote that note for me and his mama. Nobody else. What it says is personal, and that's how we gonna keep it. Personal."

Gunner wasn't satisfied with that answer—there was definitely something wrong about Danee Elbridge and Coretta Trayburn being equally protective of the note's contents, while completely at odds over what those contents said about Carlton Elbridge's death—but he could see the Digga's widow was not going to discuss the matter any further. So . . .

"And Antoinetta?"

"She ain't no friend of mine, and she wasn't none of Cee's. Only reason we even knew her is 'cause she likes to hang with some of the folks we party with. She's always lookin' for stars like Cee to get busy with so she can talk about bein' with 'em afterward."

"And the girl who was with her that night at the Westmore? You'd really never seen her before?"

"No. That was the first time."

"And Carlton never mentioned her name?"

She thought about it a moment before answering, said, "He mighta said her name once. I think he said it was Felicia. Felicia or Phyllis, somethin' like that."

Gunner gave her one of his business cards, said, "It would help me a great deal to talk to these ladies if I could find them. Maybe you could make a call or two for me, see if somebody knows their last names, or possibly where one of them lives."

Danee Elbridge took the card, showed him the courtesy of glancing at it briefly. "Why? They ain't gonna know nothin'."

"Still. I'd like to talk to them. You never know what they might have seen or heard that night that could be helpful."

"Helpful how? Cee killed himself, Mr. Gunner. Why the hell can't people just accept that and leave it alone?"

Gunner eased her gun out of the front of his pants and tossed it on the couch. "Only one reason, really, Mrs. Elbridge," he said. "Because it might not be true."

On his way out, Gunner stopped the Cobra just beyond the Elbridge estate's still-open gate, left the car parked in the driveway there to see if he could figure out why the gate wasn't closing. He was trying to pry open the system's control box just inside the grounds when a car horn began bleating incessantly out on the street, forcing him to come around to see who was making all the racket.

"Yo, man! Get the fuckin' car out the way!"

It was a young, needle-thin brother in a black-on-black Cadillac Eldorado, trying to turn up into Danee Elbridge's driveway. He was yelling through the car's open side windows from behind the wheel, giving Gunner a limited view of him, but even through the sun-dappled windshield Gunner could see he was bald, bony, and nowhere close to California's legal drinking age of twenty-one.

Gunner walked slowly over to the Cadillac's driver's-side window, peered down at the scowling kid inside. "Don't tell me, let me guess. 2Daddy sent you," he said.

"Yeah, that's right. And I'm late. So do like I tol' you and move the god-damn car!" He leaned on his horn again, hard, to prove how serious he was.

Gunner just looked at him.

"Look. You gonna move the muthafucka, or do I gotta move it for you?" the kid asked, throwing the Cadillac into gear.

"You don't wanna even think about that, june bug," Gunner said.

"June bug?"

The teenager leapt out of the car, moved to stand within an inch of Gunner's face. He was wearing a giant, fire engine–red DKNY jersey, baggy denim shorts that reached nearly to his ankles, and a gold neck chain he could have used to lock his bicycle to a lamppost. He pulled the hemline of the red jersey up high with his left hand, gave Gunner an unobstructed view of the black-skinned .45 automatic hanging loosely out of the waist-band of his pants.

"You must be lookin' to get served, old man," he snarled.

Gunner turned his head to one side and smiled—Damn, these baby hoodlums could be stupid!—then yanked the .45 out of the kid's pants, aimed it point-blank at his forehead before the kid even had a chance to blink.

"Oops," Gunner said.

2Daddy's errand boy was frozen stiff.

"You were standing too close," Gunner said. "And the piece was prac-tically falling out of your pants. You wanna show somebody you're strap-ping, youngblood, show 'em. Don't beg 'em to take your shit away from you."

The kid opened his mouth to speak, but the investigator shook his head, warned him against it.

"What's happening? Who—" Danee Elbridge asked. She'd apparently heard all the horn honking and come out to see what it meant. She was standing now beside Gunner's car, holding her robe closed tightly around her, absorbing the face-off going down in the street just outside her front gate. "Oh. It's *you.*"

Without taking his eyes off 2Daddy's friend, Gunner said, "Looks like your ride to 2Daddy's finally showed up. Maybe you recognize him."

"Yeah, I recognize 'im. That's Teepee. He ain't for shit."

"You better watch your mouth, bitch!" the kid screamed furiously.

"Hey, hey," Gunner said, tapping the nose of the .45 on the flat of the younger man's forehead. "Show the lady a little respect, huh?"

"Respect my ass! You muthafuckas're fuckin' with the wrong man! Dee say he wants the bitch brung to his crib, and that—"

Gunner slammed the butt of the .45 off the crown of his head, hard, dropped him semiconscious to the pavement like a spineless crash-test dummy. While the kid blinked up at the sky and bled, groaning softly, Gunner looked over at Danee Elbridge wryly and said, "I was getting kind of tired of all those 'fucks' and 'bitches.' Weren't you?"

nine

"Who the fuck is *this*?" 2DaddyLarge said.

The would-be gangster named Teepee shrugged, eyes avoiding the other, slightly older man's at all costs. "He say his name is Gunner. Aaron Gunner."

"Didn't nobody ask you what the fuck his *name* is. I asked you who the fuck he *is*."

The three men were standing alone in the front room of the gangsta rapper's large, tenth-floor suite at the Century City Marriott, awash in the sunlight pouring through a full-height window to the north.

"Maybe if you tried asking *me* the question," Gunner said, sounding for all the world as if he were just looking to be helpful, "you'd get a more satisfactory answer."

2DaddyLarge—a dreadlocked, broad-shouldered, dragon-nostriled young brother wearing a pair of white, loose-fitting, monogrammed silk pajamas—finally looked at his unwanted guest directly, red eyes open wide with mad dog venom. "Say what?"

"I said, why don't you try asking *me* who I am. I should know better than *him*, right?"

2Daddy rolled a thick tongue over a mouth full of gold-covered teeth, demonstrating an uncanny range of self-control. "Okay," he said after a moment. "So who the fuck *are* you?"

"I'm a private investigator. Local. Name's Aaron Gunner, like the man said. I've been hired by somebody close to C.E. Digga Jones to take a closer look at his suicide, see if maybe there's some chance he was actually murdered. I was out visiting the Digga's wife this afternoon when your boy showed up, offered to bring me around to say hello."

"That's fuckin' bullshit!" Teepee cried. "I didn't *offer* to do a goddamn thing! He *tol'* me—"

But 2Daddy turned on him, snapped, "Shut the fuck up, fool! Let the man talk!" He looked back at Gunner, said, "Go ahead, Gee. Hurry up an' get to the part what explains why I'm talkin' to *you,* 'steada the bitch I sent this nigga here to bring me."

"That happened because the lady didn't want to come," Gunner said. "And I did. And since you'd already sent a car . . ."

2Daddy looked down at the floor and shook his head, seemingly amused. "Shit," he said, laughing.

It was a sucker move Gunner had seen far too many times to ever fall for. When the big right uppercut came, its target was long gone; Gunner pivoted left to sidestep it, then threw a straight right of his own at the rapper's head, filling the hollow of the younger man's left cheek with the full weight of his fist. Teepee moved in from the side as 2Daddy reeled backward, but Gunner had the kid's .45 out from behind his back before he could take two steps. By the time 2Daddy looked up, ready to charge, Gunner was already using the gun to wave his boy Teepee over to his side of the room.

"You have any doubt I won't empty this bad boy in both of your asses, either of you tries me, I'd advise you to lose it now," Gunner said, holding the automatic straight out in front of him so that it couldn't be mistaken for a mere prop.

"Bitch, you done fucked up big-time, now," 2Daddy said, using his tongue to count all the teeth on the left side of his jaw. His face was a mask of unadulterated rage, but he stayed right where he was, impressed enough by Gunner's promise to shoot him that he wasn't up to testing it. Yet.

"Do yourself a favor," Gunner said tersely. "Find something else to call me besides bitch."

"Nigga, I'll call you any goddamn thing I *wanna* call you! Who the fuck—"

Gunner turned the nose of the black .45 downward, shot him in the outside of his left thigh, planning it so that the bullet would graze his flesh and die in the body of the large, overstuffed couch behind him. 2Daddy dropped to the floor and howled, clutching his wound with both hands to try and stem the blood flowing freely from it.

"Sorry. But it was either that or wash your mouth out with soap," Gunner said casually. He really had heard all the four-letter vitriol he could stand in one afternoon.

"Fuck!"

"Ordinarily, I'd be concerned about the noise, but what the hell. You're the loud rapper in room ten-seventeen, I'm sure the front desk gets calls about you all the time." Gunner turned now to the stunned kid named Teepee, said, "There's a movie called *The Maltese Falcon*. Ever hear of it?"

Teepee looked at him, the very model of infantile shock and confusion. "What?"

"*The Maltese Falcon*. It's an old classic, you're gonna love it. I want you to go get me a copy of it. Right now."

The kid was completely befuddled. "What?" he asked again.

"Teepee, you ain't goin' fuckin' *nowhere*!" 2Daddy cried, tears of anger streaming down both of his dark cheeks.

"He either goes or I put the next one in your goddamn ear," Gunner told him. "And then he can explain to all your fans and homies how somebody as badass as him let it happen."

He turned to Teepee, waited for him to make up his mind.

"*The Mall Tease Falcon*," the kid finally said.

"Right. I'll give you twenty minutes. You aren't back with the tape by then—or if the cops show up first, by some strange coincidence—no more 2Daddy. Next flava with his name on it's gonna have to be one of those 'In Loving Memory' greatest-hits packages."

Teepee looked at 2Daddy sadly, said, "Sorry, Dee, but this nigga's crazy."

"Stay where the fuck you are, Teepee!" 2Daddy screamed.

"I gotta go! I'll go get the muthafuckin' tape and be back, I promise!" He raced to the door before the rapper could offer any further protest, pointed a bony finger at Gunner before leaving. "It's gonna be *on* if you touch Dee again, muthafucka. I mean it. You touch 'im again 'fore I get back, you're dead."

He slammed the door behind him to bolster the empty threat, turning a deaf ear to 2Daddy's repeated demands that he return.

Knowing he had precious little time to work with, no matter what play the kid decided to make now, Gunner went straight to the nearby closet, came back with the spare pillow he found on a shelf there. 2Daddy watched him pull the pillowcase off, the rapper's leg continuing to leak blood through his hands onto the shag carpet beneath him, and said, "What the fuck's *that* for?" Sounding somewhat less imperious already.

Gunner threw the pillow aside, started tearing the case into narrow strips. "Tourniquet. To slow the bleeding. You do know what a tourniquet is, don't you?" He knotted three of the strips together to make one long one, tossed it over to the man on the floor.

2Daddy quickly wrapped the tourniquet around his left thigh, high above his wound, said, "Fuck, fuck, fuck," as he yanked it tight, then knotted it. It was clear to both of them that the injury wasn't serious, but for him, this was immaterial; what real damage had been done was psychological, not physical. Having a cap popped in him in his own crib, in front of a member of his crew, by an old man he didn't even know . . . For a player off the streets, humiliation didn't come any more devastating.

"Man, what the fuck is this *about*?" he barked, all but pleading for a straight answer.

"I told you. C.E. Digga Jones."

"Yeah, so the little bitch is dead, so what? What's that gotta do with me?"

"You were here in L.A. when he died, weren't you?"

"Man, I don't know. Maybe. I'm out here all the time."

"I was told you were here shooting a video that week."

"And if I was? What's that suppose' to prove?"

"There's an expression in legal circles called 'opportunity to commit.' Maybe you're familiar with it."

"'Opportunity to commit'? Commit *what*?"

"You put a gun in a man's mouth and pull the trigger, 2Daddy, it's called murder. Opportunity to commit murder."

"Murder? Man, stop trippin'! Homeboy served *hisself*, I didn't have nothin' to do with that shit!"

"Sure you did. You used to talk about serving him up all the time."

"Nigga, that's bullshit. Him an' me liked to wolf all the time, yeah, but it wasn't nothin' personal. It was bus'ness."

"Business?"

"That's right, bus'ness! I was talkin' 'bout servin' his little West Coast ass up *saleswise,* man, not literal, like. We was competitors."

"Oh . . . you were *competitors.*" Gunner smiled. "And the fact that he was slappin' skin with an ex-girlfriend of yours every night, that never really bothered you."

2Daddy's eyes suddenly came alive again. "You don't wanna go there, muthafucka."

"Too late. I already went. And it looks like your beef with the Digga wasn't all that businesslike, after all."

"Nigga stole my bitch! What, you think I shoulda been all right with that?"

"Danee was never your 'bitch.' Why's that so hard for you to understand?"

"'Cause she *was* my bitch, nigga! *You* don't know!"

"I know what *she* says about it. And she says you've got your nose all opened up over nothing. A couple of nights out together back in the day, that's all you ever had."

"That's a fuckin' lie! We was in *love*! *Mad* love!"

"Yeah, well, the Digga's widow doesn't see it that way, and neither did he. You thought things might be different with him out of the picture, but you were wrong. Hate to be the one to break it to you, 'Dee,' but you killed a man over a woman you're never gonna have."

"Bullshit! I didn't kill *nobody*!"

"Or maybe it was just his colors you didn't like. Him being a Crip, and you a Blood . . ."

"Man, fuck you! Homeboy served *hisself*, even his own people said so!"

"I don't care what his own people say," Gunner said, deciding it was time to throw the wounded rapper a little curve, just to see how he would handle it. "They haven't seen the tape. I have."

2Daddy scrunched his face up in a show of abject cynicism, said, "*Tape?* What tape?"

"The surveillance tape from the hotel. The one that shows everybody who went in or out of the Digga's room the night he died. *That* tape."

2Daddy didn't miss faking a lack of concern by much; his only real mistake was taking too long to reply. "Nigga, you're trippin'," he said.

"Brother named Ray Crumley showed me a copy of it before somebody whacked him trying to steal it. Was that you, or your boy Teepee?"

"Wasn't neither one of us. We don't know no nigga name Ray what you said, and we don't know nothin' 'bout no fuckin' tape."

"Yeah, you do. One of you killed the Digga and got caught on tape doing it. Then when Crumley tried to sell you a copy of the tape, you tried to jack it from his crib instead, ended up killing him too."

"No! I didn't— Man, this is *wack*! You tryin' to set me up!"

He was all but crying now, just as a man who was indeed being set up might. The distinctions between this and the behavior of someone who was merely afraid of the imminent consequences of his actions were almost infinitesimal—but Gunner knew them when he saw them, all the same, and he was certain he was seeing them here. There was simply too much surprise mixed in with 2Daddy's fear. He knew more than he was telling, to be certain—he just didn't seem to know enough to be guilty of the specific crimes Gunner was accusing him of.

Needless to say, the investigator's job had just become that much harder.

Resigned to making one last attempt to learn what it was the rapper wasn't saying, in the hope it would lead to something bigger, Gunner said, "I'm running out of patience here, Dee. And you're running out of time. Guilty or innocent, the police are gonna stick you for the Digga's murder, soon as they do what I did and connect you to Crumley and the tape. You ever wanna lay another dope track down in your life, you better talk to me, right here and now, give me some kind of chance to control the damage they're gonna do before it's too late."

"Talk to you about *what*? Man, I done *tol'* you, I don't know—"

Gunner jammed Teepee's gun back into the waistband of his pants behind his back, said, "Fine. I'm out. You wanna let the Man jam you up without a fight, more power to you." He turned and started for the door.

"Wait, wait! Hold up, goddamnit!" 2Daddy screamed.

Gunner looked back at him, waited for his follow-up.

"Look here." He paused, behaving like a man who was being forced to pull his own teeth. "I didn't kill *nobody*, all right? Not the Digga, not this Crumley nigga you talkin' about—not *nobody*," 2Daddy said. "But . . . I might know who did."

Gunner still didn't speak.

2Daddy sighed deeply, the surrender killing him, said, "Night homeboy died . . . he was with a ho' I know. Girl name Antoinetta. Antoinetta Aames." He paused again, faced Gunner directly. "We ain't tight or nothin', but I know her. Me an' her use' to party together an' shit, long time ago."

So 2Daddy knew Danee Elbridge's friend Antoinetta even better than she did. It was almost too good to be true.

"And? Get to the point, 2Daddy."

"The point? The point is, the bitch is crazy, man! She's a *fiend.* Girl's body is dope, but her head . . ." He shook his own head at the thought. "It ain't right. She's what you call one a them paranoid schizo muthafuckas. I forget what you call it."

"Paranoid schizophrenic?"

"Yeah, that's it. Paranoid schizophrenic. Like, she always thinkin' somebody's fuckin' with *her,* so she always fuckin' with somebody *first.* Cuttin' niggas up with knives, or tryin' to run 'em down in they own cars. Shit like that."

"How is it you know she was with the Digga that night?"

"How do I know? I know 'cause she tol' me, that's how. She called me an' tol' me."

"When?"

"Fuck, man, I don't know. Couple days later, I think. Somethin' like that. Bitch was all shook up 'bout bein' there, said she was scared Five-oh was gonna think she was the one shot homeboy."

"Did she?"

"Hey, fuck if I know. I asked her if she did, an' she said she didn't, but . . ." He shrugged. "She wasn't gonna tell me if she did, right?"

"What about her friend Felicia? The sister who was with her?"

2Daddy's face bunched up like the question was something Gunner had pulled from a quantum physics text. "Felicia? Who the fuck is Felicia?"

"Antoinetta was there with a friend that night, 2Daddy. It was her and a girl named Felicia, or Phyllis. One or the other."

2Daddy shook his head. "I don't know nothin' about no Felicia," he said. "Antoinetta didn't say nothin' 'bout no other bitch bein' up there with her."

Gunner processed this information for a moment, said, "So why'd she call you? Why you and not somebody else?"

"Why'd she call me?" 2Daddy asked. "She called me 'cause she needed some Benjamins to go hide somewheres, an' I'm the only nigga she knows got a dollar in they goddamn pocket. Who the fuck else was she gonna call?"

"You give her the money?"

"No. Hell no. You crazy?"

"So she could still be around somewhere."

2Daddy just shrugged.

"Where would I be likely to find her? Just to hear her side of things?"

"Her side of things? Shit, nigga, I just told you. The bitch is crazy. All she gonna do is say I'm a lie. That I was the one done the Digga, not her."

"Just the same, 2Daddy, I'd like to look her up. Where could I find her?"

2Daddy frowned, annoyed by Gunner's insistence on doing things his own way. "Maybe over by her moms' house. That's where she was livin' last time I seen her. But—"

"You have an address for her moms' house?"

"No. I told you, man, me an' her ain't been tight in a long time. Last time I was over there was a couple years ago, an' somebody else was drivin'."

"Okay, 2Daddy. We're all done. Thanks for the four-one-one, and take care of that leg, huh?"

"Fuck you," 2Daddy said, mad-dogging the investigator once more. Being reminded of his flesh wound while learning Gunner was leaving had suddenly returned him to his original state of impertinence.

"Oh, and listen. When your boy Teepee comes back with the tape—tell him I said to make a big bowl of popcorn and watch it tonight, pay special attention to a character named Wilmer. Can you remember that? Wilmer?"

"Nigga, I ain't your fuckin' secretary. I ain't tellin' Teepee shit!"

Rather than argue with him, Gunner just laughed and left him in peace.

For the second time in two days, Gunner tied up a pay phone in the lobby of a hotel he could never afford to stay in in order to conduct some business, and just like the first time, it wasn't a particularly rewarding experience.

Bob Zemic still hadn't called his office when Gunner checked with Mickey, so Gunner called him instead. It was now nearly three-thirty, well past Zemic's lunchtime, so his promised review of the surveillance tape Gunner had asked for should have been completed long ago.

"Sorry, Gunner, but it was as I suspected," Zemic said. "Ray's interest in your tape was strictly sexual in nature."

Gunner looked off to one side for a moment, resisted the urge to curse under his breath. It was the last thing he had wanted to hear Zemic say. "How's that?"

"I mean, the only thing on it worth mentioning is a little foreplay the guest in room five-oh-nine did on a ladyfriend out in the hallway before they turned in for the night. Beyond that, the tape was completely unextraordinary."

"Foreplay? What kind of foreplay?"

"Without going into all the gory details, I'll say only that it involved two women, and that someone like Ray would have probably found it highly entertaining."

"I see. And Elbridge?"

"That's also like I said. There was nothing out of the ordinary to see. The tape shows a few people entering his room, then leaving afterward. That was it."

"You recognize any of these people?"

"It was three females. All black, relatively young. First two together, then one alone. I'm not sure, but I think the one alone was Elbridge's wife. At least, she resembled the lady I saw identified as his wife on TV a couple of times right after he died."

"And the other two?"

"I couldn't tell you. Looked like a couple of groupies to me. Maybe I'm wrong."

"You'd never seen either of them before?"

"No. Neither before or since. Cameras never really caught a clear view of their faces, but I'm pretty sure they weren't familiar."

Which made it all but certain that Crumley hadn't wanted the tape for blackmail purposes after all. If the people on it couldn't be positively identified, what good was it to an extortionist?

"And you say everyone was accounted for?" Gunner asked. "That is, everyone who entered the kid's room was seen to come out again?"

"Yes. Time stamp says the two groupies went in around five-thirty, came out just before seven. The wife went in right after that, left again less than twenty minutes later. Oh, and before I forget to mention . . ."

"Yeah?"

"Elbridge himself was visible at the door on both occasions. As alive as you and I are right now."

Even over the phone, Gunner could feel the grin that had just broken out on Zemic's face.

. . .

The logo for Body Count Records was a nine-millimeter automatic hand-gun in profile, branded along its snout with five human silhouettes intended to represent five kills. Beneath the gun, graffiti-style block letters spelled out BODY COUNT in bold silver and black, with the O in each word dissected by the white crosshairs of a rifle scope. If the design struck you as clever and harmless, a visit to the label's corporate headquarters in Burbank was a painless experience. But if you saw it instead, as Gunner did, as a prime example of the hard sell of violence and mayhem the entertainment industry was doing on America's children, just to move product, thirty seconds in the building was enough to send you screaming for the exits. Because the goddamn logo was everywhere, if the receptionist's area was representative of the whole. On the glass entry doors, on the wall behind the receptionist herself, even on each and every one of the roughly three dozen gold record plaques that peppered an entire wall.

It all made Gunner almost sorry that he'd come, except for the fact that he'd had little choice. Despite the bad news Bob Zemic had just given him, Gunner still felt Antoinetta Aames and friend were two people he should talk to, and he was anxious to find them—but not until one nagging question had been answered for him. Benny Elbridge himself would have been the ideal person to ask, but he hadn't been answering Gunner's calls all day, so the investigator had decided to look up the only other person he could think of who might have the information he required: Raymont Trevor, the man Desmond Joy had described as Bume Webb's chief operations officer.

Gunner had called ahead to make sure Trevor was in, then driven straight to Burbank to wait him out, knowing Trevor wouldn't be an easy man to see without an appointment. Still, the investigator suspected that the answer he'd given the receptionist when asked what the nature of his business was—he was the private investigator Benny Elbridge had hired to clear Bume Webb of C.E. Digga Jones's murder—would demand Trevor's attention eventually, and he was right. Less than twenty minutes after his arrival, Trevor's private secretary came out front to show Gunner to Trevor's office—a large, opulently appointed room on the floor above no *Fortune* 500 CEO would have resented owning. Assuming, of course, he or she could live with all the Body Count logos scattered throughout the decor.

"Mr. Gunner? Raymont Trevor," the record exec said upon Gunner's entrance, grinning as he came around his desk to shake hands. Gunner had only seen Bume Webb in newspaper photos and video footage, but he noticed immediately that Trevor was nothing if not a smaller version of him: barrel-chested, bald-headed, and as neckless as a badly drawn cartoon character. Only scale and the full-bodied goatee Trevor wore served to separate the two men physically. "Angie said something about your being a private investigator working for Benny Elbridge?"

Gunner shook Trevor's hand, said, "That's right. And you're doing a fine job of acting like you didn't already know, if you don't mind my saying so."

Trevor almost laughed. "Excuse me?"

"I'm gonna make this brief, Mr. Trevor. Because you're a busy man, and so am I. Is Bume Webb's money paying for my services, or not? I need a simple yes or no."

The smile on his host's face slowly vanished before Gunner's eyes. "What?"

"Not to worry. It's not a deal breaker, yet. But a man needs to know who he's working for, or it's no go, right?"

"I'm sorry, brother, but it seems there's been some kind of mistake. I don't—"

"Yeah, you do. It took a couple days, but it's finally come to my attention that the man I thought was my client has been paying me with money he doesn't have. Which means he's being bankrolled by somebody else. That somebody doesn't have to be Bume, but he's the only one I can see playing that role at the moment."

"I'm still not following you."

"No? I'll wrap this up, then. I don't work for other people's front men. That's not how I operate. If you or Bume put Benny Elbridge up to hiring me, you'd better say so, and fast, because I'm not working another minute on Elbridge's behalf until I know who's behind him, and why. I'm sure you can understand."

Trevor rebuilt from scratch the charming smile he'd shown Gunner earlier, said, "I'll say it again. It sounds like there's been some kind of mistake. I'd really like to help you, but . . ." He hiked his huge shoulders up in a big man's shrug, smiled with even more dubious sincerity.

Gunner let the smile sink in, decided he disliked it greatly, and turned his back on it before he could do something to it he knew he'd only regret later.

Driving to his office at Mickey's after leaving Raymont Trevor in Burbank, Gunner was again made uneasy by the odd sense that somebody was trailing him, tracing his every move in the thick of rush-hour traffic. Three times in two days he'd felt this way now, and professional paranoia didn't generally go that far. He was being tailed, by a person or persons unknown, and the realization left him both furious and apprehensive.

Maybe being convinced someone was back there, rather than merely suspecting as much, made the difference, but this time he thought he was able to spot the vehicle shadowing his own: a silver, late-eighties Chrysler LeBaron with what looked like California plates, its front bumper listing badly to the left, damn near scraping the ground. A good fifteen car lengths behind him on the southbound Harbor Freeway—too far away to afford Gunner a decent look at the driver sitting behind the glare of its windshield—there was nothing concrete about the Chrysler he could point to as suspicious, save for the feeling he had that he'd seen it somewhere before. Not today, but recently. Sometime Tuesday perhaps, or maybe even Monday.

But where?

At just a few minutes shy of six p.m., the flow of traffic on both sides of the Harbor was its customary, lethargic self. You crept forward at ten miles per hour for a distance of fifteen feet, then stopped, only to repeat the process all over again. Gunner's Cobra was in the number three lane, the Chrysler in the number two, but they may as well have been bumper to bumper, so identical was their rate of speed. The entire freeway was one big synchronized crawl, affording Gunner no opportunity to find a slower lane, force the Chrysler to gain on him so he could get a good look at its driver.

So Gunner stopped the Cobra cold.

For appearance' sake, he got out of the car, shrugged an apology at the driver of the Toyota pickup directly behind him before moving around to the front of the Cobra to raise its hood. The double-chinned, mustachioed Hispanic in the Toyota leaned on his horn to offer his condolences, but Gunner just ignored him, feigning vague interest in the big Ford V8 stuffed into the Cobra's engine compartment as he watched the Chrysler crawl inexorably toward him, get to within ten car lengths . . . and then start merging right, making a hasty and forceful retreat off the freeway.

"Shit!" Gunner said.

He'd made a strategic blunder, faking the Cobra's breakdown here, just beyond a freeway off-ramp, rather than just short of one. Another quarter-mile, and his suspected tail would have been trapped between exits, with no avenue of escape readily available to him. But now . . . the silver car's driver was just able to make the Vernon Avenue turnoff, disappear up the ramp before Gunner could see his face or make out the license plate number on his car.

"Shit!" the investigator said again, dropping the Cobra's hood closed with a bang.

The guy in the pickup was still honking at him mercilessly, unable to go around, and several cars in back were joining in. Gunner just let them have their fun. They weren't calling him an idiot, exactly, but they would have been well within their rights if they had.

Mickey was putting the finishing touches on Joe Worthy's customary, aircraft carrier—like flattop when Gunner walked in. The two older men were alone in the shop this late in the day, and had been talking in hushed tones like a pair of women trading gossip in the church hall. Immediately, the investigator knew something was up; loud voices here always meant good news, subdued voices always meant bad.

"Man, where the hell have you been?" Mickey asked.

"Body Count Records. Two floors in a sweet-looking high-rise out in Burbank, pictures of mad-dogging young knuckleheads named Boney this and Thrilla that all over the place. Why? What's up?"

"You ain't heard?" Joe Worthy asked.

"Heard what?"

"It's all over the news," Mickey said ominously. "How could you not hear?"

"I didn't have the radio on in the car. What the hell are you two talking about? What happened?"

"That girl Sparkle Johnson? The one on the radio you almost worked for a couple days ago? Somebody tried to kill her this afternoon. Put a bomb in her car and tried to blow her ass up."

"Lucky thing you quit on her, huh?" Joe Worthy asked, grinning.

Like it was something to be proud of.

Six days earlier, when he had first approached Gunner about investigating the death threats Sparkle Johnson had allegedly been receiving, Wally Browne had given the investigator every phone number he owned: home, office, cellular, pager—even one for faxes. He'd been desperate for Gunner's help then, and wanted to make himself readily available. But not tonight. Calling Browne's home and office lines now only connected Gunner with disparate versions of voice mail, his cellular number was constantly busy, and three attempts to page him went totally unrewarded.

It seemed Gunner had made himself yet another well-deserved enemy.

And then the phone next to his bed rang well after eight p.m., and an exhausted-sounding Browne said, "Well, I guess you're happy now, huh, Mr. Gunner?"

"Never mind the sarcasm. How is she?"

"What, you don't think a little sarcasm's warranted here?"

"It's warranted. How's she doing?"

"Why don't you come see for yourself? She's staying here with me for the night."

Gunner took the address down and said he'd be right over.

According to all the news reports, Sparkle Johnson had escaped with only minor injuries the explosion that had killed her unfortunate lunch date, but it wasn't until he'd seen her for himself that Gunner would allow himself to believe it.

She was sitting on Wally Browne's living room couch when Browne showed him into his Bel Air home, wearing what had to be Browne's bathrobe and slippers, sipping something hot and steaming from a bright yellow cup. Her left hand was heavily bandaged, and a large square of blood-spattered medical gauze was taped over her right cheek, just below the eye. Her listless gaze barely moved from the floor when Gunner sat down in the chair beside her.

Gunner thought back to their first meeting four days ago, found the contrast between that Sparkle Johnson and this one more than a little unnerving.

"Doctors say she's gonna be okay," Browne said as he sat down beside her on the couch, patting her gently on the knee. "She's got a few facial lacerations from shattered glass, and a flying piece of something almost took her left thumb off, but . . . all in all, I'd have to say she got off pretty easy. *Damn* easy, in fact."

"The bastard murdered Kyle," Johnson said, still staring blankly at the floor. Tears were flowing freely down both of her cheeks.

"Bas*tard*?" Gunner asked, questioning her use of the singular.

"Jarrett. Jarrett Nance." She finally looked up at him. "We were engaged once."

"You're saying you know who did this?"

Johnson nodded solemnly. "It had to be him. Who else would it be?"

Browne was mortified. "But I thought—"

"I'm sorry, Wally. I thought he was harmless. If I'd known he was capable of something like *this* . . ."

"He's the Mr. M who's been writing the letters?" Gunner asked. "And making the phone calls?"

Johnson nodded again. "Yes."

"How do you know?"

"I know because he's the only one who ever called me that before. Topsy. It's what he started calling me after our breakup, just to hurt me."

As Browne had explained to Gunner at their first meeting, Johnson's "anonymous" Mr. M had referred to her as Topsy on more than one occasion, and though the investigator had never actually read Harriet Beecher Stowe's *Uncle Tom's Cabin,* he knew enough about the infamous Civil War–era novel to know that this had been the name of the doomed Little Eva's most beloved and headstrong slave girl.

"So where does the M come in?" Gunner asked. "That a middle initial, or . . ."

Johnson shook her head, said, "I don't know where he got the M. Jarrett's middle name is Charles—the M must've just been something he used to try and throw me off."

"I don't believe this," Browne said, angry now. "An *old boyfriend*? That's what this has all been about?"

Johnson started crying, said, "Wally, I said I'm sorry! What more do you want me to do?"

"I want you to tell me why you weren't straight with me from the beginning! Jesus, Sparkle, a man is dead now!"

"I know that! Don't you think I know that?" She tried to set her cup down on an end table beside her, dropped it over the edge onto the floor instead. Black coffee spattered across the tan carpet at her feet, almost certainly ruining it, and she cursed once, then broke down completely, burying her face in the palms of her hands.

"Oh, God. Oh, God, kid, I'm sorry," Browne said, instantly remorseful. He edged closer to her on the couch, tried to drape an arm around her heaving shoulders, but she shrugged it off, moved as far out of his reach as she could.

Unlike Browne, Gunner let her cry without interference, kept his silence for a good minute before attempting to speak to her again. "You tell the police what you just told us? That this Jarrett Nance is the man they should be looking for?"

Johnson shook her head, avoiding his gaze. "No. I couldn't."

"Why not?"

"Because I couldn't believe he'd really do such a thing! I still don't. And yet . . . I know that's just my heart talking, not my head. It had to be Jarrett."

"Then the authorities have to be notified. Right away."

"Yes." She nodded. "Of course."

"I can call them if you like," Browne said, looking for some way to make amends for having been so hard on her earlier. "I'll just say you remembered something you'd forgotten to mention earlier, and you'd like to talk to one of their detectives again, if you could."

"I think that would be a good idea," Gunner said. "And in the meantime, she and I can keep talking, go over a few questions I'd like to ask."

From the look on her face, Johnson didn't like the sound of that, but Browne nodded and left the room before she could register a complaint.

"Don't worry. I'll make this brief," Gunner said, smiling to reassure her. Johnson made a halfhearted attempt to smile back.

"This Jarrett Nance. Proper motivation aside—would he actually know how to build an explosive? Does he have any experience in that area that you know of?"

"That I know of? No." Johnson shook her head. "He's an ad buyer. He buys commercial time on television for advertisers. But . . ."

Gunner waited for her to go on.

"He's also a gun nut. Reads all the magazines, visits all the web sites. If he wanted to build a bomb, I'm sure he could learn how to very easily."

"Was the device timed, or tied to the ignition? That is, did it go off before the driver tried to start the car, or not until?"

"It was timed," Johnson said. "Kyle was just getting in the car when . . . when it went off."

"This was in the restaurant parking lot?"

"Yes."

"But you weren't in the car yourself."

"No." Johnson shook her head. "Kyle had opened the door for me, but I hadn't gotten in. I was putting on an earring that had fallen off inside the restaurant. If it hadn't been for that . . ."

"Cops have any idea yet what kind of device it was?"

"What kind?"

"Yes. Was it a sophisticated piece of work, or a crude one?"

"Someone said it looked like a pipe bomb, but that it was too early to be sure. Look. What are you asking me all these questions for? I already told you who's responsible, didn't I?"

"You told us who you think is responsible, yes. But only five minutes ago, you weren't so sure."

"Well, I'm sure now. It was Jarrett. It *had* to be."

"He hates you that much?"

"Yes."

"You said you two were engaged once. I take it you were the one who broke it off?"

Johnson nodded, said, "I all but left him standing at the altar. I thought I was in love with him, but I wasn't."

"When was this?"

"Last January. I walked away as much for his sake as mine, but of course . . ."

"He didn't quite see it that way."

"No. Would you?"

Gunner let the barbed remark slip by, asked, "So that brings us back to the question Browne asked earlier. Why wait until now to tell us he was the one harassing you? Even if you thought he was harmless—"

"I *did* think he was harmless."

"Then why didn't you shut him down yourself before now? Or let me do it for you with Browne's blessings?"

"I *did*. I *did* try to shut him down myself."

"And?"

"He wouldn't listen. He just pretended not to know what I was talking about. And I knew if I pushed him, he—"

She stopped herself cold, like someone who'd nearly tumbled over the jagged edge of a high precipice.

"He'd what?" Gunner asked calmly.

"He'd do something crazy," Johnson said, after much deliberation. Improvising.

"But if you didn't think he was dangerous . . ."

"Look. I felt I owed the man, all right? I was just trying to give him every possible chance to go away on his own before siccing somebody like you or the police on him. I can see now that was a mistake, of course, but—"

"Forget it. You're bullshitting me. Let's do this some other time," Gunner said tersely.

The comment caught Johnson off guard. She opened her mouth to offer some retort, but Browne rejoined them before she could speak, and Gunner stood to leave.

"It's all set," Browne said. "They're sending a couple of detectives over now."

"Good," Gunner said. He looked down at Johnson, added, "Maybe you'll feel a little more comfortable talking to them."

"I don't—" she started to protest.

But Gunner turned to Browne again, said, "You might want to talk to her about the importance of being honest with your friendly neighborhood policeman before the two you just called for show up. Cops can smell a half-truth a mile away, and they aren't nearly as tolerant of them as I."

Browne didn't understand. "What's he talking about?" he asked Johnson.

"I expect you'll want somebody to watch her for a while," Gunner said. "At least until her friend Nance is in custody?"

"Yes. Of course. But—"

Johnson leapt to her feet, said, "Wally, that isn't—"

"Save your breath, Sparkle. Mr. Gunner's watchin' you, and that's that."

"Actually, it won't be me," Gunner said. "But I've got a good man I can probably put in place by tomorrow morning, if that'd be acceptable to you. I'll give you a call around ten, let you know who, where, and when."

"Wait a minute. A 'good man'? You don't think you oughta handle this yourself?"

"Much as I'd love to, I can't. Previous obligation. If you don't want my man . . ."

"We don't," Johnson said.

"Right. That's what you said last time," Browne reminded her. He rolled his eyes at Gunner, said simply, "We'll take him."

"But I don't know nothin' 'bout 'surveillance,' " Jolly Mokes said early the next morning, not surprising Gunner in the least.

"Sure you do. Surveillance is just another word for reconnaissance. And you know how to do recon, don't you?"

"That was a long time ago, Gunner."

"I know it was. But some things you never forget. Big as your ass is, Jolly, I never saw a man hide in some bush like you could. You can do this job with your eyes closed—I wouldn't ask you if I didn't think you could."

"Yeah, but—"

"Look. Two days ago you said the Lord told you I'd have some kind of work for you, right? Well, the Lord's paid off. What the hell are you balking now for?"

Jolly got up off his bed, walked around the oversized birdcage that was his one-room downtown apartment, bare feet clearing a path through all the newspaper and candy wrappers on the floor as he paced. "I ain't balkin'," he said, wearing only a pair of striped boxer shorts and a stained white cotton T-shirt. "It's just . . . I guess I was hopin' you'd give me somethin' a little easier to do, that's all. Somethin' I can't mess up."

"You aren't gonna mess this up. I told you."

"Somebody already tried to kill this lady once, right? What if they try again, and I don't stop 'em? Who's gonna be responsible then?"

"I will. I'm the one the client hired to protect her, not you. If something goes wrong, the heat's all mine."

Jolly just shook his head and went right on pacing.

Finally irked, Gunner pulled the wooden chair he'd been sitting on backward out from under himself, shoved it back over near the small dinette table where he'd found it. "For Chrissake, Jolly, I'm a private investigator! What kind of work did you think I could give you, polishing the chrome on the Bentley?"

"No, but—"

"The situation is this. The lady needs somebody to watch her back, and I can't do it. I've got other obligations. Do you want the job or not?"

Jolly stopped pacing, said, "Hell yes, I want the job."

"Excellent. You have a car?"

"A car? Three weeks outa lockdown?"

"Shit, that's right. I forgot you just got out."

"I gotta have a car?"

"Yeah. You don't think you could maybe borrow one somewhere?"

"Borrow one?" The big man thought about it, shrugged. "Yeah, I guess. This brother down in Pedro I know got some extra wheels, he might lend 'em to me for a couple days if I asked."

"How about some decent clothes?"

"Clothes?"

"You're gonna have to do some of this surveillance on foot, indoors, and our girl likes to go places where you could feel like a hobo wearing Calvin Klein. You at least have a dress shirt, some slacks . . ."

Jolly shook his head.

"No. Okay." Gunner reached into his pocket, fished out the last of Benny Elbridge's cash retainer, and peeled off five twenties. Hoping instruments of the Lord like himself were reimbursed for all expenses, somewhere down the road.

. . .

He had told Raymont Trevor his work for Benny Elbridge was done until he knew exactly where the fee Elbridge was paying him was coming from, and he was prepared to make good on that promise if necessary, but privately, Gunner wasn't looking forward to doing so.

By now, he'd been on the Carlton Elbridge suicide case for three days, going on four, and in that time he'd come across enough duplicity, jealousy, and unyielding secrecy to more than hold his interest for days to come. None of it had convinced him yet that C.E. Digga Jones had been murdered, but it certainly had him wondering. Wondering enough that he wasn't ready to walk away. There was a threshold beyond which an investigation became more about his own hunger for the truth than his client's, and somewhere over the last forty-eight hours, Gunner had stepped across it.

Still, only an idiot did a puppet's bidding without knowing who was pulling its strings. Gunner had to know who the money man—or woman—behind Benny Elbridge was, or he'd be forced to quit his employ, the restless soul of Carlton Elbridge—not to mention Ray Crumley—be damned.

Having decided this question would never be answered by phone, however, as calls to Benny Elbridge's number were going as unheeded today as they had been yesterday, Gunner left Jolly Mokes only a few minutes after nine a.m. to try and visit Elbridge personally. The address his client had given him three days ago led the investigator to a tiny shack in the rear yard of an almost equally tiny house in Willowbrook, where dry, uncut grass and one weather-beaten coat of cheap white latex seemed to be the architectural dress code of the day. The roofs of both structures were shedding shingles like corpses shedding skin, and neither seemed to be standing at anything approaching a right angle; the smaller one, especially, resembled something a child might have drawn freehand.

"Yo, big man."

Gunner had almost reached the porch of the quiet little shack when the voice came, caused him to spin around with obvious surprise. Two young black men wearing business attire and Gargoyle sunglasses had apparently followed him up the driveway of the front house without him hearing, and now stood there side by side like hip-hop FBI men.

"Mr. El ain't home."

The smaller of the two was the one talking. And smiling. Both men were dark-skinned and big, but not gargantuan; more like linebackers than defensive ends. The silent one had a black Kangol hat on his head and attitude to spare; the other one just had all the white teeth he was flashing.

"Mr. L?" Gunner asked, pretending not to understand.

"Mr. Elbridge." He widened the smile, appreciating the investigator's attempt at ignorance. "Ain't that who you came to see, Mr. Gunner?"

So they knew him. Did that just make a bad situation worse, or better?

"You brothers know me?"

"Uh-huh. But you don't know us. You don't *need* to know us."

Gunner was looking for a way past or around the pair, hadn't found one yet that wouldn't in all probability land him in the morgue. Each man had some hardware wrinkling the inner fabric of his coat, and the one with the hat, at least, seemed to have the temperament to use it.

"Okay, boys," Gunner said, showing the two men the palms of his hands to inform them of his pacifist nature. "Clue me in. What the fuck's about to go down here?"

"Ain't nothin' goin' down. We just gonna take you for a ride, that's all. Come on, let's go." He gestured with one hand for Gunner to start moving down the driveway, out toward the street.

"A ride?" Despite the risks, Gunner couldn't help but laugh. "Shit. I'm not going for any *ride*!"

The smaller man's smile finally went away, metamorphosed into the same grim expression his partner wore. "You wanna bet?"

Christ, Gunner thought, *they're serious.*

"Look. It's nice to see a couple of kids who don't change the channel just 'cause the movie's in black-and-white, but you're confused. Taking people for rides only worked for Warner Brothers back in 1946, it's as fictional an occurrence today as Santa coming down the chimney."

The two brothers eyed him in stony silence for a long minute; then the smaller one sighed and told his partner, "Fuck it. Pop a cap in his leg, we'll *drag* his ass out to the ride."

Nine-thirty in the morning, the guy next door scanning the headlines of the *Times* out on his front lawn in clear view, and big man eases a SIG 9 out of its holster under his arm and points it at Gunner's left knee. Still not saying a word.

Not surprisingly, Gunner found a way to make his pulling the trigger completely unnecessary.

The California Institution for Men looked all wrong for a prison. Prisons were supposed to be unsightly fortresses of concrete and steel, giant monolithic blights on the landscape that blocked out the sun and squelched even the slightest thought of entry or exit. Instead, the CIM was a nondescript collection of cinder-block buildings spread out across a 2,500-acre parcel of land in Chino, a quiet San Bernardino County suburb forty miles east of Los Angeles. If you took away all the razor wire and guard towers, in fact, the four-facility complex could have passed for a large, if woefully unattractive, college campus.

This was where Gunner ended up at the behest of his two new friends in the nicely tailored suits, Brother Kangol and Brother Kangol-Not. Back at Benny Elbridge's place, he had thought the car they'd lead him to would be the silver Chrysler with the askew front bumper, but instead it was a brand-new pearl-white Lincoln Town Car. When he asked about the Chrysler, he didn't get an answer, though the impression their silence left him with was that neither man knew what the hell he was talking about.

And so it had gone the entire ride out to Chino. Gunner had asked maybe a half-dozen questions, starting with the most obvious, before he'd decided to save his breath and enjoy the scenery. The big man in the hat drove, his partner with the smile sat in back with Gunner, and for fifty minutes neither man said anything that was intended to satisfy the investigator's curiosity. Had he feared they meant to kill him, their reticence might have moved him to throw his door open, take his chances surviving a death plunge onto the eastbound San Bernardino Freeway, but once the route and duration of their journey began to suggest their eventual destination, the investigator felt confident that murder was not item one on their agenda.

Bringing him out to see Bume Webb *was*.

"All you gotta do is go in, give 'em your name," the talker in the backseat said when they'd found a space in the CIM visitors' parking lot. "It's all set up, they're expectin' you and everything."

Gunner knew he had to go, but he felt like he ought to at least bitch about it beforehand, lest they think him entirely spineless. "This was a lot of trouble for you boys to go to for nothing, you know. I'd have driven out here myself if you'd only asked."

The big man behind the wheel didn't even bother to turn around, and the smaller one in the back just frowned. As if to say, *Yeah, right, you would have.*

Gunner got out of the car and started walking.

Visiting a famous inmate at a maximum-security prison should have been a complex affair, but in less than thirty minutes, Gunner was face-to-face with the legend known as Bume Webb. As promised, someone had called ahead to alert the CIM authorities he was coming, and the result was a welcome incredibly short on questions and/or complications. Gunner didn't know if this was a reflection of the facility's security, or of Bume's power to get things done, but he preferred to believe the former. Bume's realm of influence was frightening enough as it was.

They met in a glassed-off room in the visitations building, where Gunner had found Bume already waiting for him. A folding table and two metal chairs were the only furniture in the room, and Bume dwarfed them all, made them look like movie props built to three-quarter scale. Even prepared to be impressed by his size, Gunner was taken aback; the man was simply immense. Almost as wide as he was tall, he had hands big enough to engulf a cantaloupe, and forearms as thick as an outdoor utility pole. If the orange jumpsuit he was wearing hadn't been specially made, it had to have come from a very small lot; Gunner imagined there couldn't have been more than three inmates in the entire California penal system who would've required clothing of equal dimension.

The baton-wielding corrections officer who'd brought him here let Gunner into the small room, then stepped just outside the door when he was satisfied Bume intended to behave himself. Gunner heard the door latch closed behind him and tried not to feel like a mouse who'd just been dropped into the python's glass case at the zoo.

"We gotta make this fast," Bume said, not getting up from his chair. "We only got fifteen minutes."

Like his body, his voice carried the weight of a Mack truck and trailer.

Gunner took Bume's lead, remained where he was. "Okay. You wanna start, or should I?"

"You wanted to know if I was the one told Mr. Elbridge to hire you. The answer's yes. You got a problem with that?"

"I don't know. Would you? You did some work for one man, found out later you were really doing it for somebody else? Would you be down for that?"

"If it was for a good reason? Yeah."

"What kind of good reason?"

"Like the man what really hired you knew you would've said no, he'd've asked you to do the work himself, straight up. 'Cause that's what would've happened, right, I'd've tried to hire you myself? You would've said no."

"Maybe," Gunner lied. "Maybe not. It might have all depended on what you wanted me to do, and why."

"Okay. So now you know all that, right?"

Gunner shook his head.

"Shit. Come on, Gunner. I want you to find out who whacked my boy Digga. What the hell you think I want?"

"I don't know. Maybe to make some people think it wasn't you who whacked your 'boy'?"

Bume's eyes grew small, even harder with menace. "Some people gonna think that no matter what. I don't give a fuck about them. All I give a fuck about is findin' out who served the Digga."

"You don't believe he served himself?"

"Hell no. Would I be talkin' to you if I did?"

"I think you'd better get used to the idea. Nobody can say why, but so far everyone seems to agree that the boy hadn't been all that thrilled to be alive lately. Desmond Joy in particular says death was almost always on his mind."

"Bullshit. Nigga just got depressed sometimes, that's all. Same as you'd be, muthafuckas like Desmond an' the Digga's moms was always messin' with your head, way they was always messin' with his."

"How do you mean?"

"I mean they was givin' homeboy some fucked-up advice, tellin' 'im he needed to leave Body Count an' start his own fuckin' label. They was only lookin' out for themselves tellin' 'im that shit, that was the worst thing he coulda done."

Gunner glanced around their stark environs, said, "Or the best thing. In case you haven't heard, Bume, things at Body Count have gotten a little funky since you went away. If the Digga had lived to stick around, he might've been the only one left on the payroll to answer the phones and open the day's mail."

"Wrong, nigga. Me an' him was a team, same as always. Soon as he signed his new contract, we was gonna have Body Count blowin' up again. Me bein' up in here wasn't gonna change that."

"New contract? What new contract?"

"One homeboy was all ready to ink 'fore he got killed, what else?

Damn, man, ain't you figured out nothin' yet? That's why the Digga got served, so he couldn't do no more records for Body Count!"

Unable to hide his surprise, Gunner finally walked over to the table where Bume sat, claimed the remaining chair there for himself. "You wanna run that by me again?"

Bume shook his head with disgust, said, "I told you. We ain't got much time in here. So listen the fuck up. Everybody be thinkin' homeboy's death was all about *him,* but that's wack. It was all about *me. I'm* the one they was tryin' to fuck with, not him."

The suggestion was not as outrageous as it initially sounded, once Gunner thought about it. If the Digga really had been on the verge of re-signing with Body Count as Bume was now alleging, no one had stood to lose more as a result of the rapper's death than Bume. No one. Even a still-undecided Digga would have offered the record mogul one last chance to raise his once proud label from the ashes of his incarceration. But with the Digga—like all the other brand-name rappers once under Bume's employ—now gone for good . . . Bume's financial ruin seemed all but guaranteed.

Could that have been something other than an inadvertent by-product of the Digga's death?

"Let me make sure I understand you," Gunner said. "You're suggest-ing that somebody murdered C.E. Digga Jones just to fuck with *you.* To put the last nail in Body Count's coffin before the Digga could make any more records for the label."

"You goddamn right," Bume said, nodding his head emphatically.

"Okay. So who was it? Who in the hell hates you so much that they'd murder someone who records for you just to jack you up financially?"

"I don't know who, fool. If I knew who, I wouldn't need you, would I?"

"You can't think of one or two likely candidates?"

"I can think of more'n that. But . . ." Bume cut a glance at the correc-tions officer standing on the other side of the glass wall, saw that his eyes

were as fixed upon him as they'd been from the moment the guard had first
let Gunner in here.

"Well?"

"By now I guess you figured out I got a few enemies. Niggas who like
to say I did this or that to 'em, busted 'em up or cheated 'em outa some
chedda, bullshit like that, right?"

Gunner nodded.

"Well. Enemies ain't all I got. I got me some 'friends' too. Maybe you
should talk to some o' them."

"Friends?"

"Specifically, some of 'em what helped me along the way. Back in the
day when I was just comin' up. I can't name no names, but some of 'em,
they got what you call a 'distorted view' of what they done to contribute to
all my success. So we been havin' this fuckin' ongoin' argument about it
lately." He shrugged, as if that were some form of elaboration.

"Are you talking about early investors?" Gunner asked.

Bume grinned. "That's what they like to *say* they was."

"Like Ready Lewis, you mean?"

Bume didn't say anything, just looked at Gunner like he'd finally found
some reason to respect the investigator's intelligence. Then the big man
turned his head to one side and nodded at the guard outside, issuing a sig-
nal that the time had come for Gunner to be taken back to where he'd come
from.

twelve

Bume's delivery boys took Gunner back to his car the same way they had driven him out to Chino: in complete silence. The radio was on, as it had been earlier, tuned to 92.3 the BEAT and bassed out enough to rattle the teeth of the dead, but beyond that, the Lincoln was again as quiet as a covered grave for fifty minutes. The difference this time was that Gunner actually liked it that way.

It was the kind of mood thoughts of his nephew Alred always seemed to put him in. He had been hoping ever since Slicky Soames dropped the drug dealer's name that he'd be able to close the Elbridge case without ever having to renew his acquaintance with the blackest of black sheep in the Gunner clan, but now he knew that wouldn't be possible. Bume Webb had just pointed a meaty finger at Alred and dared Gunner to go fetch, and that wasn't a command Gunner could easily disregard. If Bume thought his homeboy Ready was responsible for the Digga's demise, Gunner owed it to his client to examine the possibility. No matter what kind of personal aggravation such an examination would entail.

So Gunner endured another ride in the Lincoln saying nothing, trying to psych himself up for the task ahead.

In fact, the only attempt Gunner made to converse with his pair of escorts on the return leg of the trip came when they were dropping him off back at Benny Elbridge's place, where the investigator's red Cobra was somewhat incredibly still parked. He leaned in through the white Town Car's open rear window after getting out, said to the smartly dressed black man with the scoundrel's smile, "You don't think I oughta know you brothers' names? Just in case we meet again at a party or something?"

Both men laughed in unison, Brother Kangol in the front seat seemingly the most amused. He looked back at his partner, shrugged a what-the-hell, and the latter said, "I'm Jessie, and he's Ben. But folks like to call us—"

"J and B. That's cute."

"It ain't cute. It's *dope,*" Ben said. Not laughing anymore. "You wanna watch who you call cute, muthafucka."

The big man threw the Lincoln in gear as his homeboy Jessie grinned, left Gunner standing there in a cloud of the car's exhaust.

It was almost one o'clock when Gunner sat down at his desk for the first time all day Thursday. Bume Webb's enforced summons this morning had cost him half the day. He didn't need Mickey to tell him this was no way to run a business, not showing up for work until most people were finishing lunch, but Mickey told him anyway, not even waiting for the front door to close to start tearing into him. Fortunately, both Gunner's landlord and Winnie Phifer, the barber's assistant in the shop, had people in their chairs and other customers waiting, so Gunner didn't have to deal with Mickey bringing his whining into the back room after him.

Two written phone messages were waiting for Gunner when he sat down: one from Desmond Joy, and another from Steven La Porte of the LAPD. Both had come in late that morning, and were simple requests for a callback. He felt encouraged to see both messages, and was anxious to talk to each of the people who had left them, but there was one call he had to make before making any others. He just hoped it wasn't too late.

"You meet with my man Jolly this morning?" Gunner asked Wally Browne as soon as KTLK's general manager picked up the line.

"Yeah. He came in about two hours ago. I gotta tell you, Gunner, I'm not so sure he's the right man for the job here."

"Why? What happened?"

"Nothing 'happened.' It's just . . . the man seems a little rough around the edges to me, that's all. He acts like he's afraid to speak, and when he does, it's usually to say somethin' about Jesus bein' his personal savior, et cetera, et cetera. How long's he been doin' this kind of work, anyway?"

"Since eight o'clock this morning. How long do you think he's been doing it?"

"Hell, I didn't mean—"

"So how did you leave it with him, Mr. Browne? Is he out watching Ms. Johnson now, or did you send him home?"

"You mean you don't know?"

"No. Frankly, I don't. Like I told you last night, I've got another case to work—this is the first chance I've had to check in with either one of you."

Browne fell silent for a moment, still unconvinced Gunner's judgment could be trusted in this matter. Eventually, however, he said, "Far as I know, he's on the job. I gave 'im all the info he asked for, Sparkle's itinerary and the like, and he left, I assumed to start watching the house before she came in to do her show this morning."

"She went on the air today?"

"Please. Are you kidding? I begged her to take some time off till I was blue in the face, but I'd've had more luck asking an elephant to climb a tree."

"She say anything about the attempt on her life yesterday?"

"What, on her show, you mean?"

"Yes."

"She had to. How could she ignore it? But she didn't say a whole lot. Just a few words of reassurance about her condition, and about how she wasn't going to let the crazies in this world stop her from deliverin' the message. That sort of thing."

"But nothing about Nance."

"No, no. No way. Give the lady credit for havin' a little intelligence, Gunner."

Gunner asked if either Browne or Johnson had received any word yet from the LAPD about Nance's status as a suspect, and Brown said he'd called downtown less than an hour ago, was told by one of the investigating officers that Johnson's old boyfriend was being held for questioning down at Parker Center at that very moment.

"You got this cop's name?" Gunner asked. "I'd like to call him or his partner later, see how Nance's Q-and-A turned out."

"Sure. Hold on a minute." Browne found the name and number, read them aloud for Gunner to take down. "What, you don't think they're gonna hold 'im? After everything Sparkle told us about him?"

"I don't know. They will if we're lucky. If they hold him, it probably means he's our man, and we can all relax, stop worrying about somebody else trying again. Whereas if they don't . . ."

He thought better of finishing the sentence.

"He's the guy. He's *gotta* be the guy," Browne said. Trying as much to make himself believe it as Gunner.

"Yeah. Let's just hope he is," Gunner said.

"Aw, hell," Matthew Poole said, sounding over the phone like he was trying to talk with half a sub sandwich stuffed in his mouth. "I almost made it. Two weeks without any harassment from you."

"You think this is easy for me? You're the fourth flatfoot I've had to talk to in four days. Talk about a root canal without Novocain . . ."

Poole was a veteran robbery/homicide detective with the LAPD, and Gunner's oldest and most reliable contact within the department. Their friendship was tenuous at best, but persevering, and was entirely held together by a near-constant exchange of favors. For two men who had absolutely nothing of consequence in common—Poole was a jowly white man who liked Sinatra, Gunner a younger black man who liked Turrentine—it was a surprisingly efficient relationship.

"Antoinetta Aames? What the hell kinda name is that?" Poole asked, after Gunner had requested he run a trace on Aames for him. It seemed safe to say now that Danee Elbridge wasn't going to be calling with the info on Aames he'd asked for, so the authorities were the investigator's next option. He had thought briefly about asking Kevin Frick to run the trace for him, then decided against it, as Frick had made it clear the last time they spoke that he didn't want to be bothered again with anything relating to the Elbridge case until Gunner could offer him something in the way of physical evidence.

"I don't make 'em up, Poole. I just write 'em down. Sister's name is Antoinetta Aames, what can I tell you?"

"So who is she, and why should I care?"

"She's a possible wit to a possible homicide. Or maybe even a murderer, I won't really know until I talk to her. Her or her girlfriend Felicia something, if you could maybe make that connection for me too."

"I see. Got it. You wanna take a deep breath now, try to say that again in *English*?"

"Sure. You got a few minutes?"

"No. Forget about it. Gimme the exact spelling of her name, I'll run the goddamn trace."

Shortly after hanging up with Poole, Gunner got a callback on the message he'd left earlier for Steven La Porte.

"Thought it might interest you to know, you're no longer a suspect in the Crumley case," the detective said.

"I didn't know I *was* a suspect," Gunner said.

"Well, I'll admit you weren't a great one, but we had you on our A-list all the same. Lucky for you we found somebody better."

"Let me guess. It's a lady by the name of Antoinetta Aames."

"Antoinetta Aames? Never heard of her. This guy's name is Melvin Felipe, the biggest shit-for-brains you'd ever wanna see."

"Melvin Felipe?"

"He's a crackhead with three other aliases, but none of 'em are important. What's important is, his prints were all over Crumley's apartment, and we can't seem to locate 'im to ask 'im why. Looks like he's a runaway."

"And his motive for doing Crumley?"

"You mean besides the fact Crumley caught 'im robbing his crib? He hasn't got one. You really think he's gonna need two?"

Gunner ignored the rhetorical question, asked the cop if he and his partner, Chin, had any physical evidence outside of Felipe's fingerprints to link him to Crumley's murder.

"Not yet," La Porte said. "We traced 'im to his sister's place out in South Gate, but there was nothin' there to see by the time we came by to look for 'im. He hadn't been home since early Tuesday morning, the sister said, and he cleaned out his room when he left. I wonder why."

"Then my tape didn't turn up over there, I guess."

La Porte found that worth a chuckle. "You and your friggin' tape. Get over it already, will you? Crumley gettin' whacked had nothin' to do with your suicide case, this was a simple B and E gone bad."

"We can't be sure of that yet, La Porte. Just because your suspect's a crackhead—"

"He's got two priors on similar beefs, Gunner. And the MO on those was the same as it was here—entry through a bedroom window, nothing but small items taken. Cash, jewelry, silverware, et cetera. Only difference this time was, he got caught with his hands in the cookie jar, had to hurt somebody to get away."

It was a convincing argument. The BHPD's Kevin Frick had been saying all along that Crumley's murder and Carlton Elbridge's apparent suicide would turn out to be unrelated, and maybe he was right. As bad as Gunner wanted the two to connect, the pieces just wouldn't fit. A surveillance tape that couldn't be used to blackmail Elbridge's hypothetical killer; the lack of a second VCR in Crumley's apartment for making copies; now a murder suspect with a history of committing similar crimes entirely devoid of hidden subtext.

"You ask the sister if she ever saw Felipe with a tape?" Gunner asked, not one to let go of an unfeasible idea easily.

"No. But not because we didn't think of it. Lady seems to have the same appreciation for rock cocaine her brother does, we were lucky she could remember she had a brother at all. Hey listen, Gunner, is that about it? I'm being a good guy here, callin' to let you know you were off the hook. I'd've known you were gonna question me all fuckin' day about this shit . . ."

"Okay, okay. But do me one last favor, will you? Let me know when Felipe turns up. You're probably right about this being a dead horse I'm beating, but if I'm still working this case when you collar him . . ."

"Yeah, yeah, okay. Assuming he's still breathing when we find 'im, you can have a few words with 'im soon as Pete and I have had ours. What the hell do I care?"

Gunner didn't know it until the dial tone sounded in his ear, but that was the man's way of saying good-bye.

Desmond Joy wanted to do a late lunch. He wouldn't discuss his reasons over the phone, just asked Gunner to meet him in an hour down at Coley's Kitchen on Crenshaw and Vernon in Leimert Park. Gunner had actually had other plans for his afternoon, but he found a way to change them so that both Joy's and his own needs were met.

He was walking out of his office to leave when Benny Elbridge met him at the door, a hangdog look on his face. He wasn't near tears, but Gunner had seen less remorseful-looking people begging for a judge's mercy down at the county courthouse.

"Well, well," the investigator said. "Look who finally remembered I'm alive."

"I come here to offer you an apology, Mr. Gunner," Elbridge said, man enough to meet Gunner's gaze without flinching. "I lied to you."

"Yes. You did, didn't you?"

"But Mr. Trevor says you're still on the job. That you're gonna keep on lookin' for my boy's killer, even though you know now it's really Bume you been workin' for all this time."

"That's right. At least, I'm not ready to give up yet."

"Good. God bless you. I mean that." He reached out to take Gunner's right hand, swallowed it up in both of his own.

"Forget it," Gunner said, easing his hand away uncomfortably. "A fee's a fee, right? What difference does it make where it comes from?"

"If it's comin' from a man like Bume, it can make a lotta difference. I know me, I had a hard time doin' what he asked me to do, hire you with his money to find out what happened to Carlton. I'd've had just a few more dollars in my pocket when Mr. Trevor called . . ."

"Sure thing, Mr. Elbridge. I've been there myself, it's okay."

"No. It ain't okay. Mr. Trevor said now that you know the truth, I don't really have to talk to you no more, that he can handle everything with you from now on. But I didn't wanna just go 'way and leave you thinkin' I only did what I done for the money. That Bume Webb cared more about Carlton than his own father did."

"There's no need to explain, Mr. Elbridge."

"Still." Elbridge took his left thumb, smeared a tear across the breadth of his left cheek. "I just wanted you to know. I'd've had the money, I would've hired you myself, for real. I didn't need Bume Webb to tell me to do that."

Gunner wasn't sure the old man deserved to be let off the hook so easily, but Elbridge's need for forgiveness was too great to deny. He took a bribe to front for Bume Webb, that was all; a dishonorable deceit, to be sure, but not a particularly destructive one. Surely there was nothing to be gained now by making him feel like the only client who had ever successfully run a game on Aaron Gunner.

"Far as I'm concerned, Mr. Elbridge, you're still my client," Gunner said, patting the old man's left shoulder softly. "You're the man who hired me, and you're the man I intend to keep reporting to. That all right with you?"

Elbridge couldn't believe what he was hearing. "Sure, sure. But—"

"If Mr. Trevor has a problem with that, he can call me. He's got the number."

Elbridge grinned, stuck his hand out to shake Gunner's with great enthusiasm. "All right then! You want I should call you, or . . ."

"I'll call you tonight, say around six, give you an update on what I've found out so far. Just make sure you're by the phone when I call this time, huh?"

"Oh, you got it. I'll be there, don't worry."

It was another ten seconds before he stopped shaking Gunner's hand.

thirteen

At two-thirty that afternoon, Gunner found Desmond Joy sitting at a table in the middle of Coley's Kitchen's small main dining room, already digging into the restaurant's rich Jamaican fare like a man who'd last eaten a week ago. In less than three hours, a cluster of people waiting for tables would be making it impossible to enter Coley's through the front door, but this early in the day, Joy and Gunner practically had the place all to themselves.

"So what's up?" Gunner asked, as soon as he'd sat down and ordered the jerk chicken and a bottle of ginger beer from a waitress only too eager to please him.

"I understand you're still working for Mr. Elbridge," Joy said, dabbing at the corner of his mouth with a napkin.

Gunner nodded. "That's right. Today makes three whole days. What, was I supposed to have lost interest by now?"

"That wouldn't have surprised me. But that's not the reason I ask." He refilled his glass from his own bottle of ginger beer, said, "I ask because I'm about to do something it only makes sense to do if you're going to continue on with this thing. If you're close to wrapping it up, there's really no point in my saying anything."

Gunner shook his head. "Sorry. Way things look right now, I may not be done for a few more days, at least." He made a gesture to indicate it was Joy's move. "So . . ."

"I've done some checking on you, Brother Gee. Trying to find out how legit you are. And the four-one-one I get is that you're all that and more. Your homie Slicky in particular assures me I can trust you with even the most sensitive info without worrying about where it might go from here."

"Slicky's a good man."

"As are you, apparently. Which is why I'm going to take a chance here and tell you something you really have no right to know, in the interest of helping you reach a quick and satisfactory conclusion to your investigation."

Gunner smiled. "That's very generous of you, Brother Joy. A quick and satisfactory conclusion to my investigation would be quite welcome."

"You joke, Brother Gee, but it isn't funny. If I'm wrong about you, the Digga's rep could be damaged beyond all repair, and his family would bear the brunt of that."

"All right. This is serious business, I get it."

Joy waited for their waitress to set Gunner's beer down in front of him, then disappear again, before continuing. "You asked me the other day what reasons the Digga could have had to take his own life, and I declined to give you an answer. Since you're still pursuing the possibility that he was murdered, I can only assume his wife and mother did likewise. Is that correct?"

"It is. I couldn't get either one of them to say two words on the subject."

"Then neither of them told you what was in his note."

"His suicide-slash-rap-lyrics note? No. Not hardly."

Joy nodded, finally left with no choice but to say what he'd come to say. "About ten months ago, out in Philly, the Digga had a girl up in his room. Somebody he'd met at a club the night before, I don't even think he knew her name. Sad to say, but there was nothing unusual about it, that was just the Digga's way on the road. Anyway, the way he explained things afterward, they got down to business rather quickly. She gave him some head, asked him to give it to her from behind. So he did. Then, afterward—"

"He found out she wasn't a she," Gunner said.

"Yes. How did you know?"

"I've heard that story before. It always starts the same way. First some head, then some backdoor action."

"Yeah. I'd heard it before myself. Unfortunately, the Digga hadn't. He didn't know the score until the damage had already been done." He shrugged. "And of course, a young brother's ego being what it is, he didn't take the shock too well." Joy looked around the room to make sure he wasn't being overheard, then said, "He almost killed the poor bastard. The only reason he didn't was because I happened to have the suite right next to his that night, broke in through the adjoining door to stop him." He sipped his beer, watched as Gunner's plate was delivered. When they were alone again, he said, "As it was, the young 'lady's' hospital bills came to a little over ten grand, and it cost us another fifty to buy his silence in the matter thereafter."

"Sixty grand? He walked away for that?"

"Yeah, I know. We got off cheap. But the damn kid was a fan, what can I say? He actually blamed himself for what happened to him, not the Digga. Only thing he really asked for afterward was the reassurance that the Digga didn't hate him for the game he'd played on him."

"And did he get it?"

"He was led to believe he did. That, and the monetary compensation we offered, was the best I could do for him, I'm afraid."

"In other words, the Digga wasn't ready to kiss and make up."

"No. Not even. He looked upon what the guy had done to him as rape. The idea that he'd had his jimmy inside a man's mouth and ass . . . It just wiped him out. Drove him crazy."

"And that's why he wanted to kill himself? Because he'd once had sex with a man?"

"You telling me you find that surprising? That a straight, healthy young black man with a wife and two kids would have a hard time dealing with being tricked into getting jiggy with another man?"

Obviously, the answer was no. Gunner knew as well as anyone how pervasive homophobia was among young African-American males, and how lethal that homophobia could sometimes become. Raised as they generally were in fundamental Christian households, black men were conditioned from a very early age to consider homosexuality nothing less than an abomination in the eyes of God, and so rejected the practice with great prejudice. And aside from the moral aspects of the issue were the strictly practical ones. In a cultural setting where a young man's ability to meet any physical challenge was constantly being tested, no charge could bring him more grief than that he was somehow more a woman than a man. That was the kind of label that, on the street especially, could make one's daily existence a living nightmare.

"I can see how he might've taken it pretty hard, sure," Gunner conceded. "It's just . . . This isn't just any young brother from the hood we're talking about, is it? It's C.E. Digga Jones. A media superstar who could've bought you and me, and all the people we'll happen to meet over the next five years, with what he earned on an average payday."

"And if he was? What difference should that have made?"

"Maybe none at all. I'm only saying that, considering everything else he had going for him, you'd like to think the kid could've found a way to overlook the indignity of having had a single, inadvertent gay experience."

"That's easy for you to say, Brother Gee. You aren't the one who had to live with it."

"No. That's true, I'm not."

"What you need to understand is that it wasn't just the guilt the boy had weighing on him. It was the fear as well. He was terrified the guy in Philly would go back on our deal and start talking, that sooner or later, the word would get out about what the two of them had done to each other in that hotel room together. But of course, word never did get out. The guy never opened his mouth, just as I always told the Digga he wouldn't. And that's the real tragedy in all this, you see. The Digga killed himself for nothing. That kid who played him back in Philly was *never* gonna talk."

"But how could you have been so sure of that? You said yourself the money he took to go away was chump change. If somebody had gotten an inkling of what had happened that night and offered him big dollars for his story . . ."

"Nobody *knew* his story," Joy said. "I told you. I fixed everything. I set it up so that no one would ever know what really happened out there but me, the Digga, and him. The cover story for his injuries I invented satisfied everybody who heard it—the police, the hotel, even the hospital where he was taken. Only way somebody else could have found out the truth about that night was if the kid said something, and I don't think he would've ever done that, like I said. I've got a sense for people, brother, and my sense was that this boy cared more about the Digga than he did himself. Sounds pitiful as hell, I know, but that's just the way some of these kids are today."

"Still. I should probably talk to him, don't you think? Just in case he's driving around Pennsylvania in a brand-new Jaguar you don't know about?"

Joy shook his head, said, "Out of the question. The agreement we made was that he wouldn't out us, and we wouldn't out him. You wanna talk to him, Gee, you're gonna have to go find him on your own."

"All right. Let's just assume he didn't talk, then. Word could have still gotten out some other way. Or am I mistaken in thinking the Digga's wife and mother also knew what happened to him that night?"

"You're not mistaken. Of course they knew. The kid had been half crazy with guilt ever since, it was inevitable that he'd tell his wife and mother what happened."

"Then one of them could have leaked the story. If not deliberately, accidentally."

"Right. Like they leaked it to you, you mean?"

Joy had Gunner there. The investigator had seen firsthand how protective both women were of the information in question; the likelihood that one of them had shared it with somebody else, even inadvertently, was remote to say the least.

"There was no leak, Brother Gee," Joy said. "I would have heard about it if there had been, the Digga would've told me."

"Even if he'd been instructed by a blackmailer not to?"

"*Especially* then. I'd saved his ass once, he would've expected me to do it again. That was my job."

Gunner ate in silence for a few moments, letting Joy's story take root in his mind. After he'd heard Joy order another ginger beer and ask that their check be brought with it, Gunner said, "What about the note? Both you and the kid's wife say it explained his reasons for contemplating suicide in some detail."

"Depending on your ability to understand the language, yes. It did."

"Was there any indication when it was written? That is, could he have actually written it sometime before his death, rather than immediately preceding it?"

Joy thought about it, shrugged. "I suppose it's possible. There was no date on the note as I recall. But it was lying right next to his body on the floor when we found him, so we just assumed he'd written it that same night. Why—"

"I'm wondering if someone could have read the note before that weekend, found out about his misadventure in Philly that way."

Joy shook his head again. "I don't think so. The Digga guarded his music pretty carefully, it would've never been left around for somebody to see." His beer and the check arrived at their table, and he sent the waitress on her way again with the check and what looked like a Platinum American Express card. "Face it, Gunner. The Digga committed suicide. His love for the ladies finally got him into something too heavy for his ego to handle, and it killed him. It happens to people that young sometimes."

It was an oddly rational attitude for a man to take about the loss of a million-dollar meal ticket, but it wasn't entirely without merit. Gunner had been waiting three days for someone to provide him with the one thing missing from the ubiquitous C.E. Digga Jones suicide theory—a viable motive—and now he finally had one. Coupled with a complete lack of evidence to the contrary, it was the perfect excuse to go back to the Body Count home offices tomorrow, tell Raymont Trevor his boss's suspicions about the Digga being murdered were unfounded, if that was what Gunner wanted to do.

But . . .

"You make a good case for suicide, Brother Joy," he admitted. "And I'll take what you've told me under advisement. But that's all I can promise you right now. I'm sorry if you were hoping for something more."

"You're damn right I was. I told you I wanted to see you wrap this thing up, before it explodes in all our faces. We had an understanding, I thought."

"I'm afraid we didn't. I'd like to put this case to bed just as quickly as you'd like me to do it, but there's a number of loose ends I need to clear up first. Starting with who killed Ray Crumley, and why."

"Crumley? The security man out at the Westmore?"

"You remember him, huh? Yeah. That Crumley. I meant to mention it earlier, but I never got the chance. He was murdered Monday night sometime. The police think by a crackhead he caught jacking his apartment, but I suspect there was more to it than that."

Joy set his beer glass back down on the table, his staid veneer showing a sudden hairline crack. "How's that?"

"Well, it's a long story, but the short version is, I think he was blackmailing somebody. He'd taken a surveillance tape shot at the hotel the night of the Digga's death home with him for a couple of days, then returned it, and I can't imagine why he would have done that other than to somehow use it for extortion purposes. Doesn't that make sense to you?"

"I don't know," Joy said dully. "I imagine it would depend on what was on the tape."

"What was on the tape was the hallway outside the Digga's door between the hours of four and eight p.m. the Saturday he died. I've never seen it personally, but among other things, I understand it shows everyone who came in or out of the kid's room throughout that length of time."

"I don't understand. So it showed who his visitors were before eight. The cops say the Digga died around midnight, how could Crumley have used that tape to blackmail anybody?"

Gunner shook his head, said, "I don't know. The blackmail angle's just a guess, like I said. But it's one of the things I'd like to explore a little deeper before I stick a fork in this case and call it done. There's one or two more, but I won't bore you with them right now."

Joy looked disappointed, opened his mouth to protest, when Gunner cut him off to say, "Excuse me," waved somebody behind Joy over to their table.

"Desmond Joy, I'd like you to meet my cousin, Del Curry," the investigator said when Del had reached them, apparently feeling a little sheepish about the interruption. "Hope you don't mind, but I asked Del to meet me here after we were through. We *were* through, weren't we?"

Joy shook Del's hand, not particularly happy, said, "Sure, sure."

"I could sit out front if you two need another couple of minutes," Del offered. "I'm actually a little early."

"No, no. It's cool, it's cool." Joy stood up, eyed Gunner with no small measure of ire. "I'm sorry you've decided to go ahead with this, Brother Gee. Danee and Ms. Trayburn have been through hell and back these last three weeks. It'd be a shame if your indifference to reality caused them to suffer even more."

He met their waitress returning to their table, signed his bill and retrieved his credit card, and left. Del watched him go before taking his seat, asked, "Was it something I said?"

"In case you didn't recognize him, that was the Digga's manager. He's been a little on edge lately."

"No shit."

Gunner asked his cousin if he'd like something to drink, and when Del said no, got right down to the business he'd called him here to discuss.

"Forget about it," Del said when Gunner was through. "I'm not interested."

"Del, I wouldn't ask if I had some other alternative. You've got to do this for me, man."

"Sorry, Aaron. I haven't talked to Alred in six years, and I'm not gonna start talking to him now. You have something to say to him, you're gonna have to say it yourself."

"I intend to. All I'm asking you to do is get me a meeting with him. Call him and say you need to talk to him, set a time and place for the two of you to get together tonight. I'll take care of the rest."

"Why can't *you* make the call?"

"Because he won't come if I do. The last time I talked to him, we exchanged some words, basically promised we'd never come near each other again. I had my way, we'd leave it at that, but he's become a key player in the case I'm working, there's some questions I've got to ask him."

Del shook his head in disbelief, astounded by the position Gunner was putting him in. "Damn," he said. "I hate the fool just as much as you do. Why do *I* have to deal with his worthless ass?"

"Because his mother was your first cousin, same as I am," Gunner said, referring to his late sister Ruth. "He's as much family to you as he is to me."

Del made a face, said, "Lucky me," and asked Gunner for suggestions as to where and when his meeting with Alred Lewis should take place.

Jolly Mokes's first day on the job as Sparkle Johnson's babysitter was proving an uneventful one, much to Gunner's relief. Gunner met with Jolly at four at the Deuce, right after leaving Del at Coley's, and listened attentively as the big man told him what a bore it all had been from a stool at the uncrowded bar.

"Ain't nothin' happened the whole day," Jolly said, as if he hadn't been hoping for precisely that result when Gunner first assigned him the job that morning. "She went to work, she went to lunch, then she went back to work. Gang of reporters and TV people followin' her everywhere."

"She ever talk to you?"

"Once. In the lobby of the station she works at. She came up to me and said I wasn't foolin' nobody, actin' like I was just in there readin' the newspaper or somethin'. She said my bein' there wasn't servin' no purpose, that she'da been you, she wouldn'ta hired me to keep an eye on a dead tree."

Gunner grinned. "Fitting name for her, isn't it? Sparkle?"

"The Lord says thou shalt not kill," Jolly said. "Nobody knows that better than me. But if He could ever forgive a man for puttin' somebody in a box and nailin' it shut . . ."

"You don't want to talk like that, Jolly. Not even in jest."

"Hey, man, I didn't—"

"You don't have the right. Or do you think Grace would disagree?"

Jolly shook his head, suddenly and appropriately contrite. Gunner was right: the murder of his late wife would forever make Jolly an unfitting source of such misogynistic levity.

"So what do you want me to do now?" he asked.

"Go back and start again, what else? Watch her until she goes home to Browne's place tonight, I'll relieve you from there. That'll probably be somewhere around seven, seven-thirty or so."

"I don't get it. You said the cops got the man put the bomb in her car, right? Why do I still have to watch her?"

"Because I'm not convinced the man they have in custody *is* the one who put the bomb in her car. I've got a call in to the detectives who've been questioning him this afternoon. As soon as one of them calls me back—"

"Yo, Gunner! Phone call!" Lilly said, standing at the other end of the bar holding a cordless telephone receiver up in the air.

Gunner turned back to Jolly, said, "That must be them now. Hold on a minute." He walked over to where Lilly was standing, reached across the countertop for the receiver in her hand, but she just drew it back, all but hissing like an angry snake.

"How many times I gotta tell you about receivin' calls in here?" she asked. "A thousand? Fifty thousand?"

"That would be a very conservative estimate. It's gotta be more like a million. Can I have the phone, please?"

"Two dollars," Lilly said, holding her free hand out, palm up.

"Two dollars? You must be crazy."

Lilly started to take the phone back into her office.

"All right, all right, here, damnit!" He reached into his right-hand trouser pocket, freed two one-dollar bills from his money clip and handed them to her. She smiled, practically threw the handset at him in return, and walked away.

As Gunner had thought, the man waiting on the other end of the line was one of the two LAPD robbery/homicide detectives he'd been waiting to hear from. This cop's name was Jay Peers, and despite having earlier received Wally Browne's urgent request that he cooperate with Gunner in full, he was by far the least personable law enforcement officer the investigator had spoken to all week. It was the law of averages; five cops in four days, one of them was bound to be a humorless automaton.

Still, the content of Peers's replies to Gunner's questions bothered the investigator far more than the reluctance with which he presented them. With only a few clipped words, Peers essentially reported that the interrogation he and his partner had performed on Sparkle Johnson's rejected lover, Jarrett Nance, that afternoon had served only to suggest that Nance might know who Johnson's attempted murderer was, but was not himself that person. And worse yet for Gunner, what little evidence in the case the cops had so far been able to piece together seemed to bear that out.

"So who does he say did it?" Gunner asked.

"I'm not at liberty to say," Peers answered.

"But he gave you a name."

"Yes and no."

"Yes and no?"

"He gave us a name, but not of an individual. More than that I can't tell you, Gunner, I'm sorry."

Gunner paused, feeling the very planets of the universe starting to turn against him. "You aren't talking about the Defenders Of the Bloodline?"

Now it was Peers who fell deathly silent. "You came up with that on your own. Make sure you remember that if anybody ever asks."

He hung up without saying another word.

"Well?" Jolly asked when Gunner rejoined him, a look of grave concern coloring the investigator's face.

"You've gotta go back now, Jolly. Right now, I don't want Ms. Johnson left alone again for a minute."

"What did the cops say?"

"I'll explain all that later. Get back over to the station before she leaves for the day and stay by her side—no more watching her from a distance. I'll relieve you tonight out at Browne's place just as soon as I can, like we discussed earlier."

He needed more convincing, but eventually Jolly obeyed the order and took off, left Gunner alone to rue the prospect of becoming reacquainted with his old friends, the Defenders Of the Bloodline.

The DOB, as the group was most commonly known, was an underground, highly secretive band of urban terrorists intent on purifying the African-American community of the so-called "traitors" in its midst: those black men and women who failed to meet the Defenders' guidelines for proper sociopolitical conduct. Anyone who had ever been accused of being either an Uncle Tom or the female equivalent due to their less than liberal viewpoints on subjects relevant to race was open to targeting by the Defenders—high-profile right-wing conservatives like Sparkle Johnson being a prime example—and people so honored all too often ended up dead as a result.

It had been roughly six months ago, while he was working the case Yolanda McCreary had hired him for, that Gunner had had his first and only run-in with the Defenders. Yolanda's brother, Elroy Covington, had disappeared in Los Angeles under mysterious circumstances the previous year, and in trying to determine what had happened to him, Gunner learned the DOB had sanctioned the missing man's assassination. It turned out that while Covington had indeed been murdered, the Defenders were not actually to blame, but this only became apparent after Gunner had been kidnapped and threatened with death himself by the infamous clan. Had there been any real closure to that experience—most specifically, the arrest and incarceration of all the individuals involved—it might have been easily forgotten. But with only one exception, the Defenders Gunner had dealt with were still out there somewhere, as faceless and anonymous as shadows on the sidewalk, and so were free to make good on the promise they had made him that he would now and forever be under their watchful eye, on the off chance he should someday foolishly choose to lock horns with them again.

So far, that day had failed to come. Not because Gunner had actively avoided it in any tangible way, but because fate had merely deemed it so. Now, however, a second meeting with the Defenders seemed a very likely eventuality. He had been able to dismiss Wally Browne's initial suspicions that the DOB was behind Sparkle Johnson's harrassment without much difficulty, baseless as they had been at the time, but now those suspicions would have to be reassessed. Jarrett Nance had seen to that.

It wasn't a pleasant thought.

Gunner called Lilly away from the other customers in the house, and when she came back around the bar to reach him, told her to pour him something lethal.

"It's like that, huh?" she asked, eschewing a shot glass to fill a tumbler halfway to the top with Wild Turkey.

"Oh, yeah. Bad news doesn't come any badder." He grabbed the glass before she could push it toward him, downed a good swallow of the bourbon like it was Diet Coke.

"Should I bother to ask what the problem is?"

Gunner shook his head. "You don't wanna know."

"Would a little good news help?"

Gunner grunted. "Good news? What's that?"

Lilly grinned, took a business card out of her apron pocket and handed it to him. "Lady said to give this to you next time you came in. Maybe you remember her."

The name on the card belonged to Brenda Warren, and it identified her as the public relations manager for a company in Torrance called Digiphonics. A short note was scribbled in blue ink on the back:

Sorry I missed you! Was hoping for some more stimulating "conversation"...

This was followed by her signature and what Gunner could only assume was her home phone number.

He stared at the card for a long while, Lilly having a wonderful time watching him wrestle with his conscience.

"When was she in?" Gunner asked.

"Last night. Came in around seven, I think, didn't leave till about eleven. When it was obvious you had other plans for the evenin'."

"She say anything else?"

"No. What the hell could she say? 'Can you tell me when that big, handsome nigga I'd like to screw the pants off of might be in again?' " She threw her head back and laughed like a madwoman.

It was an amusing quip, but Gunner was in no position to appreciate it. He had had more than one extended thought about Brenda Warren since their meeting two nights ago, and discovering the feeling was mutual was not going to help him leave things at that. He had tried to tell Del and Lilly they were crazy to question his ability to remain faithful to Yolanda McCreary, unavailiable as she was to him for weeks at a time, but the truth was, they had known exactly what they were talking about. Yolanda had instilled in Gunner a need for sexual contact he hadn't known in years. The last thing he needed now was to be actively pursued by a fox like Brenda Warren.

"What's wrong, Gunner?" Lilly asked, her laughter having finally wound down to a mere grin. "That didn't make your day?"

Gunner looked at her, wondering why it was he considered this woman a friend, and not his worst enemy. "You're a very fat woman, Lilly. I ever tell you that before?"

The insult only cracked her up again. "Yeah, I know I'm fat. But I also know I'm beautiful, least to some people."

"Sure you are. You've got that special kind of beauty. The kind woolly mammoths had before the Ice Age came and wiped 'em all out."

"Ha! Fuck you!"

The big bartender waddled away, chuckling, not such a hard-ass that she couldn't see the humor in a joke made at her expense.

. . .

Gunner's meeting with his nephew Alred Lewis took place in the coffee shop of the Holiday Bowl bowling alley on Crenshaw Boulevard and Rodeo Road a few minutes after six that evening, just as he'd asked Del to arrange it. He expected this to be the last bit of work he would do on the Carlton Elbridge suicide case before turning his full attention to Sparkle Johnson and the Defenders Of the Bloodline. Tomorrow, barring a miracle, he would call Benny Elbridge and resign, saying he'd come to the same conclusion the police had about C.E. Digga Jones's death at the Beverly Hills Westmore Hotel two weeks ago: the kid had killed himself. Now that Desmond Joy had given the Digga a motive, that appeared to be all but a certainty, especially since no evidence existed to suggest otherwise.

Gunner was still intrigued by Ray Crumley's homicide, to be sure, but he no longer believed it was connected to the Digga's death. That possibility too had so far proven to be unfounded, and therefore seemed to beg no further active investigation. Unfortunately, ready as he finally was to move on, Gunner had one last lead to pursue before he could close the Elbridge case with a clear conscience: Bume Webb's assertion that Alred Lewis had had the Digga murdered just to put a stake in Bume's heart.

It was a theory rife with improbability, but Gunner did the right thing and endeavored to explore it anyway. His drug-dealing nephew drove a canary-yellow Porsche Carrera a nearsighted man could spot eight blocks away, and the investigator sat in his Cobra across the street until he saw Alred park the car in the Holiday Bowl parking lot, then saunter slowly inside. Alone, as requested.

After giving Alred enough time to enter the coffee shop, take a seat, and not find Del there waiting for him, Gunner went in himself and spotted his nephew sitting in a corner booth with his hands crossed in front of him, looking as out of place in a bowling alley as a tuxedo at a square dance.

Tall, hairless, and strikingly handsome, the twenty-six-year-old was dressed from head to foot in black, in clothing that fit him to perfection and cost the equivalent of a pro athlete's monthly income, and the expression on his face, as always, promised nothing but trouble to anyone who dared even mildly annoy him.

He saw Gunner coming almost immediately, but didn't move, just watched him advance with a searing disdain. He let his uncle sit down in the booth across from him, then smiled, asked calmly, "What the fuck are you doin' here?"

"My league starts rolling in an hour. I saw you come in, thought you might like some company."

Alred's smile shifted to the other side of his mouth. "That's funny. But I didn't come here to be amused. What the fuck is goin' on? Del said—"

"Del won't be coming. He only called you because I asked him to. I'm the one who needs to talk to you, Alred, not him."

Alred glared at him, letting the smile slowly ease off his face as he tried to figure out if he should leave now, or wait a little longer. "I thought we agreed last time we saw each other, Uncle. We don't owe each other shit no more."

"This isn't about what we owe each other. I'm not—" He cut himself off as a short, cheerful Asian waitress materialized beside their table to ask if they were ready to order. Gunner asked her to bring him some pork fried rice just so they could keep their table—great Chinese food being the coffee shop's atypical specialty—then turned to his nephew again when she departed. "I'm not looking for any favors this time, Alred," he said. "This time I just want some answers to a few questions. Questions about you and Bume Webb."

Alred hadn't been expecting that. "Bume who?"

"Come on, Alred. You're gonna pretend you don't even know the man, we're gonna be here all damn night."

"Okay, so I know 'im. Bume Webb, lord of the record bus'ness. What about 'im?"

"I went to see him out at Chino this morning. He says the two of you are in business together."

"Me an' Bume? Bullshit. That nigga's *yesterday's* news, what do I wanna be in business with his ass for?"

"He was actually speaking in the past tense. According to him, you were the money man who helped him get his label Body Count off the ground."

Alred laughed. "Shit. He's delirious. Bein' locked down must be fuckin' with his mind."

"You're saying he made the whole thing up?"

"I'm sayin' I don't give a fuck what the nigga has to say about me. And neither should you."

"I'd be inclined to agree with you, Alred, except I'm not so sure what he says isn't true. An enterprising young millionaire like yourself has to put his money somewhere, and the stock market isn't always the answer. If Bume came around looking for a key investor in his recording company a while back, I could see you pitching in a few dollars to help rather easily. Just as I could also see you taking some serious offense later when he tried to deny you what you felt was a fair return on your investment."

Alred grew quiet, offering no denials.

"The reason all of this concerns me, in case you were wondering, is that someone hired me earlier in the week to look into the death of Bume's boy the Digga, and Bume seems to think you'd be an excellent place for me to start."

"What?"

"Basically, the man said you wanted more credit for Body Count's success than you were due, and that having the Digga killed was your way of thanking him for not giving it to you. It's a little far-fetched, I know, but you can't honestly say it could never happen."

Alred was furious now. "It's bullshit," he said. "And that's all I'm gonna say about it. In here with you, anyways."

"What? You don't trust me to be discreet?"

"I don't trust you, period. You been ridin' my ass since I was ten years old, there ain't nothin' you wouldn't do to try an' fuck me."

"If you're trying to say you think I'm wired here, you can rest easy. I'm not. Busting you on racketeering charges is a job for the Feds, not me. My only interest in you is finding out whether or not you had something to do with C.E. Digga Jones getting the back of his head blown off two weeks ago."

"I already told you, I didn't. And you're a goddamn fool if you need me to tell you that shit."

"Yeah? Why's that?"

"Because the Digga was worth more alive to me than he was to Bume, that's why. I'm the one lost out when the nigga shot hisself, not Bume."

"Sorry, Alred, but you're losing me."

"Talk to the Digga's manager. Desmond Joy. Ask 'im who the Digga was gonna be recordin' his next three records for. Body Count, or New Millennia."

"I already know how Joy would answer that. He'd say New Millennia. He told me two days ago they were just waiting for the Digga to sign the contracts when the kid died. But what's that got . . ." His voice trailed off as his mind raced forward, answered the question he was about to ask before he could even state it.

The smallest of smiles appeared on Alred's face.

"*You're* New Millennia. The Digga was getting ready to sign up with *you*."

"I got some good people runnin' things for me, but yeah. That's right," Alred said. "You just said it yourself, Uncle. A man's gotta put his money somewhere. And the stock market don't always do."

Their waitress chose this moment to deliver Gunner's rice, and he was happy to have the interruption. He hadn't figured Alred would freely confess to the Digga's murder, but this was an even greater surprise.

"Does Bume know?"

"What? That I own New Millennia?"

Gunner nodded.

"Naw. Don't nobody know. I was gonna wait till the Digga signed the deal, then show up at the press conference to announce it, get my face in all the pictures so Bume wouldn't have no choice but to see me." He laughed.

"Bume doesn't believe the kid would've gone through with it," Gunner said. "He says the deal was all in Joy's mind, that the Digga was too much Bume's boy to ever leave."

"He does, huh? Well, he don't know. The Digga was *already* gone, he couldn't wait to do bus'ness with me." He watched Gunner run a fork around in his rice listlessly, taste it like a kid forced to eat creamed spinach. "What's the matter, Uncle? Lose your appetite?"

Gunner didn't even look up from his plate, just said, "You can go now, Alred. Sorry I bothered you."

"Oh no. Not yet. I ain't had a chance to ask *you* no questions yet."

"Questions? What do *you* need to ask questions for?"

"'Cause information's a big part'a my business, Uncle. That's why. You say somebody hired you to look into the Digga's death. What the hell's that mean? *They* think I whacked his ass too?"

Gunner sighed, seeing his nephew was determined they converse like two people who could actually stomach each other. "You or somebody else. They've got the idea he was murdered, and they wanted me to prove it. Only you can't prove something that never happened, can you?"

"No. You can't. I coulda told you that when you first got started."

"Yeah, well. Forgive me for not consulting you sooner."

"I mean, if anybody was gonna serve that nigga, it was his wife. Danee. On accounta how homeboy played on her ass mornin', noon, and night. I seen some brothers run some games on their ladies, but the Digga, god-*damn* . . ." He shook his head just thinking about it.

Gunner stopped eating, studied Alred intently. "Yeah, I've heard all about it. He even had some girls up in his room the night he died. Maybe by chance you know them."

"I might. Who was it?"

"Couple of sisters named Antoinetta Aames and Felicia something or other, I don't have a last name for Felicia yet."

"You ain't talkin' about Felicia White?"

"I just told you. I don't know. Am I?"

"That's the only Felicia I know. Felicia White. She use' to be one of my man Rocket's bitches. 'Fore she got sick, anyways."

"Sick? Sick how?"

"Sick with the AIDS, man. What else? Felicia's a first-class ho', Uncle. Rocket use' to have her ridin' every dick in San Bernardino County, it was just a matter of time 'fore she got the virus."

Gunner put his fork down now, shoved his plate all the way to one side. "Hold it a minute, Alred. Let's back up here a little."

"Back up? What for?"

"This Felicia White you're talking about. Does she have a girlfriend named Antoinetta, or not? Because if she doesn't—"

"Yeah, she got a friend name Antoinetta. Least, she introduced me to a girl by that name up at the club once. She was a freak just like Felicia. Two of 'em'd fuck a doorknob they thought it was gonna feel good to 'em."

"But if this Felicia's HIV-positive . . ."

"Yeah. That's right. The Digga was lookin' to catch the shit hisself, he was gettin' busy with her like you say. 'Less he was wearin' a hat, which I seriously doubt."

Gunner stood up from the booth, tossed a twenty-dollar bill on the table under his nephew's nose. "You have an address for this Felicia White, Alred? Or a phone number?"

"No. Hey, what's up? Where you goin'?"

"What about her pimp? This guy Rocket you mentioned?"

"I got a number for him, yeah. Out in the car. But—"

"You're gonna have to give it to me. Come on, let's go."

It was the worst possible ending to their meeting, and the one Gunner had feared above all others. Alred "Ready" Lewis, his insufferable, crack-selling nephew, telling him something useful, and thereby doing him yet another favor.

A favor he knew he would someday, somehow, be expected to repay.

fifteen

"I don't understand you, Poole," Gunner said. "If I'd've wanted you to come, you'd've told me to go fuck myself."

Poole laughed. "Yeah. I probably would've. I've gotta get myself a hobby, huh?"

They were sitting in the LAPD detective's unmarked olive-green Crown Victoria, watching nothing happen outside of Antoinetta Aames's Culver City apartment building from a half-dozen parking spaces down the street. It was a few minutes past nine Thursday evening, and dark. Quiet. Both men held a cup of coffee in an AM-PM cup in one hand, while a set of faxed mug shots featuring Aames and Felicia White, respectively, sat on the bench seat between them. Gunner had looked the photos over when Poole first handed them to him, then had put them down, disgusted. He couldn't remember the last time he had seen two women look more indifferent to being busted. White, in particular—fair-skinned, long-haired, and Asian-eyed—seemed to be grinning at the police photographer with all the come-on she knew how to manufacture.

Gunner wondered if she'd looked at Carlton Elbridge that way, just before going down on him.

"What time is it?" the investigator asked Poole.

The cop glanced at his watch, yawning, said, "Twenty-one-oh-nine. We're goin' on two hours here."

Gunner nodded, fixed his eyes on the front entrance to Aames's building again. They'd already gone up to her apartment twice, received no answer when they rang the bell. It wasn't proof she wasn't home, of course, but the darkness behind her windows seemed to suggest that was the case.

"You wanna tell me again why we're doin' this?" Poole said. "Not that it's likely to make any more sense the second time around, but . . ."

"You didn't have to come, Poole. You invited yourself, remember?"

"Sure, sure, I remember. I'm just askin' for a little clarification, that's all. I came along hopin' to learn somethin' about how *real* law enforcement officers like you do your job, but if you aren't gonna bother to *explain* anything . . ."

"We're here because the address you had for White turned out to be an old one, and she isn't in the book. Okay?"

"Not okay. Why do you you wanna talk to either one of these yahoos? What are you expectin' them to tell you?"

"I told you. I don't know. Something."

"Something?"

"The tape Ray Crumley removed from the Westmore only showed three people visiting the Digga's room the night he died, and Aames and White were two of them. Crumley's boss at the Westmore says his only interest in the tape was a pair of ladies it caught getting nasty on each other out in the hallway, but I don't buy that. That's too easy. I think Crumley wanted that tape for something it showed either White and Aames doing, or Danee Elbridge, the Digga's other visitor that night."

"So why aren't we talkin' to Danee Elbridge?"

"Because I've already asked her about Crumley, and she didn't bat an eye. She's a pretty cool customer, Poole, but I don't think she's that cool."

"Still. My comrade La Porte told you to forget about the Crumley homicide, you said. He's got a perp, he's got a motive, and the whole enchilada's got nothin' to do with C.E. Digga Jones."

"Nobody's saying it does. I'd just like to be sure it doesn't, that's all. 2DaddyLarge said Aames was all freaked out that she was gonna somehow get blamed for the Digga's death. Before I put my toys away and go home on this one, I think I should ask her why, don't you?"

Poole shook his head, drank some more of his coffee. "You already know why. Because she took a girl up to the kid's room to do a three-way with 'im she probably knew had AIDS. You and I wouldn't make a murder rap outa that, but we're not crazy. Aames is. She's a bona fide psycho-ward beauty queen, Gunner, just like your friend 2DaddyBig, or whatever his name is, told you, and her arrest jacket clearly confirms that."

"Fine. So let her prove it. Let's put the question to her personally, and see what she says."

Poole sighed heavily, showed Gunner a smile full of unabbreviated condescension. "Okay. You're the boss. But I tell you one thing . . ." He turned away, tossed the remainder of his coffee out the open side window of the car onto the street. "Next week I'm buying myself a fuckin' dish, order every sports channel they've got. Better I should be at home watchin' Eastern Montana Tech kick the shit out of Gomer Pyle U than spendin' my free nights like this."

"Tell you what, Poole. You can leave at any time. I can do this just as easily on my feet as I can sitting here with you."

Poole just ignored him, reverted almost subconsciously to his cop-on-surveillance mode. Silence flooded the car as the two men studied the entrance doors to Aames's apartment building again, waited for something even remotely worth their interest to appear in the vicinity. Gunner didn't know how Poole was passing the time, but his own mind drifted back in time two hours, when he'd gone out to Wally Browne's home in Bel Air to check on Jolly Mokes as promised.

Browne had answered the door, but Jolly was standing just behind him, watching Browne's back like any good bodyguard would. Sparkle Johnson was in the den reading, out of Gunner's sight, and never came out while he was there. Which was just fine, because he'd really only come to speak to Browne and Jolly, individually and in that order.

"I gather from the new orders you've given your man that you heard what Sparkle's friend Nance had to tell the police today," Browne said after leading Gunner to a first-floor library adjacent to his kitchen and closing the door behind them. The look on his face wasn't a smug one, exactly, but it could easily have been mistaken as such.

"I heard," Gunner said.

"I hate to say I told you so, Mr. Gunner, but I did say from the beginning that those bastards were involved in this. Didn't I?"

"There's still no guarantee that they are, Mr. Browne. I only moved Jolly inside as a precautionary measure."

"Come on. Who're you kidding? The Defenders Of the Bloodline are behind Nance, and you know it. He said so himself."

"Did he?"

"Sure he did. They didn't tell you? He's been workin' for 'em all along. He told the cops he's not a Defender himself, but the guys who've been giving 'im his orders are."

"And his orders were to harrass Ms. Johnson?"

"Yeah. He said all the letters and the phone calls were their idea, not his. And of course, the bomb in her car yesterday. According to him, he didn't have anything to do with that."

"No. Of course not. I don't suppose he was able to give the cops any names?"

Browne shook his head. "He told them he doesn't know any names. They never gave him their names, or showed him their faces. All his orders came over the phone, he said, except on two occasions when he and the people he met with were completely in the dark—he couldn't see a thing.

Which is fairly common for the Defenders, right? Isn't that how they always operate?"

Unbeknownst to Browne, Gunner could vouch personally for the fact that it was. In his own previous encounter with the DOB, he had come in contact with no less than four men who had done the Defenders' dirty work, yet he'd survived the experience knowing the name of only one: Byron "Blue" Scales, a lean and mean young brother who was presently serving a thirty-year sentence up at Folsom on, among other things, a kidnapping conviction pertaining to Gunner himself. The remaining three Defenders Gunner had run into were still at large and unidentified, including the one who had ostensibly ordered the investigator's kidnapping so that they might meet, Gunner bound to a chair and blindfolded at some unknown site all the while.

"Ms. Johnson still think Nance was working alone?" Gunner asked.

"She says she does. But I don't think she really believes it. It's just what she has to say in order to blow off my concerns for her safety. She wants to keep pretending everything's okay."

"Yeah? Well, wait until the Feds call. That could change her mind quick."

"The FBI? What have they got to do with this?"

"The Defenders are a pet project of theirs. The DOB's a national enterprise, not a local one, so that automatically makes them the Bureau's business. If they haven't taken over the LAPD's investigation into last night's bombing yet, they will soon. You can bet on it."

"Jesus," Browne said. "I hadn't thought about that. The FBI! Sparkle's gonna have a coronary!"

"Don't knock it. Once they get involved, they'll cover her like a blanket twenty-four/seven, and my friend and I will be able to go home."

"Yeah, but until then . . ."

"We'll be here. Of course."

But Browne went right on worrying. Jolly still wasn't his first choice as a bodyguard for Johnson, and he wasn't shy about reiterating the fact. The big man was physically imposing enough, he said, but he doubted Jolly had the temperament necessary to resort to violence, should circumstances ever call for him to do so.

The irony in that was laughable, of course, but Gunner never told Browne as much, just reminded him again that, for another twenty-four hours at least, it was either Jolly or nothing. Browne seemed tempted to go with nothing this time, but eventually relented when Gunner wouldn't budge.

A few minutes later, Gunner's large friend entered Browne's office in the radio executive's stead, Gunner having asked Browne if he could have a word with Jolly in private.

"I want you to start carrying this," the investigator said, pressing a .45 caliber Para-Ordinance P10 firmly into Jolly's right hand.

Jolly looked at the gun as if it were a live tarantula. "What for?"

"Because the game's changed, and you may need it. Has Browne talked to you at all about what's going on?"

Jolly shook his head.

"Ms. Johnson's boyfriend's claiming he's been harrassing her under orders from a group called the Defenders Of the Bloodline. Ever hear of 'em?"

The big man took so long to answer, Gunner was beginning to think he hadn't heard the question. "The Defenders?"

"Yeah. Also known as the DOB. They're a bunch of black crazies who think conservatives like Johnson are the scourge of our people and should be wiped off the face of the earth. Which would be somewhat amusing, except that they aren't just talking. They've already killed a number of people here and elsewhere, and the Feds have been getting nowhere trying to stop 'em."

Jolly paused again, came back with a simple shrug this time. "I don't get it."

"Get? There's nothing to get. Johnson's boyfriend could be full of shit for all we know, but just in case he isn't, we've gotta prepare for the worst here. If the Defenders really are involved in this like he says, Jolly, size and strength alone aren't gonna cut it against 'em. Even you are gonna need a little gentle persuasion to sweet-talk 'em with, they make another move on the lady while you're watching her, and that means I want you strapped from here on in. No ifs, ands, or buts."

"Yeah, but . . ."

"You're worrying about violating your parole, don't bother. You use that thing to take a Defender down, the cops are gonna be too busy planning the parade route to even think about busting you on a parole beef. Believe me."

"Sure, sure. I just . . ."

"What? The Lord's not telling you you can't protect yourself properly, is he?"

"No. It ain't that."

"Then?"

"Hell, I'm just thinkin' 'bout *you,* that's all. I mean, this ain't your only piece, is it?"

"My only piece? No." Gunner couldn't help but find Jolly's concern slightly touching. "That's just a spare I had lying around the house. Don't worry about me, Jolly. Worry about yourself, and Ms. Johnson. And please, not necessarily in that order."

Shortly thereafter, he left Jolly to it.

But their conversation stayed with him for some time afterward. Jolly's question about the Para-Ordinance being the investigator's only weapon had led him to start giving some serious thought to a possibility he hadn't cared to fully acknowledge before, namely that the Defenders Of the Bloodline had finally decided to make good on their promise to keep him under some form of surveillance. Up to this point, he'd written that off as a hollow threat, just something the Defenders had said in parting to make him lose a little sleep, but now he wasn't so sure. Now he had to wonder if the silver Le Baron that had seemed to be following him for the last several days was relevant to something other than his efforts in the Carlton Elbridge case.

Could inserting himself and Jolly into their plans for Sparkle Johnson have finally put him back on the Defenders' hit list?

It was probably best to consider it likely, and operate accordingly. So he sat in Poole's car now, down in Culver City, one eye looking for Antoinetta Aames and the other for the silver Chrysler, hoping like hell to see the former first. Because once Aames was out of the way, he could concentrate on Johnson and the Defenders. Aames and her girlfriend Felicia White were the only holes in the Elbridge investigation left to fill, as far as the investigator was concerned.

Unfortunately, neither lady was anywhere to be seen.

Aames's apartment building was a two-story number on Barrington Avenue that dated back to the sixties, the kind of ubiquitous structure that featured a carport out front and a giant starburst on its face, the latter mounted just above the ridiculous name its builders had pretentiously bestowed upon it: Seacrest Manor. In two and a half hours, Gunner and Poole saw a grand total of four people pass through the Manor's unlocked doors, three men and one woman, and none of them resembled either Aames or White in the least.

After the last of this quartet had disappeared inside—a young, brown-skinned man with a ratty beard and ponytail to match—Poole turned to his right and said, "Okay, Gunner, you win. Get outa my car, I'm goin' home."

He braced himself to hear Gunner argue, but the investigator lacked all incentive. "I'm with you," he said, nodding. "This is a bust—take me back to my car."

"You're givin' up?"

"Not giving up. Just regrouping. I'll either come back later or try to draw a line on White instead. Her old pimp answers the phone the next time I call, he might be able to give me a new address for her."

Poole started the car without comment, pulled the Ford slowly away from the curb. A more patient man might have kept going south on Barrington, circled the whole block to get back to Washington Boulevard and the 405 Freeway on-ramp he sought, but Poole just turned the unmarked cruiser into the first driveway on his left, backed out again to reverse his field. Seeking the shortest distance between two points, as was so often the cop's wont.

Meanwhile, Gunner took one last look at Antoinetta Aames's apartment building, saw the ponytailed man they'd seen enter earlier come out again, moving as if something big with sharp teeth would soon be hot on his heels.

"Hold up a minute, Poole," Gunner said.

"I see 'im."

Poole slowed, watched first through his side mirror, then his side window as the guy hustled past them on the left, built a slight lead on his way out to Washington. Gunner had never seen him before, but he knew the type; hype or crackhead, rummie or stoner, addiction always gave them the same look of anxious desperation, clothed them in the same thin layer of sour sweat.

Gunner opened his door while the car was still moving, stood up to yell something out to the guy as Poole, surprised, hit the brakes.

"Hey, Marvin!"

Marvin Felipe never turned around, just took off at a dead sprint at the very sound of his name.

Gunner jumped out of the car to follow him on foot, snapped at a startled Poole to head him off in the Ford. Felipe already had a half-block head start on them both. He was younger than his pursuers, and fast, but his health was shot, and that made the difference. Over the next four blocks, along the quiet residential streets just north of Washington, Felipe stumbled twice, then fell altogether before Gunner and Poole collapsed upon him, the cop from the north, the investigator from the south.

Gunner reached him first, had to duck a few wild punches Felipe threw at his head before a hard right of his own put the bearded man down again, eyes rolling around in their sockets like dice being shaken in a cup. Gunner watched as Ray Crumley's alleged killer retched onto some poor devil's perfectly manicured lawn, then snatched him up by the back of his neck and marched him over to Poole's car. It sounded as if every dog in the neighborhood was barking in applause.

"What the fuck is this, man? I didn't do nothin'!" Felipe cried, as soon as Gunner tossed him into the Ford's backseat and got in right behind him.

"I take it this is La Porte's suspect? Marvin what's his name?" Poole asked Gunner, turned around in the car's front seat so as to take a good look at their quarry.

"Marvin Felipe," Gunner said. "Yeah. Unless he just takes off running every time he hears the name."

"I don't know what you assholes are talkin' about! My name is Julian!" Felipe cried. "Julian Ashby!"

"Julian Ashby. That's a good one. You got any ID on you, Mr. Ashby? Something with your picture on it, specifically?"

The man with the ratty ponytail just blinked at him, mouth nervously chewing on something completely imaginary.

"No. I didn't think so." Gunner took out the Ruger he'd been carrying since he picked up the Para-Ordinance for Jolly, trained it more or less in the direction of Felipe's midsection. He then turned to Poole again and said, "Let's go back to Ms. Aames's apartment, see if we can't figure out why he was so anxious to leave."

Felipe's mouth flew open to object, his eyes wide with fear—but he decided at the last minute to hold his tongue instead. He sat back, stared straight ahead as Poole turned the cruiser's engine over, drove them all back to Antoinetta Aames's apartment building on Barrington Avenue.

The door to Aames's apartment was standing open when they reached it, but both Gunner and Poole had known bad news awaited them long before that. They'd had to take turns ordering Felipe out of the car before he agreed to come along, wearing Poole's handcuffs now, and they recognized his reluctance as the reaction of a man who did not want to view the same nightmare twice.

"I didn't have nothin' to do with this, I swear to God," Felipe said, starting to cry.

Gunner and Poole traded glances, their respective weapons already out and at the ready, then gently pushed the crackhead forward to lead their way inside.

Compared with that of the late Ray Crumley, Antoinetta Aames's homicide was damn near antiseptic. Blood was at a minimum, and physical dissarray was nonapparent. Aames's killer had simply arranged for her to lie facedown on her living room carpet, then put a single bullet in the back of her head. No muss, no fuss. From the lack of markings on her fully clothed body, it appeared Aames had cooperated with her murderer all the way.

By the time Steven La Porte and his partner, Peter Chin, arrived on the scene in answer to Poole's call, the Culver City Police Department had already descended upon it in full force, rendering Gunner and Poole mere observers to their investigation into the Aames homicide. La Porte and Chin's only interest here was Felipe, but the CCPD wouldn't let them anywhere near him. This was Culver City's case, and Felipe was their perp, and nobody from the LAPD was going to talk to him until the CCPD had talked to him first. All night long, if necessary.

"Fuckers," La Porte said, striking a match to light a cigarette when he, Chin, Gunner, and Poole had all gathered in the parking lot behind Aames's building.

"Hey, SOP," Poole said in commiseration. "If we were in their shoes, we'd do the same thing."

La Porte appraised Poole carefully, said, "With all due respect, Lieutenant, what's *your* interest in this? You workin' a connected case?"

Poole shook his head, slightly embarrassed. "Not at all. I was just giving Mr. Gunner here a hand on my off hours, as I'm prone to do from time to time. You might say it's my own unique way of giving somethin' back to the community."

Gunner cut his friend a look that Poole pretended not to notice.

"Okay," La Porte said to the investigator, letting the nature of Poole's relationship with him lie for the time being. "Why don't you take me and Pete through this from the top."

"Sure thing. In a nutshell, La Porte, I was right and you were wrong. Looks like your homicide and my suicide *are* connected."

"Yeah? How so?"

"Same way I've been saying all along. Felipe went into Ray Crumley's apartment Monday night to get my hotel surveillance tape. Seems he and Aames were close friends, they've known each other for years, and Monday afternoon, she offered him fifty dollars to break into Crumley's place and get her every blank tape he owned. She was only interested in one, he said, but she told him to take everything, just in case."

"Very interesting. He happen to say why?"

"The surveillance tape Crumley had showed her and a girlfriend named Felicia White visiting C.E. Digga Jones a few hours before the kid died, and Aames was terrified Crumley might use it to broadcast the fact. White's an ex-pro who's apparently got full-blown AIDS, and Felipe says Aames had it in her head that taking the lady up to the Digga's room that night was some kind of prosecutable offense."

"You're joking," Chin said.

"No. It sounds screwy, I know, but Aames was a certified paranoid schizophrenic, she had a history of mental problems longer than your arm. Worrying about getting ten years to life for introducing the Digga to a sex partner with AIDS wouldn't have been all that unusual for her."

"Yeah, but even if that were true . . ." La Porte started to say.

"How could Crumley have known about White?" Chin asked, completing his partner's thought.

"That I couldn't tell you," Gunner said, "and neither can Felipe. Unless he knew the lady personally, blackmailing Aames with the tape should have never even crossed Crumley's mind."

"All right, all right. Enough about Aames already," La Porte said. "What I wanna know is, does Felipe admit killing Crumley, or not?"

"He didn't admit it to us, no. But his denials made it pretty obvious he did. Impression I get is that he did Crumley by accident, just like you always said—in a panic after Crumley discovered him in his apartment—and if our friends inside are any good at what they do, they should probably turn him over to you with a signed confession to that effect."

"And Aames?" Chin asked. "What about her?"

"He cops an innocent plea there too. He said she only gave him half the fifty she promised him when he delivered the five tapes Crumley had Tuesday morning, told him to come back tonight to get the rest. Only when he got here . . ."

"She was dead," La Porte said. "Naturally."

"Call us stupid, La Porte, but Poole and I believe him," Gunner said. "One, because he genuinely seems to have loved the lady, and two, because this murder seems way out of his league. Killers change their MOs all the time, sure, but this guy's not that bright. Beating a man's brains out with a blunt instrument is a job he can handle, but killing a lady with one shot without leaving a mess of any kind behind?" Gunner shook his head again. "Very unlikely."

"Besides, we were on top of him the minute he broke to leave," Poole said. "There's no way he could've ditched a weapon somewhere without one of us seein' it."

"Okay. Not that my partner and I really give a rat's ass, you understand," Chin said, "but seeing as how we're here with nothin' else to do but ask you guys questions until we get to talk to Felipe ourselves . . . If *he* didn't whack Aames, who did? White?"

"For lack of a better suspect, yeah," Gunner said. "For all we know, she was as spooked about Crumley's tape as Aames was. Maybe more. If it turns out the tapes Felipe says he gave Aames aren't in her apartment somewhere, I'll have to assume her killer lifted them on his or her way out the door, the same way Felipe did over at Crumley's place, and right now, I can't see anyone else doing that besides White."

"You tell CCPD that?" Chin asked, breaking the ying-yang rhythm he and La Porte had going by opening his mouth twice in succession.

"Of course. They put a call in before you boys got here, there should be an APB out on her now."

"Then your busy day is done," La Porte said.

"Yeah. I guess it is. I'm gonna go back inside now, see if your friends'll give me their blessings to leave. Unless there's anything else you gentlemen would like to know?"

La Porte and Chin both shook their heads at him.

"Good. Come on, Poole, let's go."

"Do me a favor, Gunner," La Porte said as the two men started off, flicking his spent cigarette away like it was the last he would ever smoke. "Give them a message for me, huh?"

"Not on your life, Detective," Gunner said, neither stopping nor turning around. "You want a policeman to fuck you, you're gonna have to tell him so yourself."

"So what now, hotshot?" Poole asked, as he was dropping Gunner off at his car.

And the truth was, Gunner didn't know. Nothing had happened tonight that seemed relevant to anything other than Ray Crumley's murder, yet he still couldn't convince himself it all didn't somehow tie in to the death of Carlton Elbridge.

The theory he'd just laid on La Porte and Chin regarding Antoinetta

Aames's interest in Crumley's surveillance tape seemed sound enough, except that it didn't explain how Crumley could have known to hold it over Aames's head (and possibly Felicia White's as well). For Crumley to recognize the tape as something he could blackmail either of the women with, its value in that regard should have been obvious to him, which White's HIV status almost certainly couldn't have been, or Aames would never have dared bring her along to Elbridge's room in the first place.

Gunner decided Crumley must have seen something more incriminating on the tape than Aames had led Marvin Felipe to believe—and that something could only have pertained to her or White's involvement in Carlton Elbridge's alleged suicide. Nothing else made sense.

Being the first to find White and talk to her was the most obvious way to learn if this last was true, but now that Gunner had made the lady a prime suspect in an open Culver City Police Department homicide investigation, he was legally obligated to back off and leave her apprehension to the professionals. Which was probably for the best in any case, because his leads on White were few and far between. Thanks to Poole and Alred Lewis, respectively, he had an old address for White and the name and phone number of a pimp she used to turn tricks for out in San Bernardino County. That was it. Even if he felt like risking the CCPD's wrath by looking for the prostitute at the same time they were, Gunner sure as hell was in no mood to drive all the way out to San Bernardino just to hear a grown man named Rocket say he didn't know where Felicia White was, and more important, didn't give a damn.

So his work on the Elbridge case was once again in a holding pattern. Without White, there was no obvious next step for him to take. He could have gone out to Wally Browne's to relieve his man Jolly, but he didn't think that would be either wise or necessary; it was well after midnight, and Gunner was dead on his feet, and the FBI had probably already dispatched a surveillance team of its own to watch Browne's place, in any case. Tonight he'd just drive home, call Browne to make sure all was well, and then turn in.

Or maybe he'd make the call from the Acey Deuce instead.

When this thought occurred to him less than three blocks from home, even as tired as he was, it seemed innocent enough. He often made such late, spur-of-the-moment appearances at Lilly's before retiring.

But tonight it wasn't just the vision of warm, amber bourbon being poured into a glass that moved him to make the turn leading to the bar's front door. Or the promise of a good laugh or two, should Eggy Jones or Harold Gaines be in the house, throwing their customary verbal jabs at Lilly like poisoned lances. Tonight, the Deuce's draw upon Gunner was something else entirely, and he knew what it was soon enough to have time to avoid it, go home to bed like he'd originally planned, if that was his choice. All he had to do was turn the Cobra around one more time.

Mindful that a woman named Yolanda McCreary would want him to do precisely that.

All too often, like so many things in life, the reality of making love to a woman fell far short of a man's fantasies. The heat and energy, the kinetic power anticipated, never quite materialized; her flesh felt cool rather than warm to the touch, or his approach left her apathetic, gave her no reason to give more than she was getting.

On this night, it wasn't like that with Yolanda McCreary.

Tonight, her body was everything he had hoped it would be—full, smooth, exquisitely colored and balanced—and their pairing every bit as fervent and needful. They even made the right sounds together: deep sighs and urgent proddings, laughter in small, joyful doses.

Details of the room she and Gunner lay in were lost to him; her form was the only thing he could see in the darkness. The tiny mole on the outer rim of her navel; the soft white glow of her teeth against his skin; the pebbled texture of her dark, imperfectly round nipples—even cloaked in waves of shifting shadow, all these things filled his eyes and drew him to her, over and over again.

And then, suddenly, they were done, spent and satiated, and she was walking him to the door of her suburban Chicago townhouse. In the dead of night, they stepped out of her living room onto her front porch, where she threw her arms around him to kiss him one last time.

Only afterward, as Gunner was making his way across the damp lawn toward the Cobra improbably parked at the curb, did he see the car sitting in his woman's driveway: a silver Chrysler Le Baron with a bent and twisted front bumper.

He didn't know how he could have missed the car before, and he didn't much care. All he knew now was that he had to move, and quickly. He set himself, started to turn back around . . . and something hard and cold pierced his back, just below the left shoulder blade, instantly turning his legs to ice. His assailant forced the knife in as far as she could make it go, then stepped back to watch him fall, clutching at a wound he would never reach. He thought she would laugh as he lay there dying, unable to call for help for all the blood filling his lungs, but she didn't. All she did was gaze down upon him, no longer wearing the face of Yolanda McCreary, to study his suffering with the cool, detached interest of a moonlit automaton.

"Allah is on our side," Brenda Warren said.

seventeen

It had only been a dream, but it had deep roots in possibility.

Gunner awoke Friday morning realizing this fact immediately. Getting stabbed by Brenda Warren in the middle of Yolanda McCreary's front yard in Chicago may have been the stuff of pure fantasy, but Warren's role as the driver of the telltale Chrysler he was convinced had been following him lately was not. Her dogged interest in him was too flattering not to invite some suspicion, and the timing of her appearance at the Deuce coincided all too well with his first concerns about having someone on his tail. If the Defenders Of the Bloodline had indeed wanted him watched as a result of his work for Sparkle Johnson, as he had already begun to fear, who better to do it than a seductive beauty like Warren?

It was a question he had the option of asking Warren herself, as the business card she'd asked Lilly to give him Wednesday night seemed to provide him with all the means necessary to contact her, save for a home address. But confronting her directly would be complicated. First, because he couldn't imagine how to broach the subject without effectively accusing her of something she only *might* be guilty of, and second, because he didn't want to approach her at all if he could avoid it. Last night, on his way to the Deuce in search of her, he'd found the will to reverse his field and go home, his fidelity to Yolanda McCreary intact, but he didn't know if he could get close to Warren again and pull off a similar feat of resistance.

Besides, he had more important things to do with his time. He was long overdue to more personally supervise Jolly's efforts as a bodyguard for Sparkle Johnson, and his work for Benny Elbridge and Bume Webb remained unresolved. Less than twelve hours earlier, he'd been ready to call the Elbridge case a lost cause, but the light of a new day had given him a renewed determination to actively pursue a satisfactory conclusion to his investigation on his own, with or without Felicia White's help. There were only two ways of going about this he could think of, and neither seemed very promising, but both appealed more to his sense of duty than simply waiting around for White to show up and answer all the questions he needed answered in order to tell Benny Elbridge with a reasonable amount of certainty that yes, his son had indeed taken his own life twelve and a half days before.

But Jolly and Sparkle Johnson came first.

"Have the Feds contacted her yet?" Gunner asked Wally Browne around nine Friday morning, having reached the radio executive at his KTLK office.

"They're here talking to her now. Agents Smith and Leffman. They tell me they're old friends of yours."

"We know each other, yeah." Carroll Smith and Irv Leffman were the two FBI men Gunner had done business with during his first spate of trouble with the Defenders. Smith was black and almost human, but Leffman, his white partner, had all the warmth and sensitivity of a large, rotted tree stump. "Have they confirmed the Defenders' involvement yet? Or are they being tight-lipped about it?"

"They haven't confirmed it for me, no. But they've promised to have someone start watching Sparkle by early this afternoon, just like you said they would, and that tells me they're relatively certain the Defenders are involved. Otherwise, I can't see them bothering."

"You're probably right. Do you know if they've had any conversations with Jolly?"

"Jolly? I saw one of 'em say a few words to him earlier, sure. Agent Smith. Why?"

"Feds have a way of spooking some people, that's all," Gunner lied. "I was just wondering how Jolly was taking it."

"Looked like he took it fine."

"Good. Any objections to our backing out of this thing as soon as they have their people in place? I'm sure they'd prefer Jolly and I were out of the picture anyway. Makes for fewer bodies in their lines of sight."

"At the rates you're chargin'? I'd have no objection to that at all."

That left Gunner free to concentrate on the Elbridge case in full.

Over a fast-food breakfast at a restaurant near his home, he chose a course of action. He probably wasn't going to find a copy of the hotel surveillance tape he believed Ray Crumley had duplicated in either Crumley's apartment or that of Antoinetta Aames, but the time had come for Gunner to look for one all the same. Relying on the Westmore's Bob Zemic's description of the original tape's contents for him just wasn't going to cut it anymore. In order to finally determine what, if anything, the tape had to say about the demise of C.E. Digga Jones, Gunner was going to have to locate Crumley's copy and view it for himself, and the dead man's apartment—rather than the inaccessible crime scene Culver City PD had no doubt made of Aames's residence by now—was the only logical place to seek it out.

At least, that's what Gunner had thought back at the restaurant. A full hour into his search of Crumley's apartment, he was beginning to wonder if he hadn't picked the wrong horse. He'd had little trouble gaining access to the premises, as he had expected—the landlord of the building couldn't have been more impressed by his PI's license had it borne the official U.S. presidential seal—but unless Crumley had found a way to make a standard blank videocassette look like something else, the one Gunner was after simply wasn't here.

Someone had already started the process of packing up Crumley's belongings, and Gunner went through each and every box and bag, painstakingly replacing every item just as he'd found it, never coming across a blank tape of any kind. He found eleven prerecorded videotapes, and popped each one in Crumley's still-connected bedroom VCR, but none of them was anything other than what its packaging specifically implied.

Then, finally, Gunner found something else to hold his interest.

It was a large photo album at the bottom of one box. Mounted on its pages were assorted color prints recording a number of episodes in Crumley's recent past, friends or relatives with and without the portly security man by their side. All of them were strangers to Gunner save for one: Antoinetta Aames. Images of the woman whose corpse the investigator had seen only the night before were sprinkled throughout. She was a little younger and a little thinner here, but it was Aames without question, and her role in Crumley's life was equally obvious: she had once been his woman.

Now Gunner knew Crumley not only had had some connection to Aames, but may indeed have had reason to blackmail her as well. The photo album gave no clue, but if his relationship with Aames had ended poorly, he might have felt he owed the lady some small measure of grief, and blackmail would have been a fine way to deliver it.

But blackmail over *what*?

Again, that seemed to be a question only a copy of Crumley's surveillance tape could answer.

Gunner toured the dead man's apartment one more time, then reluctantly conceded defeat. The tape wasn't here. He was moving through the front of Crumley's apartment on his way to the door, ready to leave, when something in the dining area caught his attention. It was a desktop computer sitting on a drawing table against one wall, a printer perched atop a stand just beside it. Gunner had already turned the machine on once, scanned through Crumley's files without finding anything relating to Aames, White, or blackmail, but now the thought occurred to him that the

PC might have warranted a closer look. He walked over to it, noticed now that there was a small, blue slab of hardware extending off one of the computer's output ports in the back, onto which the printer's cable was installed. He examined the device closely, saw several open connectors that looked like video input and output jacks running along one side.

"Wait a minute," Gunner said out loud, turning the machine on again.

He didn't have much experience with such things, but having a PC of his own at the office for nearly a year now had made him just computer-literate enough to be dangerous. Running certain types of programs was beyond him, but recognizing their general purpose was not; he was often able to tell what a program did just by looking at its name and icon alone. If the hunch he was playing was right, he would find an icon/program name on Crumley's Windows desktop that would relate to the curious blue box mounted to the computer's parallel port, and when he double-clicked on the icon to start its associated software . . .

"Thank you, Jesus," Gunner said when the PC booted up.

The name of the video-editing program was the same one emblazoned on the piece of blue hardware that had no doubt come with it—"ZapIt"—and the contents of its home screen made the pair's function crystal-clear. Gunner had always wondered how Crumley could have copied the Westmore surveillance tape without two VCRs, and now he knew: by computer. It wouldn't have been the fastest way to do it, but it would have been the most state-of-the-art.

Gunner quickly checked the list of files under the ZapIt directory, thanked God again when he spotted the one Crumley had named simply "July11"—the date of Carlton Elbridge's death at the Beverly Hills Westmore. The investigator was smart enough to know Crumley could never have saved the entire contents of a two-hour surveillance tape in one digitized computer file, but the brevity of this one surprised him all the same. In a video clip that lasted less than fifteen seconds, Antoinetta Aames and Felicia White stepped out of Carlton Elbridge's fifth-floor suite at the Beverly Hills Westmore, then moved down the hallway toward the camera, the behavior of both women perfectly innocent throughout. They appeared neither hurried nor particularly nervous, and Elbridge himself was never in view.

Gunner didn't get it. What would Crumley have wanted with this?

There were only seven other files in the computer's ZapIt directory, and Gunner proceeded to view them all. None of them had anything to do with the Westmore clip. They were just snippets of various porno movies Crumley had apparently found it necessary to save in digitized form.

Gunner went back to the original file, started playing it over and over, looking for whatever it was he was missing. He watched Aames and White leave Elbridge's room and traverse the corridor again and again, taking all of twenty-five steps between them, and still he remained puzzled. There was nothing incriminating here. Two ladies of the evening leaving an unseen john's hotel room, that was all the clip had to show. Gunner was at a loss to explain it.

Until he remembered one small detail he'd forgotten. He shouldn't have been able to see their faces.

Bob Zemic had told him two days ago that the surveillance tape he had viewed at the hotel that afternoon could not have been used by Crumley as an instrument for blackmail because the faces of Aames and White were never visible. And yet, here were the pair's faces: unobscured, turned to the camera, completely recognizable.

At first, Gunner could think of only two explanations for the discrepancy: either Zemic had lied about what he'd seen on the tape, or Crumley had created his own abbreviated version of it here, pasting the faces of Aames and White into a sequence that otherwise did not reveal them, before transferring the doctored scene to another cassette. But there was a third explanation as well, simpler and more feasible than the others—and as he continued to think about it, examining it from every angle, he could see there was really only one thing wrong with it, one reason alone not to embrace it wholeheartedly.

It turned his view of two murders entirely upside down.

. . .

"Brother, I don't even know you," the falsetto-voiced pimp named Rocket said. "Why the fuck should I tell you anything?"

The minute he'd walked into Mickey's, Gunner had called his number for the fourth time since Alred gave it to him, and finally, Felicia White's former pimp had picked up the line. "Because Ready Lewis says you can."

"Ready? Shit. I hardly know his ass either."

"Look. The Man's looking for your girl Felicia because he thinks she may have murdered somebody, but not me. I'm thinking she could get whacked herself here pretty soon, if I or the cops don't find her before somebody else does."

"Aw, man, this is bullshit . . ."

"Don't hang up! *Listen* to me! Five-oh's already talked to you about this, right?"

Rocket grunted. "What do *you* think?"

"Then you already know the score. Sister's in some deep shit. If she murdered her girl Antoinetta, she brought it on herself, but if she didn't—"

"Felicia didn't murder nobody. She ain't like that. Never has been, never will be."

"All right. So if she didn't do it, she probably knows who did. And that's what's gonna put her in the morgue right next to Antoinetta if you don't help *me* help *her*."

"*Help* her? Help her how? By droppin' a dime on her ass?"

"No. By seeing she doesn't take the fall for something she didn't do. Or worse. Guilty or innocent, at this point I don't care. All I wanna do is talk to her. I'll do it over the phone, if necessary."

"Yeah, well, I'd like to help you, brother, but I can't. Like I told Five-oh, I ain't seen or heard from Felicia in almost a year."

"Okay. Just do me one more favor then, huh? Give Ready a call. Tell him everything I've just told you, and see what he says. Considering Felicia's medical problems, I'd say she's got enough to worry about these days. Maybe together, you and I can do something to lighten the load for her a little."

Twenty minutes later Gunner's phone rang, but it wasn't Felicia White calling. It was Carroll Smith of the FBI.

"I was wondering when I might hear from you boys," Gunner said.

"Yeah. I would've called sooner, but I've been a little busy." He sounded particularly unhappy.

"So I've heard. You're calling to ask me to withdraw the troops, I imagine."

"Not quite. I'm calling to find out where the hell the troops are with our surveillance subject. They both seem to have disappeared."

"What?"

"Ms. Johnson left KTLK about thirty minutes ago, just before our people were scheduled to start watching her, and your man Mokes went with her. Nobody here's seen or heard from either one of them since."

"Johnson didn't tell anybody where she was going?"

"No. Apparently, that would have run counter to her intentions. Her boss Browne says all the attention was driving her stir-crazy, he thinks she may have made herself scarce deliberately."

"Shit."

"I guess that means you don't know where they are either."

"No. Unless Jolly left a message for me I haven't received yet . . ." He called Mickey into his office, asked him if he'd heard from the big man at all today. Mickey shook his head and said no.

"Don't mean to be critical, Gunner, but this is what happens when you ask an amateur to do the work of a professional," Smith said. "Our information is that Mokes is an ex-con who's no more qualified to be watching Johnson than a twelve-year-old kid. What the hell were you using him on this detail for?"

"Don't blame Jolly, Smith. If Johnson took a powder on you, and Jolly followed after her, he did what I would have wanted him to do."

"Yeah, but—"

"Jolly's okay. He'll call in, don't worry."

"If he's still breathing, you mean. If the Defenders go after Johnson and he gets in the way, it's not gonna bother them at all to kill him too. In fact, they'll probably take him out just for the hell of it."

"You're satisfied the Defenders are mixed up in this?"

"Reasonably so, yes. We've been talking to Johnson's friend Nance for two days now, and he hasn't changed a word of his story yet. If he's lying about the Defenders setting him up, he put a lot of time in at rehearsal."

Gunner asked Smith what he could do to help.

"Let us know as soon as you hear from Mokes, of course. And if you've got a description and license number of the car he's driving, we wouldn't mind having 'em on file."

"I can help you with the first part, but not the second. He's supposed to be driving a friend's car—he never told me whose or what kind."

"Fine. Just make the call then. The minute you hear from him, Gunner, don't do anything else first. Are we clear on that?"

"We're clear. Now how about you boys doing something for me?"

"Such as?"

"There's a strange lady who's been hanging around my local dive lately, showing more interest in me than you would think I deserve. Name's Brenda Warren. Sound familiar?"

"Brenda Warren? No. Is there a reason that it should?"

"If she's a known Defender collaborator, yeah. Otherwise, no."

"You think she's working with the Defenders?"

"Let's just say the thought's occurred to me. Can you run a check on her for me, make sure my concerns are unwarranted?"

Smith hesitated before answering, just in case Gunner was starting to take him for granted. "I guess I can do that. Sure."

Rocket never called Gunner back, but Alred did. His flesh-peddling homie out in San Bernardino had done as Gunner asked and given him a call, seeking some assurance that the investigator could be trusted, and Alred wasn't happy about it. Gunner let him vent for a while, figuring he was entitled, then came within seconds of hanging up on him before Alred finally arrived at the real point of his call.

"Rocket told me to give you a message," he said.

The content of that message brought Gunner to the food court of the gargantuan Del Amo Mall in Torrance thirty minutes later, where a pre-lunch crowd was already starting to fill space like water gushing from a broken dam. Rocket's instructions had demanded the investigator sit alone at a table near the ubiquitous Hot Dog on a Stick, the front page of the *L.A. Times* folded into quarters before him, and Gunner followed those instructions to the letter, doing what he could to look innocuous as the minutes slowly ticked by. First ten, then fifteen. Then twenty. He was reading a *Times* story on the latest MTA Metro Rail construction shutdown for what had to be the fifth time when a black woman in her early twenties pushed past the flow of foot traffic surrounding his table, stopping just out of his reach, and in a voice he could barely hear, asked, "Your name Gunner?"

"That's right."

Felicia White took a final look around, failed to see the makings of a trap, and sat down to join him. She had a green knit cap on her head that swallowed her hair whole, and her clothing was Wal-Mart–grade unprovocative, but other than that, she wore nothing whatsoever in the way of a disguise. In fact, had she not lost what Gunner guessed to be about fifteen pounds since, she would have looked just like she had in the mug shots Poole had shown him the night before: tiny, doll-faced—and scared as hell.

"First thing you gotta know, I didn't kill nobody," she said. Not asking him to believe it, but stating a known fact.

"Okay."

"I didn't even know Antoinetta was dead till I seen it on TV. She was onea my best friends, I wouldn'ta never done nothin' to harm her."

"All right. So who did?"

"I don't know. I swear to God, I really don't. But . . ."

Gunner raised an eyebrow to urge her on.

"I think it was 2DaddyLarge. The rapper. You know who he is?"

"I know." Only four hours ago, Gunner might have been surprised to hear this, but not now. It was what he'd come here halfway expecting White to say. "What makes you think it was him?"

White checked her back briefly as someone passed behind her with a tray, then turned around again and said, " 'Cause Antoinetta kept sayin' he set us up. That me an' her was gonna get blamed for what happened to the Digga, an' it was all on accounta 2Daddy."

"How was that?"

White shook her head. "I don't know. Antoinetta was always talkin' some crazy shit, I thought she was just trippin', same as usual. But then I started thinkin' 'bout all the money she gave me, an' I realized she might be for real. Maybe 2Daddy *did* set us up."

"What money was this?"

White lowered her eyes, finally hearing a question she wasn't comfortable answering. "The money we got from the Digga," she said, making it sound like a confession of some kind. "We was up in his hotel room the night he died. You knew that, right?"

Gunner nodded.

"Well. He gave us a thousand dollars afterward. Five hundred each. An'

Antoinetta let me have all of it. Just handed me the money in the elevator as we was leavin', didn't keep a dime of it for herself."

"She say why?"

"She said she didn't need it. Just bein' with the Digga was enough, she said."

"She was that big a fan?"

White shrugged. "I guess. I know she liked homeboy's music." She shook her head again. "But still. I shoulda known somethin' was up. Girlfriend never did nobody without gettin' paid *somethin'*. That's why I figure maybe it was true what she said. About it bein' 2Daddy what paid us to be up there."

The ramifications of this suggestion moved Gunner to silence, but they appeared to have gone right over White's head.

"And why do you think he would have wanted to do that?" Gunner asked her eventually. "He and the Digga couldn't stand each other."

"I know. That's what I always thought too."

She wouldn't say any more than that.

"When you and the Digga were getting busy," Gunner said, "was he wearing a hat?"

"Yes. Hell yes," White said. Answering too fast to give it any semblance of truth. "I make everybody I get with wear a hat."

"You mean since you've been diagnosed?"

White's face collapsed. "Diagnosed? What—"

"I know about your medical problems, Felicia. So there's no need to talk to me like I don't."

White stared at him, both eyes tearing up at once. She looked off to one side, said, "Who told you?"

"It doesn't matter who told me. The point is, I know. And I sympathize, really. But if you went up to the Digga's room that night with the specific intent of infecting him with AIDS—"

"No! I didn't! I *tried* to make 'im wear somethin', but he wouldn't! Antoinetta said—"

She cut herself off abruptly.

"Antoinetta said what?" Gunner asked.

White evaded the question for several seconds, then: "She said it wasn't necessary. That she couldn't never feel nothin' when a man had a rubber on, an' they didn't really do nothin' anyhow."

"And the Digga went along with that?"

She tilted her head to one side apologetically, said, "He was all set to go. Niggas don't ever wanna put one on anyways, he sure as hell wasn't gonna argue with her about it."

"But if you'd told him about your condition . . ."

"Antoinetta said he already knew. She said he'd been with a lot of girls like me, he didn't have no fear of gettin' infected."

Gunner started to ask if she had really believed that, but the answer was obvious: Absolutely.

"How did you end up going with her that night? Did she invite you along, or did someone else tell you to go?"

"She invited me. She called me up that mornin' an' asked if I needed a date, an' I said yeah. I didn't even know who it was with till we got to the hotel."

"You ask her why she picked you? Over all her other girlfriends in the trade?"

"No. Why should I? She knew I been hurtin' for work lately, she prob'ly—" She stopped, finally catching on to what he was getting at. "Oh. You mean why like *that*."

"You should be retired, Felicia. You pose a health risk to everybody you get with, and Antoinetta would've known that. You didn't think it was at all strange that she chose you to double-team the Digga with that night?"

"No. Antoinetta was my friend. If you're tryin' to say she—"

"When you two went up to the Digga's room—did he act like he'd been expecting you? Or did he seem surprised?"

"Was he surprised?" She took a moment to think back, said, "I guess so. I remember when he come to the door he asked Antoinetta what we was doin' there. But what—"

"Then he couldn't have asked her over himself."

White just responded with a small shrug.

"And someone did ask her over, because she knew he was there. Or was that just a guess?"

"A guess?"

"His room number, for instance. She have to ask somebody at the front desk for that, or did she already seem to know?"

"She didn't ask nobody nothin' at the desk. We just went straight up."

Gunner looked away, feigning interest in the mass of people around them, so that White couldn't see how disgusted he was by the picture she was slowly piecing together for him. Somebody had used her lethal viral condition as a murder weapon with the aid of Antoinetta Aames, and she was either completely oblivious to the fact, or in some serious denial about it.

"Did you know Antoinetta's friend Ray Crumley?" Gunner asked when he faced White again.

"Ray? You mean the one what worked at the hotel?"

"Yeah. That one. Did he see you two there the night you were with the Digga?"

"Did he see us?" White was playing stupid now. "No. But . . ."

"You saw him."

She nodded.

"As you were coming in, or going out?"

"When we was goin' out. Antoinetta saw 'im in the lobby an' damn near died. I didn't get what the big deal was, but seein' homeboy there like to scared her to death."

"Why was that?"

" 'Cause she thought he'd seen us, and was gonna call the cops. I was like, so what if he does, the shit's over with now, right? But she made us run outa there anyway, drove like a fool the whole way back to my crib. Girlfriend was *trippin'*."

"You know Crumley's dead now too, don't you?"

White tried and failed again to appear nonplussed. "Yeah. They said on the news he got killed by somebody tryin' to jack his crib or somethin'. That's a damn shame."

"In other words, you had nothing to do with it."

"Say what?"

"The man who killed Crumley was in his apartment that night because Antoinetta sent him over there. You trying to say you didn't know that?"

"No! I didn't—"

"You want me to help you, Felicia, yet you're sitting here jerking me around. Now, I'm gonna ask you just once more, before I walk out of here and leave you to save your tight little ass all by yourself. Did you know Antoinetta sent a guy named Marvin Felipe out to rob Ray Crumley's place, or not?"

White stared him down, gauging his resolve, then slowly nodded her head again.

"Okay. Tell me why," Gunner said.

"She thought he had some kinda tape. What showed me an' her at the hotel. An' Antoinetta thought he was gonna show it to somebody. Either the cops or the newspapers, one or the other."

"So what if he had?"

"That's what I kept askin'! Who cares if he shows it to somebody, we didn't do nothin'. But Antoinetta just kept sayin' we was both gonna be fucked if anybody found out we was with the Digga that night. Like it was *our* fault homeboy killed hisself, or somethin'."

"Go on."

"So she went over to Ray's crib to talk to 'im. You know, to ask 'im not to say nothin' 'bout us bein' at the hotel."

"She went to see *him*? When?"

"The next day. She was on a paranoid tip, like I said, wasn't nothin' I could tell her to make her believe homeboy wasn't gonna out us. So she looked 'im up, to see if they couldn't work somethin' out."

"And?"

"And they did, of course. That nigga loved Antoinetta, he woulda done anything to get back with her."

"Including borrow a hotel surveillance tape for a couple days so he could edit your faces out of it."

"Yeah. That's right. How'd you know?"

"I saw the outtakes. Only they weren't on videocassette like Antoinetta thought. They were on his computer."

"His computer? No shit?"

"No shit. He changed the tape just like he promised, but he kept a copy of the parts he cut out for himself. I suspect that was so he could blackmail you ladies with it later, but maybe I'm wrong."

"Blackmail? Ray?" She shook her head. "No way. That's what Antoinetta was afraid of, but Ray didn't have nothin' but love for her, like I said. She got that poor nigga killed for nothin', sendin' that fool you was talkin' about before—Marvin—over to his crib to steal some tapes. Hell, he didn't even know we been over at the hotel till she told 'im!"

And there it was: confirmation that Gunner's view of Crumley had always been ass-backward, just as the video clip on the dead man's computer had recently brought him to suspect.

"Okay, Felicia, I think I've heard enough for now," Gunner said. "Would you like something to eat before we go, or are you ready to jet?"

White looked at him as if he'd lost his mind. "Jet? Jet *where*? Where've *we* gotta go?"

"To see Five-oh, of course. We'll go in together, it's gonna be all right."

"What?" She started to push away from the table.

Gunner reached out to place a hand on her arm, said, "I told you I'd help you if you leveled with me, and I meant it. But I can't do anything for you if you remain a fugitive. Most especially, keep you alive."

"Let go of me!" Her head swiveled from side to side now as she sought some avenue of escape.

Gunner got to his own feet, tightened his grip on her carefully. "Listen up. You act like you don't understand what went down, but I think you get it just fine. You're an accessory to a murder attempt, Felicia. 2Daddy or somebody had Antoinetta use you to try and infect the Digga with AIDS, and now he or she is serving up everyone who knows about it."

"No!"

"Antoinetta was first, and you'll be next if you walk out of here without me. You can take that to the bank. Is that what you want?"

It took her a few seconds to admit it, but eventually she realized it wasn't. She'd come here because she already knew that what he'd just told her was true, and she didn't have the strength to go on running from the fact anymore.

Living with AIDS was as close to death as Felicia White ever wanted to come.

eighteen

They had to throw a few *You've gotta be fuckin' kiddin' me*'s and *I don't fuckin' believe it*'s around beforehand, but the Culver City PD detectives working the Antoinetta Aames homicide case eventually came around to buying the story Gunner and Felicia White had to tell them. White was a cooperative witness, and her testimony was generally consistent, and it soon became obvious that she wasn't the murdering kind, just as her former pimp, Rocket, had assured Gunner earlier that day.

Still, like Gunner, the detectives were initially loath to believe that one man would try to kill another by using an unsuspecting AIDS sufferer as a murder weapon. It just didn't seem possible that anyone could be that twisted.

Gunner had been allowed to observe White's interrogation, and was greatly relieved to hear her tell the authorities exactly what she'd told him, except in greater detail. White was by no means a complete innocent, but the way Aames—and whoever had put her up to it—had attempted to use White like a disposable syringe had moved Gunner to pity her, and he hadn't wanted to see her say or do anything now to prove him a sucker for feeling that way.

Afterward, the cops had looked to Gunner to make sense of it all, and the investigator was only of marginal help; his own account of things was in its own way as incomplete as White's. He was, however, able to clarify one point for them that was of critical importance to their case: 2DaddyLarge was probably not the man they were looking for.

If anyone could have had a motive to commission Antoinetta Aames to make the bizarre attempt on C.E. Digga Jones's life that Gunner and White were alleging she had, it was 2Daddy; Gunner had heard enough people say it over the last five days to know that the rapper had indeed hated his chief rival and desired his woman. Furthermore, had he used Aames in this manner, it also followed that 2Daddy might have preferred to see her dead than capable of someday testifying against him in a conspiracy-to-commit-murder trial.

But Wednesday afternoon, back at his hotel room at the Century City Marriott, 2Daddy had admitted to Gunner that Aames had been with the Digga the night he died. Surely he would never have volunteered this information knowing she would only turn the investigator's attentions back around to him, providing Gunner could find her. He could have been planning to silence Aames first, but that didn't add up either, because Aames had not been killed until Thursday evening, in her own apartment, and 2Daddy would not have waited over twenty-four hours to deal with her.

Luckily, though, Gunner thought he knew who might have.

He asked the Culver City PD detectives if they knew yet what kind of weapon had been used on Aames, and when he heard their answer, his hunch was confirmed: they weren't sure, the cops said, but they thought it had been a .45 auto of some kind.

The very handgun of choice of 2Daddy's not so bright errand boy, Teepee.

As Gunner explained it to his interrogators, the pair's relationship was such that anyone 2Daddy hated, Teepee almost certainly hated as well. They were both East Coast to the bone, and as hardened by the streets as young black men could become. It wasn't much of a stretch to envision the gangsta rapper's loyal yet dim-witted handyman not only sharing his jealousy of the Digga but possessing the initiative to try and murder him on 2Daddy's behalf. Gunner felt relatively confident that Teepee was both that stupid *and* that bold.

Predictably, neither 2Daddy nor his henchman could be found at the Century City Marriott when the Culver City PD called asking for them. According to the hotel staff, both men had returned to New York that morning, just in time to escape any fallout from Aames's murder. Neither Gunner nor the cops took this to be a coincidence.

The at-large status of Teepee notwithstanding, then, Ray Crumley's homicide was now a closed book, and Gunner no longer had to wonder if Crumley's death had somehow been connected to that of Carlton Elbridge. It hadn't. The individual orbits of the security man's murder and the rapper's suicide had merely intersected, they weren't one and the same.

Gunner was finally free to get off the Elbridge case merry-go-round.

As soon as the Culver City PD released him, he called Benny Elbridge and asked for an early-evening meeting at the Deuce, in lieu of the telephone call he'd promised but never made the day before. Next, Gunner called Mickey to ask if he'd received any calls from Jolly, and was happy to have his pessimism shattered when Mickey said yes, he had.

"So where are they?" Gunner asked his landlord.

"He didn't say," Mickey said.

"But I told you—"

"I know what you told me. But the man wouldn't answer me. He only wanted to talk to you."

"What about the Feds? You tell him to call them like I said?"

"I told 'im."

"And?"

"He acted like he took the number down, but he didn't say if he was gonna call or not. He just grunted, said to tell you he'd call back again in an hour, then hung up."

"Damn! How long ago was this, Mick?"

" 'Bout fifteen minutes ago. Right after your boy from the FBI called. Agent Smith."

This last meant that Smith, and probably Wally Browne as well, still didn't know where Jolly and Sparkle Johnson were, unless Jolly had done as Mickey instructed and called Smith at FBI headquarters. Gunner glanced at his watch, saw that it was well past two o'clock. If Jolly hadn't made the call to Smith, both the federal agent and Browne would have to be foaming at the mouth with worry by this point.

"Listen to me, Mickey. I'm coming in now, but if he calls back before I get there, don't let him hang up without getting at least a phone number from him. Do you understand? I've *got* to find out where he is."

"I hear you. But if he don't wanna tell me . . ."

Gunner made the drive from Culver City to his office in South Central—one which normally took thirty minutes—in a little over fifteen, shunning the unpredictable flow of freeway traffic for the less stressful access of the surface streets. Mickey had the TV on when he arrived at the shop, tuned as usual in the afternoon hours during the week to the Classic Sports channel, and Mickey, Winnie, and a small group of customers were cheering Muhammad Ali on like they didn't know the butt-whipping they were watching him lay on Joe Frazier was on tape. It was all Gunner could do to hear his own voice as he asked the barber if Jolly had called back yet. Mickey just shook his head, went right back to encouraging the champ to victory.

Gunner went back to his office and closed the door he almost always kept open behind him, seeking some shelter from all the racket out front he knew a beaded curtain alone would never grant him. He walked through the suddenly pitch black room to his desk, turned on his desk lamp . . .

. . . and nothing happened.

Thinking the bulb was out, he went to get a fresh one from the bottom drawer of his desk, caught some movement just behind him as he pulled the drawer open. He tried to turn, but too late: something that felt more like a medieval battering ram than a human fist hit him on the right side of his face, sent him crashing to the floor with breakneck speed. He remained conscious for several seconds, just long enough to see that the back door to Mickey's shop was letting more light into the room than any locked door had a right to.

Then he let the pain and darkness take him where they would.

"Where are we, Jolly?" Gunner asked.

"Somebody's house. I don't know who."

Gunner had awakened to find himself lying on the carpeted floor of what looked like a dark, empty bedroom, his hands bound behind his back, Jolly sitting on an aluminum folding chair before him. They appeared to be alone.

"Somebody's house where?"

"I ain't supposed to tell you. I ain't even supposed to be talkin' to you."

"The silver Chrysler with the fucked-up bumper. That was yours?"

Jolly nodded after a long pause.

"Where's Ms. Johnson?"

"Hey, man, I told you—"

"It's okay to talk to me, Jolly. Your friends have their way, I'm not gonna be around to repeat what you tell me later. You understand that, don't you?"

"They ain't my friends. They ain't nothin' but instruments of the Devil, every one of 'em."

"You're not a Defender yourself?"

"No. Hell no!"

"Then what is *this*?"

Jolly didn't say anything.

"Where's Ms. Johnson?" Gunner asked again.

"In the other room. Same as you."

"You haven't hurt her?"

The big man shook his head. "No."

"Good. How'd you get her here?"

"Why you wanna know that?"

"Just tell me, Jolly."

After another pause, Jolly said, "She tried to sneak off this mornin', but I followed her. She went somewheres down by the beach, I think she was gonna go shoppin'. Anyway, I caught her gettin' outa her car in the parkin' lot, used this stuff they give me to put her to sleep. Then I brung her over here, like I done you."

"The stuff you used on her. You talking about chloroform?"

"I think that was it, yeah. They said put it on a rag and cover her mouth with it, and that's what I did."

"Who's 'they,' Jolly? These Defenders have names?"

"I don't know nobody's name. I don't *wanna* know nobody's name. Only reason I even know what they look like's 'cause I owe somebody a favor."

"Yeah? Who's that?"

"Man what saved my life back in the joint once. Couple Aryan Nation boys was beatin' on me pretty good, prob'ly woulda killed me if he hadn't jumped in to help. I told 'im I could ever do somethin' for *him,* all he had to do was ask." He shrugged. "So just 'fore they sprung me, he did."

"He told you to keep an eye on me."

"Yeah. That was all I was supposed to do. He said you was messin' in Defenders bus'ness again, and they needed somebody to watch you."

"Then all that talk about you being born again . . ."

"Was the truth. I wouldn't lie about nothin' like that, man. Thing is . . . I owed the brother, like I said. And he wasn't askin' me to do nothin' to hurt nobody. Least—"

"Not at first."

Jolly nodded. "But then you went and put me to work watchin' Ms. Johnson, and everything got all messed up. My man's friends started tellin' me I had to help 'em to kill her, or else they was gonna tell you I was workin' with 'em, get me locked down again."

Gunner strained to glance about, asked, "So where are these brothers now? Are any of them here?"

"No. Ain't nobody here right now but us." Jolly stood up. "I was supposed to kill both of you today, but I couldn't. I done killed somebody once, not countin' all the gooks I done in 'Nam, and I ain't never gonna do it again. So I just brung you here. I didn't know what else to do. They give me this address and told me where they keep the key out front, said I should hang in here if I ever needed somewhere to hide."

"Do they know we're here, Jolly?" Gunner asked, hoping to God the big man would say no.

But Jolly nodded again, said, "I called 'em and told 'em. They're on the way now."

"How long ago did you call?"

"I don't know. 'Bout fifteen, twenty minutes ago, maybe."

Gunner felt his stomach begin to churn. Twenty minutes was probably ten more than they would need.

"Cut me loose, Jolly. We don't have much time," the investigator said.

Jolly shook his head. "I can't, Gunner. I wish I could."

"You *can*. Get your ass over here and cut me loose before they make you an accessory to a goddamn multiple homicide!"

"I ain't gettin' locked down again. I *can't*. I'd rather be dead than go back inside."

"Jolly, for Chrissake—you've already got the blood of one innocent woman on your hands! You wanna be responsible for *two* now?"

Jolly just stared at him.

"You can't do this. You're a different man than you used to be. You have God on your side now. Your Lord and Savior, Jesus Christ, remember?"

Still, Jolly remained silent. Gunner watched his face, saw it slowly soften. The big man started to step forward . . .

And then they both heard the sound of a key being jiggled in a lock out in another room.

Jolly froze as an unseen door opened, closed behind a series of foot-steps announcing the arrival of visitors. Gunner listened intently as they approached, guessed it was two people at least, maybe as many as four.

It turned out to be three.

They were all men, black, two in their twenties and one at least thirty. The older man was fair-skinned and wore a beard; his companions were darker-complexioned and clean-shaven. Gunner knew all this because the trio's only form of disguise was gloved hands, which was the most clear-cut indication yet that the investigator's fate was sealed. Jolly's and Sparkle Johnson's, as well. The Defenders occasionally showed someone their faces without killing them afterward, but it wasn't something they made a habit of.

The bearded man, who had led the others into the room, looked Jolly and Gunner over for a long time before he spoke, the very picture of parental disapproval. "What's going on here, Jolly?" he asked.

And Gunner immediately knew he'd heard his voice before, while sit-ting in a chair secured to the floor of an unidentified room, a strip of duct tape covering his eyes.

"I ain't gonna kill 'em," Jolly said with admirable backbone. "So I brung 'em here. What you wanna do with 'em now is your bus'ness."

The Defender glanced around, said, "Ms. Johnson is here too?"

"In the other room."

The bearded man turned his head, nodded over his shoulder at one of the men standing behind him, who slipped quietly out of the room. Gunner could only pray he was leaving simply to see if Johnson was there, not to execute her.

Finally, the elder Defender turned his attention to Gunner and smiled.

"You should have a gag in your mouth, Mr. Gunner. Please forgive your friend Jolly here for neglecting to provide you with one."

"It's not the gag I miss as much as the chair bolted to the floor. I don't suppose you brought that along with you?"

"Ah. Recognized the voice, did you?"

"Of course. Some things you never forget."

"Good. Then you'll also recall we gave you fair warning that something like this might happen to you, if you ever sought to impede the will of Allah again."

"You boys don't work for Allah. Wake up and smell the coffee. You're homicidal ideologues, nothing more. Hiding behind Allah will never change that."

The younger, darker-skinned Defender who had gone to check on Johnson reentered the room, nodded at the man who had given him the order.

"I will not debate with you the sanctity of our mission," the bearded man said to Gunner, his smile a thing of the past. "I tried that once, and failed. I will say only that our people will be rid of the self-loathing, assimilation-promoting serpents in our midst, whether you choose to see that as Allah's command or not."

"Oh, that's right. Allah speaks to you personally, doesn't he? Did you know that, Jolly? That the boss man here is divinely inspired?"

Jolly didn't answer him, placed in an awkward position, but his expression made it clear that he found the question troubling.

"You wanna kill *me,* kill me," Gunner said to the elder Defender. "But let Johnson go. She's a radio talk-show host, for God's sake. Only thing she's guilty of is voting with her tax bracket in mind, not conspiring to commit genocide."

"She professes to be a black woman, yet she broadcasts her advocacy of all things white to millions of Americans daily. That is vile and shameless treason, Mr. Gunner, and it must not be allowed to go unpunished." He looked at Jolly again. "I expect he had a weapon when you brought him here. Give it to me, please." He held his right hand out toward the big man, palm up, and waited.

Jolly turned to Gunner, already grieving over what he was being forced to do, and lifted the front of his shirttail up to draw the investigator's Ruger cautiously out of his belt.

After that, his right hand was a blur.

The first shot he fired hit the man with the beard point-blank in the chest; the next four went to the men behind him, two rounds for each. It was five rounds in rapid succession, so close together they almost rang in Gunner's ears as one. One of the younger Defenders had managed to get his own nine-millimeter out before going down, but that was as close as any of them got to saving themselves. The younger men died instantly, while the oldest lay on his back and coughed up blood, struggling in vain to move something other than his spasming left leg.

"God Almighty," Gunner said, when his heart finally decided to start beating again.

The Ruger fell from Jolly's grip without the big man ever noticing, so engrossed was he in the crimson-spattered battlefield he had just created. He stumbled more than stepped over to the aluminum chair nearby, dropped himself onto the seat like his legs wouldn't hold his weight anymore.

"Damn, Jolly. What in hell you gonna do *now*?" he asked himself.

nineteen

The house Gunner almost died in was in Long Beach. It was a single-story, two-bedroom ranch-style that had been vacant and on the market for seven weeks. The realtor to whom it was registered told the Long Beach Police Department its owners now lived somewhere in Florida, and she didn't know how or where the Defenders could have gotten a set of keys to the front door.

Up to now, Gunner had been extremely fortunate. Over the last four days, bodies had been piling up around him like snowflakes in a blizzard, yet none of the law enforcement officers he'd had to deal with regarding them had given him much in the way of a hard time. But a man could only tempt fate so long. You kept showing up in places where fresh corpses lay about, sooner or later one cop or another was going to shake your cries of innocence off and press his thumbs into your neck until you copped a plea of some kind. And that was how it was with the boys of the Long Beach PD. As far as they were concerned, Gunner and Jolly were part of a five-man ring which had kidnapped Sparkle Johnson, and the three brothers on the bedroom floor were simply the result of an argument they'd all had as to how many ways the ransom money they were soon to demand for her return should be divided: five or only two.

Still, Gunner was lucky. Had Johnson not been found safe and sound, the LBPD might have really gotten ugly, actually tried to force a confession out of him and Jolly, rather than merely insist upon one. But Johnson *was* alive and cognizant, an able witness to their investigation, so no physical force was ever exerted by them on anyone. In this way, the cops were lucky too, because the call Gunner had asked them to make to one Carroll Smith of the FBI actually bore fruit, and soon Big Brother himself was on the scene to further observe their actions.

"You're one lucky sonofabitch, Gunner," Smith said, shaking his baby face from side to side. He'd brought his partner, Irv Leffman, along tonight, and the three of them were huddled in the kitchen alone, away from the madding crowd of the LBPD's still-ongoing investigation. "Your pal Mokes doesn't have a last-minute change of heart . . ."

"Bang-bang, you're dead," Leffman said. It was the closest thing to a joke Gunner had ever heard the bald, heavyset white man say.

Gunner nodded. "Question is, did he do the right thing? Or would he have been better off going along with them?"

"Are you asking can we cut him a deal?" Smith asked.

"You said yourself he saved my life. Johnson's too. That should be worth something, shouldn't it?"

"The man's on parole for murder-two," Leffman said. "And he's the only reason you and Johnson were in danger in the first place. How do you figure that's worth a deal?"

"I figure it because it matters more to me what he did than what he almost did. Bottom line, Agent Leffman, Jolly risked his life for ours when he had at least an outside chance of simply walking away. You wanna see the poor bastard do another thirty years for *that*?"

"If the courts decide that's what he deserves—"

Gunner turned to Smith before Leffman could finish, said, "If nothing else, he just gave you clowns three less Defenders to worry your little heads about. And a key one at that. You gonna tell me that's not enough to buy him a little slack?"

Smith produced a small, noncommittal shrug. "That could depend. How sure are you again that the man with the beard in there was the one you dealt with earlier?"

"As sure as it's humanly possible to be. He all but admitted it to me, we talked about old times."

"And he was the one giving all the orders?"

"Now, same as then. Yes."

Smith glanced at Leffman, received a skeptical frown in return. To Gunner, he said, "If we can identify him, and establish the fact that he was, as you suggest, a key link in the network . . . we might be able to do something for Mr. Mokes. Assuming your faith in him proves warranted."

"But we're not promising anything," Leffman added.

Gunner smiled at him, thankful for small favors. "Fair enough," he said.

At seven o'clock that evening, Gunner met with Benny Elbridge at the Acey Deuce for what he intended to be the last time.

The two men sat at the same table they'd occupied four days earlier, when Elbridge had officially become the investigator's client, and did their best to hold a conversation despite all the people who kept interrupting them to pat Gunner on the back and tell him how great he looked on TV. The Sparkle Johnson kidnapping story had been all over the news for hours, and on-camera interviews with all of the principals, save for Jolly, were still being telecast over several channels. Outside the house in Long Beach, Gunner had merely mumbled a few words to a group of reporters on his way to Smith and Leffman's car, but Johnson had treated the event like a press conference called in her honor. She said some nice things about him and the Long Beach PD, but what she talked about most was herself, and how determined she remained, despite the Defenders' attack upon her, to speak the truth about America for all who cared to hear it.

"A lot of black people don't want to *know* the truth," she said. "But Sparkle Johnson's going to tell it to 'em anyway."

It must have made Wally Browne happy enough to burst.

As for Gunner, Johnson's egomania was behind him now, leaving Benny Elbridge as his last remaining piece of unfinished business. He knew Elbridge would have problems with his final report, conflicting as it did with the older man's view of his son's death, but he had come to the Deuce prepared to stand firmly by it, no matter what Elbridge said.

Or so Gunner thought.

"I'm sorry, Mr. Gunner, but you're wrong," Elbridge said, tossing the investigator's hastily written report back over to his side of the table. "There ain't no way Carlton killed himself."

"I'm sorry too, Mr. Elbridge, but I'm afraid that's the way it is. There isn't a shred of evidence anywhere that anyone other than your son was responsible for his death. At least, none that I can find."

"Then you just gotta keep lookin'."

"There'd be no point in that."

"Why not?"

"Because Carlton committed suicide. I know that's a hard thing for you to accept, but it's true."

Elbridge shook his head like a nine-year-old refusing to eat. "No."

"Look. You told me four days ago he would've had no reason to contemplate suicide, but that wasn't entirely accurate. Fact of the matter is, he'd been thinking about it for some time. And depending on your point of view, perhaps justifiably so."

"What the hell are you talkin' about?"

"I'm talking about what happened to him out in Philly several months ago. Or didn't you know about that?"

The older man blinked, tried to remember how to make his mouth work. "Who told you what happened in Philly?"

"That's not important. What is is that it's something else I would've liked to know when you hired me, but had to find out later for myself.

Honesty hasn't exactly been the cornerstone of our relationship, has it, Mr. Elbridge?"

"Shit! Why would I wanna tell you about somethin' like that? That was a private matter, it didn't have nothin' to do with you!"

"It did if the boy took it as hard as you obviously did."

"What?"

"What happened to Carlton wasn't his fault, Mr. Elbridge. And it wasn't the end of the world either. But you're acting right now like it was both. If Carlton knew you felt that way, he couldn't have found much comfort in the knowledge."

Elbridge fumed in silence for a moment, his anger gradually dissipating. "I never told the boy how I felt."

"Maybe you didn't have to. Sons have a way of sensing their father's disapproval. It isn't something they have to see or hear to know it's there."

"If you're tryin' to say it was my fault the boy shot himself . . ."

"Something drove him to it. Why couldn't it have been the loss of his father's respect over a onetime, accidental sexual experience with a man?"

" 'Cause he didn't give a damn for my respect, that's why. He didn't *need* it. Only thing that boy cared about was his wife and children. Nothin' else was important to him. Not his money, not his fame—nothin'."

"You're forgetting about Coretta, aren't you? His mother?"

"I ain't forgettin' about Coretta. He loved her too, of course. But not like he loved Danee and his kids. What he felt for them was somethin' special."

Gunner had never heard him sound so certain about anything. "Special how?"

"I can't explain it," Elbridge said. "The boy just lived for those three, that's all. Especially Danee. Carlton loved that girl so much it like to make him sick sometimes."

"He had a rather odd way of showing it, don't you think? Spreading himself around like he did?"

"Didn't matter. You can't get a woman to understand it, but some men can do that, Mr. Gunner. *Make* love to a hundred women, but only *be* in love with one. That's how it was with Carlton. Sex was one thing, and love was another. And the only woman he could ever *love* was Danee." He tossed down a swallow of his drink, shook his head. "Now, if he ever thought he was about to lose *her* respect . . . That's somethin' mighta shook 'im up, for sure."

All around them, the Deuce had come alive with noise, overlapping voices and music from the radio, but Gunner couldn't hear a note of it.

He was already too deep in thought to acknowledge anything else.

Saturday morning, Gunner drove up into the Hollywood Hills to visit Danee Elbridge again. The front gate was working now, so he'd had to ring the bell to reach the house. Her Lexus was missing from the carport this time—thirty bullet holes in its trunk lid, she would've had to put it in a body shop somewhere eventually—but the winged nude at the center of the fountain remained. She still wasn't talking, however.

It was ten o'clock sharp, and the lady of the house was dressed to go out, forgoing the diaphanous nightgown for a pale beige jumpsuit that made her look good enough to eat. In fact, the only thing marring the perfection of her appearance was the bluish-black bump riding high on her forehead, which Gunner had left her with at their previous meeting.

"Allow me to apologize for that again," he said, when they'd taken their customary places in her spacious living room. He could hear the voices of small children, and one female adult he felt it safe to assume was their nanny, moving about on the floor above them.

"Forget about it," Danee Elbridge said, smiling, rubbing her small injury gently with one hand. "Hardly even hurts anymore."

"Still."

"I don't mean to rush you, Mr. Gunner, but the kids and I were on our

way out to the park when you called. And they get a little antsy waitin'
around. So . . ."

"Get to the point. Sure." He unfolded the sheet of paper he'd brought
in with him, said, "I told your father-in-law yesterday that my investigation into your husband's death is closed. And I thought you might like to
hear what my findings were."

"I don't need to hear what your findings were. I already know. Cee
killed himself, like I always said."

"Basically, yes."

"Basically? What do you mean, basically?"

"I mean that I don't think it was as clear-cut as all that. I used to, right
up until I saw Mr. Elbridge last night, but not anymore. I can see now that
there's at least one major question about Carlton's death that still hasn't been
answered, and I've decided you're the only one who could possibly answer
it for me."

"Me? Why me?"

"Because you were the last person to see Carlton before he died. Isn't
that right?"

"Yes. I guess so. But—"

"This is a copy of the note he wrote that night. The 'suicide' note you
didn't want me or anyone else to see. It took a lot of doing, but I managed
to convince Coretta last night that she should finally allow me to read it.
Listen . . ."

Gunner began to read:

"He ain't never been a quitta,
   But his heart lies heavy,
   Tears been flowin' like water from a levee,
   Fame and chedda made the nigga's head spin,
   So fucked up he thought out was in . . ."

"I don't wanna hear this," Danee Elbridge said. "Coretta didn't have no right to give you that!"

"Hold on a minute, I'm almost through," Gunner said. And then he started reading again, quickly before she could stop him:

"Don't wanna die, but he don't wanna live,
Some won't forget, and some won't forgive,
Used to be a playa on top of his game,
Now he ain't nothin' but a goddamn shame."

Gunner stopped reading, looked up at the Digga's widow. "And that's it. That's all it says. He didn't even sign his name at the bottom."

"I *know* he didn't. I saw the note myself, remember?"

"I remember. I just read it again to you now because I thought it might be best to refresh your memory of it before I ask you to explain a few things for me."

"I already told you, Mr. Gunner. That note—"

"Alludes to your husband's unfortunate incident in Philadelphia several months back. Yes, I know. I should have told you I'd been made aware of that fact earlier, I'm sorry."

Danee Elbridge was incensed. "Coretta *told* you about that?"

"Actually, no. I knew about it before I went to see her last night. But since you'll notice I've made no effort to make the information public, why don't we forgo all the questions about who *did* tell me and continue on with the business at hand?"

"We don't have any business at hand. Whoever told you about Cee's note had no business doin' it, but now that you know about it, you can't possibly have any more doubts about what happened to him. Can you?"

"None that the police would care to hear. No," Gunner said.

"Excuse me?"

"In Carlton's note, Mrs. Elbridge—when he says, 'some won't forget and some won't forgive'—who do you suppose he was referring to, exactly? His mother? Or his father?"

It took several seconds for Danee Elbridge to answer. "His mother or his father? I don't—"

"I think he was talking about you. His beloved 'Dee.' Yours was the only opinion that really mattered to him. Mr. Elbridge told me that yesterday evening, and your mother-in-law backed him on it an hour or so later. The Digga liked to spread himself a little thin, it's true, but his heart and soul belonged to you."

"Shit. His 'heart and soul.' That's all you niggas ever think we—" She quickly silenced herself, aware that she was about to take off on an emotional tangent she didn't want Gunner to witness. "Look, Mr. Gunner. My children are waitin' for me. We're gonna have to do this some other time, I'm sorry."

"I'm almost done. Give me one more minute, please," Gunner said.

The Digga's widow acquiesced by way of silence.

"The night Carlton killed himself. You arrived at his hotel room about nine p.m., is that correct?"

After a beat: "I think so. Yeah."

"Had you been at the hotel for some time before that, or did you go straight up to his room immediately upon arriving?"

"I went straight up. Why?"

"Because the two women he'd been with earlier—one of whom you identified for the police by name—left the hotel a good hour before you showed up. Time stamp on the hotel surveillance tapes clocked them out around ten minutes to eight."

"So?"

"So how did you know they'd been there, Mrs. Elbridge? Those specific women? Surely Carlton didn't tell you?"

Danee Elbridge didn't know what to say. She bit her lip for a moment, then said, "Maybe I was wrong about the time. I seen 'em leavin', so I must've been there earlier than I thought."

"Or else somebody called you to say they were there. Somebody who might've gotten a kick out of seeing you go over there all pissed off and in a rage, ready to take a knife to Carlton like you had once before."

"That's bullshit. Nobody called me to tell me nothin'."

"You got set up, Mrs. Elbridge. 2Daddy's boy Teepee was doing the boss all kinds of favors that weekend, and tipping you off to Antoinetta Aames and Felicia White being in Carlton's hotel room was one of them. The other was sending Antoinetta and Felicia over there in the first place, though I imagine he failed to mention that."

Danee Elbridge thought it over, no doubt trying to recall what the anonymous voice had sounded like on the phone that night, and said, "You're talkin' crazy, Mr. Gunner." Clearly having realized he wasn't.

Gunner got up and walked over to the big-screen TV and VCR sitting inside a large cabinet nearby. "May I?" Without waiting for an answer, he inserted the videocassette he'd brought along with him into the VCR's mouth.

"This was something else I had to beg for," he said, putting the machine in play, then turning the television on. "It's one of the hotel surveillance tapes I just mentioned. I'd been trying all week to get security there to allow me to view this one, but they kept turning me down until last night. Just goes to show you perseverance pays off in the end."

The tape started rolling and the fifth-floor hallway of the Beverly Hills Westmore Hotel appeared on the television's oversized screen. "This is the hallway just outside your husband's room the night he died. Maybe you recognize it."

Danee Elbridge said nothing.

"I've cued the tape up to just before the time you left him. You'll notice the time stamp shows it was around nine twenty-five p.m., just over thirty minutes after your arrival."

On the tape, an animated Danee Elbridge suddenly opened the door to room 504 and stepped outside into the hall, turning her back to the camera to face somebody inside.

"There you are. Your body language alone makes it pretty clear what's going on. You're jumping in your husband's ass with both feet. And who could blame you, considering what he'd just done, right?"

"I don't wanna see this shit! Turn it off!"

"In a minute." Gunner used the VCR remote to pause the tape just as the image of the Digga's widow turned and started moving away from the door to leave. "There. Through the open door. The Digga wasn't visible up to this point, but if you look close now, you can see him, inside the room."

"I told you to turn it off!" Danee Elbridge cried, running now to snatch the remote from his hand.

But Gunner held her at bay, forced her to deal with the frozen image on the screen.

"Describe what you see for me, Mrs. Elbridge," Gunner said. "What does it look like Carlton's doing there to you?"

Danee Elbridge gazed at the television as he demanded, eyes filling with tears of anger and remorse. "He's *beggin'*," she said, her voice a small yet razorlike whisper. "On his *knees.*"

There had been an unmistakable trace of delight in this last.

"That's right," Gunner said. Chilled to the bone.

"He was always apologizin'. 'I'm sorry, baby.' 'She don't mean nothin', baby.' Like that was supposed to make some kinda fuckin' difference!" She thumped her chest with a fist, said, "*I* was the one havin' his goddamn children! *I* was the one stickin' by 'im when other men was promisin' me the world to be with 'em!" She shook her head, began biting her lip again. "But he didn't appreciate that. Oh, no. He had to have me, and every bitch in the world too."

Gunner gave her a few seconds to compose herself, then said, "So you brought him to his knees that night."

She nodded.

"How? What did you say to him?"

Nothing.

"Never mind. I think I can guess. I think you told him he was a faggot. That he could screw every woman he wanted for the rest of his life, and it wouldn't change the fact that he'd once gotten busy with a man."

The Digga's widow was glaring at him now.

"And then I think you told him you were gonna make sure all his adoring fans found out about it. Just for good measure."

Danee Elbridge still didn't say anything.

Gunner stopped the tape and removed it from the machine. "I told you I came by to ask you the only question about Carlton's death I hadn't been able to answer until now. So I'll let you hear it, and then leave.

"If a man goes up on a ledge to kill himself, Mrs. Elbridge, but somebody pushes him off before he can jump—is that still suicide? Or is it murder?"

twenty

"Oh, yeah, I remember that movie," Winnie Phifer said. "*Tick . . . Tick . . . Tick . . .*"

"Which one was that again?" Mickey asked.

"He was a newly elected sheriff in a racist southern town," Gunner said. "George Kennedy was the old sheriff he beat out for the job."

It was early Monday evening just before closing time, when no one needing a haircut was ready to get one, and Gunner and the two barbers were the only people in the shop. Winnie had started talking about movies, and somehow the Jim Brown film Gunner had seen earlier in the week on television had become the subject of discussion.

"George Kennedy?" Mickey asked.

"Yeah, you know," Winnie said. "The one who was in *Cool Hand Luke* with Paul Newman."

"Oh, yeah. Him. Now I know the movie you're talkin' about."

"Gunner's right. It was good."

"He died at the end, right?"

"No," Gunner said, shaking his head.

"He didn't die in the end? Jim Brown?"

"Not in that one," Winnie said. "At least, I don't remember him dyin'."

"He didn't," Gunner said. "He lived."

"Jim Brown? The football player?" Mickey asked.

"Yes, Mickey. Jim Brown the football player. How many other Jim Browns do you know?"

Mickey took a seat in his own chair, said, "Well, only reason I'm askin' is 'cause that's highly unusual, an early Jim Brown movie where the man didn't die at the end. Made twenty-two pictures when he first started out, and they killed him in damn near all of 'em. Think about it."

Gunner and Winnie did. *The Dirty Dozen, The Dark Side of the Sun, Butterfly* . . .

"You might have a point there, Mick," Gunner said.

"Not might. I *do*. They killed that brother every chance they could get." He paused. "But I guess that's only right, considerin' all the white men he killed playin' *football*."

He busted up laughing, and Gunner and Winnie did likewise. You only had to see Brown play once to understand the meaning of the joke.

They were still chuckling about it when the bell over the front door sounded, and two mismatched black men stepped in from the street. Winnie took one look at the ebony-clad pair and began to frown, while Mickey stood up from his chair and readied himself to throw down.

"How you doin', Mr. Gunner?" Bume Webb's delivery boy Jessie said, smiling as was his wont. His larger partner, Ben, just nodded behind him, his trademark Kangol hat—a blue one this time—affixed as if with glue to the top of his head.

"Let's get something straight right now, boys," Gunner said, staying seated. "I'm not going for any rides today."

Jessie laughed, Ben smirked.

"You know these guys?" Mickey asked.

"The one with all the teeth is Jessie. The bigger one with all the personality is Ben. They go by 'J and B,' but don't tell 'em that's cute. Ben will rip your face off."

"Damn right," Ben said.

"They work indirectly for Bume Webb. And if they came all the way over here to invite me to go see him again . . ."

"Naw, naw," Jessie said, shaking his head. "It ain't like that at all."

"It isn't?"

"No. Thing is—"

"I've got it. You two are big 2DaddyLarge fans looking to give me some grief about his boy Teepee getting busted yesterday."

The NYPD had picked up 2Daddy's overzealous henchman out in Brooklyn the day before, and as half the world knew by now, was holding him on murder charges for extradition to Los Angeles.

"Who, him? That little—" Jessie cut himself short, glancing over at Winnie, and said, "Naw. This ain't about him either. It's about you and Mr. El. Mr. El came to see Mr. Trevor this mornin', told 'im you weren't workin' for him and Bume no more."

"That's right. My case is closed. What about it?"

"Mr. Trevor made some calls. To make sure you ain't breakin' out early on 'im."

"And?"

Jessie looked back at Ben, took a fat yellow envelope from his partner's hand. Handing it to Gunner, he said, "Mr. Trevor says even though things didn't work out the way Bume thought they would, you did an all right job on his behalf. So . . ."

Gunner accepted the envelope, lifted the unsealed flap to peek inside. "How much is this?" he asked shortly.

"Mr. Trevor didn't tell us that." Jessie winked. "But it looks like about ten G's to me."

"Holy Jesus," Mickey said.

"Mr. Trevor says thanks. From him *and* Bume."

Gunner thumbed through the bills in silence, trying to feel all the strings he feared were attached.

"Gunner, if you're thinkin' what I think you're thinkin' . . ." Mickey said.

"You're gonna give it back, right?" Jessie asked. "'Cause you're too noble to take it, some shit like that."

Gunner looked up at him and grinned. "Tell Trevor I said he's welcome. Bume too."

"Now you're talkin'," Mickey said.

Less than five minutes after Jessie and Ben were gone, Gunner was on the phone booking a flight to Chicago to see Yolanda McCreary.

First-class all the way.